Don Chambers

About the Author

PEARL CLEAGE is the author of the novel *What Looks Like Crazy on an Ordinary Day*, which was both an Oprah's Book Club selection and a *New York Times* bestseller. She is also the author of *Mad at Miles: A Blackwoman's Guide to Truth*, and *Deals with the Devil and Other Reasons to Riot*. An accomplished playwright whose stage works include *Flyin' West* and *Blues for an Alabama Sky*, she is also a contributing writer to *Essence* magazine and frequently performs her work on college campuses. Cleage is the mother of one daughter, Deignan. She lives in Atlanta with her husband, Zaron W. Burnett, Jr.

i Wish i Had

A NOVEL

a Red Dress

Pearl Cleage

Perennial

An Imprint of HarperCollinsPublishers

A hardcover edition of this book was published in 2001 by William Morrow, an imprint of HarperCollins Publishers.

I WISH I HAD A RED DRESS. Copyright © 2001 by Pearl Cleage. All rights reserved. Printed in the United States of America. No part of this book may be used or reproduced in any manner whatsoever without written permission except in the case of brief quotations embodied in critical articles and reviews. For information address Harper-Collins Publishers Inc., 10 East 53rd Street, New York, NY 10022.

HarperCollins books may be purchased for educational, business, or sales promotional use. For information please write: Special Markets Department, HarperCollins Publishers Inc., 10 East 53rd Street, New York, NY 10022.

First Perennial edition published 2002.

Designed by Nicola Ferguson

The Library of Congress has catalogued the hardcover edition as follows:
Cleage, Pearl.
I wish I had a red dress / by Pearl Cleage.—1st ed.
p.   cm.
ISBN 0-380-97733-8
1. African American women—Fiction.   2. Women social workers—Fiction.
3. Middle-aged women—Fiction.   4. Michigan—Fiction.
5. Widows—Fiction.   I. Title.
PS3553.L389 I2 2001
813'.54—dc21   00-054620

ISBN 0-380-80488-3 (pbk.)

02 03 04 05 06 WB/RRD 10 9 8 7 6 5 4 3 2 1

For Zaron W. Burnett, Jr.,
husband, highwayman,
one cool-lookin' dude ...

"And I further swear that the members of the Guild of Free Amazons shall be to me, each and every one, as my mother, my sister or my daughter, born of one blood with me, and that no woman sealed by oath to the Guild shall appeal to me in vain."
—The Oath of the Free Amazons,
Marion Zimmer Bradley, *Thendara House*

"We are family/
I got all my sisters with me."
—Sister Sledge, "We Are Family"

CONTENTS

PART THREE

ACKNOWLEDGMENTS

Thanks first of all to my daughter, Deignan Cleage Lomax, for her love, support, and friendship. *There would be no books without you!*

Special thanks also to Lynette M. Lapeyrolerie for lending me her name! I also thank my family and friends, especially my sister, Kristin Cleage Williams, and James Williams of Idlewild, Michigan, and their family, Jilo and Olubagla, Ife, Tulani, Ayanna, James, Cabral, Abeo, Osaze, and Tatayana; Karen and A. B. Spellman, and the North Carolina beach crowd, Toyin, Kaji, Zenzi, Soyinka, Rev. E. Edmonds and Bernice; Carolyn, Omari, and Jamal Monteilh; BarbaraO; Elijah Huntley and Hanifa McClendon Huntley; the Broadway and Burnett families; Valerie Boyd; Ingrid Saunders Jones; *The Mongo;* Cecelia Corbin Hunter; Walter Huntley; Maria Broom; Jill Nelson; Michael Lomax; Pam Burnette and Miss Nyla; Curtis and Barbara Jackson; Tayari Jones; Susan Elizabeth Phillips;

Andrea Hairston; Jondre Pryor; Zaron W. Burnett, III; Meghan Skylar, and Josh Underwood; Margo Perkins; Don Bryan; Ray and Marilyn Cox; Kirk and Keith Bagwell; Marc and Elaine Lawson; Jimmy Lee Tarver; Susan L. Taylor; Granville Edward Freeman Dennis; Monique Greenwood and the members of *The Go on Girl Bookclubs;* Jan Peterson; Nia Damali; Johnnetta Cole; Kenny Leon; Melanie Lomax; Woodie King, Jr., Pat Lottier, and *The Atlanta Tribune;* and the brothers and sisters of The Shrines of the Black Madonna of the Black Christian Nationalist Church. I also send much love to my father, Jaramogi Abebe Agyman, my father-in-law, Zaron W. Burnett, Sr., warrior-woman extraordinaire Debbie Thomas-Bryan, and my best friend, William D. "Billy Bob" Bagwell, who made their transitions during the writing of this book. *I still feel you!*

Thanks also to Carrie Feron, Denise Stinson, and Howard Rosenstone for their assistance and support.

part

one

ONE

Joyce

I WISH I HAD a red dress. I've been wearing black for so long I feel like one of those ancient women in the foreign movies who are always sitting around, fingering their rosary beads and looking resigned while the hero rides to his death on behalf of the people, or for the sake of true love, which is really six of one, half dozen of the other, when you think about it.

I never cared much about clothes. My basic requirement is comfort, which automatically cuts out high-heeled shoes, push-up bras, panty hose and strapless evening gowns, but could theoretically still leave room for a range of colors, fabrics and even a stylish little something or other for special occasions.

The *convenience* of all black used to appeal to me. I loved the fact that I could reach into my closet and know everything I touched was going to match everything else I touched with absolutely no effort on my part, but it can be a little depressing sometimes. Even to me.

I didn't consciously start wearing black as a sign of mourning, even though at some *subconscious* level, I probably did. My husband, Mitch, died five years ago, which is when I really started noticing it, but he was just the last of a long line. My father passed when I was sixteen. My mother committed suicide on my wedding night a year later. My son got hit by a car walking home from school when he was six and my daughter didn't make it to her first birthday. I think she was the hardest one for me to deal with because I barely got to know her and she was gone.

It was just the opposite with Mitch. We'd been together since I was fifteen and we were so close I made the mistake of thinking we were the same person until he fell through that hole in the ice and drowned and *I didn't die*, even though for a long time I wished I had.

My baby sister, Ava, says it's hard to keep your body looking good when you know nobody's going to see you naked. She could have added that when you know your primary audience *when clothed* is preschoolers, some distracted teenage mothers, a few retirees and a government bureaucrat or two, it's equally difficult to get up much enthusiasm for earrings that dangle and skirts that swirl like you're standing in a little breeze even when you're not.

I'm a social worker. I used to be a teacher. Then one day I looked around and realized that what I was teaching and the way I was teaching it were completely irrelevant to my students' real lives. They were just ordinary kids from around here; young and wild and full of the most complicated human emotions and not nearly enough facility in any language to articulate those feelings to each other or to anyone else. But one day I saw them, *really saw them*, and everything changed.

It was a public high school and my classes were coed, but it was the girls who kept drawing my attention. There they'd be, balancing their squalling babies on their hips in the grocery store, slapping their toddlers at the Blockbuster, rolling their eyes and tossing their extensions, considering exotic dancing as a career option, falling in love with the wrong guys, being abused, getting AIDS and steadily having kids the whole time, and they were so absolutely confined and confused by their tiny little fear-based dreams that I looked out at them one day while I was trying to teach a poem by e. e. cummings, and they broke my heart. I started crying and had to dismiss the class so I could get myself together.

That's when I knew there had to be a better way to communicate with these girls than the one I was using. I decided that finding that better way was going to be my life's work because I don't think a group of people can survive if the women don't even have enough sense to raise their children.

That's why clothes are usually the last thing on my mind. Black pants and a black turtleneck without applesauce showing anywhere are about the best I can hope for at the moment, but somehow I can't get that red dress out of my mind.

TWO

trust me

"*OH-H-H-H-H-H!*"

The intensity of the orgasm shook me awake and I called his name out loud.

"Mitch!"

Once my heart slowed down, I looked at the clock—five-thirty. The sun wasn't even up yet. Plenty of time for a fast forty winks. I pulled the covers over my head to see if I could will myself back to sleep and was hit full blast by the loamy smell of my own pleasure. *Sweet Mitch.*

This was a good sign. He always comes to me like this when I'm getting ready to do something really important. Sort of like a kiss for luck. It's not the only time I dream about him, but it's the only time the dreams are X-rated. I don't know why. I don't try to conjure him up this way, but I don't kick him out of bed either.

I used to feel guilty about it and then one day I thought, well, hell, if the widow can't ease her permanent heartache by self-pleasuring in her sleep to dreams of her late husband, then what's the poor woman to do? It's not like I took a vow of celibacy or anything. It's just that Idlewild is a very small town and all the men are old enough to be my father or young enough to be my son, or they used to go fishing with my husband and trying to date me just makes them miss him more. So I make do with the memories and a little self-pleasuring every now and then.

I think *self-pleasuring* sounds infinitely sexier than *masturbation*. I got the term from one of Sister Judith's books. It had a whole chapter on sacred self-pleasuring rituals, featuring photographs and testimonials gathered from what the book described as "active women's collectives throughout Northern California." Personally, I don't think everything needs its own ritual, but these women are living in the Bay Area. Rituals are their life.

By now, I'm pretty much resigned to the ways things are, but sometimes when I think about the fact that I'm only forty-something and there is a very real possibility that I might never make love again, *I can't breathe*. But just for a minute, then I'm okay.

I might as well get up. It was going to be a long day. I had to drive over to the state capital and try to buttonhole enough bored politicians to make sure they vote to fund the proposal I'd spent the last three months of my life working on. I knew it was a long shot. They think the girls in my program are a bunch of wild women whose insanity does not deserve the support of Michigan's hardworking taxpayers, but I've seen the changes these girls can make in their lives once they have a working definition of what it means to be a *free woman* and that's the whole point, right?

This is one of those moments when I really miss my sister, Ava. She did a lot of fund-raising with me, but she and her husband, Eddie, are spending the next couple of months traveling around the country in a little camper. They got it from one of the old guys up here who hadn't used it in years but who couldn't stop talking about the good times he had with his wife when they drove it to California every summer *back in the day*.

My daughter, Imani, went with them. I miss her a lot, but Ava and Eddie are her parents as much as I am, even if my name is the only one on the adoption papers, and they wanted to take her as much as she wanted to go. I'm flying out to meet them when they get to San Francisco and we'll all drive back together. Hopefully, by that time, I'll have raised the rest of the money we need to keep my program open, but *from where?*

Sister Judith would probably remind me that the beginning of doubt is the end of faith. I hate it when she says stuff like that. There's something about her *certainty* that makes me want to argue even when I agree. Plus, discussions of faith always make me nervous. Not that I'm cynical. Just realistic.

Here's what I believe: Life is much harder than anybody can possibly tell you, but it doesn't matter because even if they could, you wouldn't believe them and what good would it do anyway? You've still got to get up in the morning and figure out how to spend the next sixteen or seventeen hours before you can legitimately go back to bed, pull the covers over your head and rest up for the next round, which is what I was busy doing when Mitch woke me up with the memories.

Not that I'm complaining. *No way.* There are a lot worse ways to greet the day than being warmed by memories of the sweetest love you ever had. *Trust me.*

THREE

stepping on angels

MY FAST FORTY WINKS turned into a slow half hour, and by the time I took my shower and toasted a raisin bagel for the road, I was already running late. I dashed out the back door, slammed it behind me and stopped in my tracks. A spotless blanket of new-fallen snow covered everything from my porch steps down the slope to the frozen lake at the foot of my front yard. It looked like a Christmas card.

I grew up in this house, and I inherited it when my parents passed. In the days when Idlewild was a thriving Negro resort, this kind of lakefront property was prime. Nowadays, a lot of these houses are boarded up. My few remaining full-time neighbors are mostly retirees struggling to stay independent and stave off the moment when they will be gently forced to move into that back bedroom in the house of a well-meaning son or daughter.

I tipped back my head and opened my mouth to catch some of the soft flakes on my tongue and resisted the impulse to throw myself on the ground and make snow angels. I was tempted. Ava and I used to cover the ground with them and then spend all winter stepping carefully around each one since my mother said any fool knows it's bad luck to step on an angel.

I turned on my car to warm it up a little and walked down to the dock for a last quiet minute before the madness of the day. It's easy to get distracted once I get to Lansing. Politicians are really only interested in two things: votes and money, not necessarily in that order. I'm always babbling at them about making the world safe for babies, and they're always lecturing me about budget shortfalls. After a few hours of that, it helps to be able to close my eyes and remember mornings like this when the snow makes everything look clear and clean and possible.

My parents relocated here from Detroit when I was in high school. My father was tired of working at the post office and my mother had fond memories of summers they spent here in the fifties, before integration. *The glory days.* There were cottages for rent, and supper clubs with floor shows, and restaurants that took reservations and bathing beauties who gave Lena Horne a run for her money. It was, in the words of an early brochure, "a vacation paradise for colored people."

They would be amazed at what this place has become. The land is still beautiful, but it's a ghost town now, populated mostly by people too old, or too poor, to go anywhere else and a few romantic reformers like me and Sister who still think there's a way to make it work. Integration was supposed to be a good thing, but up here, it was the kiss of death. Black folks running from each other left behind some of the most beautiful real estate for miles around and never looked back. Sometimes I think I ought to pack up and move too, but that's a self-fulfilling prophecy, like believing there will always be wars. If enough of us want to fix this place, we'll fix it.

Look at The Sewing Circus. That's my program. When Mitch died five years ago, I used the money from his life insurance to create it from scratch because I felt like the way we were doing things when I was working at Social Services was just making people more depressed and more dependent. I thought I had a better idea. Now I *know* I do.

The formal name of my program is the Albert B. Mitchell Sewing Circus and Community Truth Center, but we usually just call ourselves The Circus. We tried using initials, but saying *ABMSCCTC* took too much time, plus the younger kids couldn't remember all the letters and the rest of us didn't want to.

I like calling us The Circus because it references our history. We started out meeting at Salem Baptist Church on Wednesday nights, the same time as the Ladies Sewing Circle and the Senior Choir, but our discussions got kind of loud and there were always lots of kids around being kids, so one night when we had disturbed the peace one time too many, the organist told the choir director that I was running a three-ring circus down in the Fellowship Hall and the name just stuck.

I can't deny it. I work mostly with young women and their kids. Not all of them have babies, but most of them do and all of them will. We just celebrated our second anniversary, and we've got eight regulars with ten babies between them. We offer the usual assistance—job counseling, GED classes, day care—but I think the most important thing we offer is an active, ongoing *conversation*, the stated purpose of which is to "develop the capacity for critical thinking as part of the overall process of becoming a free woman."

I'm a big fan of stating your intentions up front as clearly as possible. Saves a lot of confusion and wasted time later, especially in a group like this one. They rarely read and most of them don't know how to analyze information that's presented to them any better than their kids do. The events of their lives and the relentless cacophony of the popular culture just sort of wash over them, and sometimes they catch the wave, but more often they don't. They need a way of decoding the world at least as much as they need basic computer skills.

So we meet for potluck dinners, *and we talk*. We watch movies, *and we talk*. Sometimes I know I get on their nerves and they accuse me of spoiling the simple pleasures in life by over-analyzing every little thing, but when you're trying to teach people how to think in a completely different kind of way, you have to talk a lot, otherwise you run the risk of assuming that everybody agrees on the issue at hand when, in truth, they're just confused or intimidated or overwhelmed by a bunch of ideas they've never heard before. When this happens once you leave the room, things go right back to business as usual, which is rarely the best option.

That's really what The Circus is about, I guess, *options*, and at this point, mine do not include spending the rest of the morning watching the snow pile up on the frozen surface of Idlewild Lake, although that certainly would be my first choice. My job today is to get in my car, drive two hours to the state capital at Lansing and convince the members of the Human Resources Committee that not approving our grant is tantamount to stepping on angels *and I know their mamas did not raise no fools.*

FOUR

black ice

THEY CROSSED THE LINE! You know that line you have to be real clear about in your own head so that when people step over it, you can be ready to bring their inappropriate behavior to their attention by whatever means necessary? Well, Senator Busbee and his buddies definitely crossed it and I definitely brought it to their attention, but whether or not the end justified the means remains to be seen.

I merged into the traffic leaving Lansing and flipped on the radio, trying to calm down. Aretha Franklin's voice came pouring out like sombody had cued her.

"All I'm askin' is for a little respect!"

And the backup sisters wailing "Just a little bit! Just a little bit!"

Sing it, Ree! I thought, but I was still too agitated to sing along. Politicians don't know anything about respect! I should have known this was not a good place for me to be when I walked into the meeting room this morning and saw the guys on the committee all sitting up on a raised platform behind a gigantic oak table with one tiny chair out front for the humble citizen who's coming to ask for their stamp of approval. That big old table and that little bitty chair are supposed to make you feel *small,* like Dorothy and the Scarecrow coming in to see the Wizard of Oz. The wizard didn't really have to *be* powerful. He just had to *look* like he was.

I think all negotiations should take place at a round table and everybody should have to rotate counterclockwise once an hour so that even the perception of head of the table, or foot, are ritually obliterated. It's not good to sit still longer than an hour in meetings anyway. Pools the blood and encourages the territorial spreading of notes, expensive pens, leather-bound legal pads and a variety of electronic devices aimed at keeping in constant touch with the world outside of the room in which the meeting has been convened.

Politicians are especially good at this. I don't know whether they believe that an overcrowded desk is just the thing to impress a constituent or what, but I've been in meetings with these guys where they spread out so much stuff in front of them that it terminally clutters your brain if you even glance down at it. Sort of like being turned to stone for sneaking a glance at Medusa.

"Re, re, re, re, re, re, re, re—spect!"

The car skidded suddenly on a patch of black ice and I realized I was driving too fast. I turned off the radio and took a deep breath. The sun was already on its way down and all the snow that turned to slush during the day would be frozen solid in a few more hours. This was not the time to be careless. This was the time to review the events of the day and figure out *what went wrong?*

I thought the proposal was perfect. Visionary without being mystical. Specific without being exclusionary. Optimistic yet firmly grounded in reality. Practical and passionate, it was, *if I do say so myself*, a fine example of the best kind of sixties rhetoric grafted onto the new millennium's requirement that we "cut to the chase."

Maybe I should have taken better notes in that grant writing class. I can't believe I actually took a *class* in saying what you don't really mean so you can get money they don't really want you to have. The instructors kept telling me the key to raising money was to maintain a "businesslike tone," like I'm supposed to be ashamed of the fact that I tend to get excited when I'm talking about things that are important to me. As a true sixties *voodoo child*, I know I am *required* to bring passion to the table just like this generation is required to bring technology and rap music.

That's my legacy, but when I protested all this focus on what I regarded as style over substance, they gently suggested that I adopt a more civil *tone* when voicing my objections. At that point, I informed them on my way out the door that toning down is of zero importance to me. I would instead simply commit to the passionate telling of the complete, unvarnished truth.

Seems like a simple statement, right? But it gets tricky. First of all, there's the problem of presuming that everybody thinks it's always a good idea to tell the truth when there's really nothing to suggest that we all agree on that. In fact, there's overwhelming evidence that we don't, including the fact that as soon as most of us read a statement advocating universal truth-telling as a goal worthy of pursuit, we start thinking of exceptions immediately.

> *Sure,* we think, *truth is great,* except when:
> —it's your boss;
> —it's your lover/mate/partner/spouse or kid;
> —it's scary;
> —you might lose money/power/love/your job;
> —you might get killed for it.

The thing is, once you start allowing for exceptions, everything becomes relative and people start talking about absurd notions like "everybody's got a right to their own truth," as if there can be more than one real truth, and the next thing you know, they're putting up fences and assembling armies and we're right back to where we started.

But it couldn't be my *tone.* The chairman even complimented me on the quality of our application and told me we'd have no problem being approved. At the appropriate time, they allowed me to make a three-minute statement and I used my time to stress the importance of self-sufficiency, since I know politicians are big on self-sufficiency and I am too. I worked in phrases like "breaking the cycle of poverty" and "taking personal responsibility for correcting societal ills."

I even handed out copies of our basic Circus credo, which I wrote at my kitchen table when we were brand new:

Ten Things Every Free Woman Should Know

1. How to grow food and flowers
2. How to prepare food nutritiously
3. Self-defense
4. Basic first aid/sex education and midwifery
5. Child care (prenatal/early childhood development)
6. Basic literacy/basic math/basic computer skills
7. Defensive driving/map reading/basic auto and home repairs
8. Household budget/money management
9. Spiritual practice
10. Physical fitness/health/hygiene

The professional grant-writing people told me it was a pretty radical statement for general distribution so I agreed to leave it out, but at the last minute, I made enough copies to hand out anyway. I wanted to give these guys a feeling for how seriously we're trying to impact the totality of these young women's lives.

Secure in my delusion, I chattered on for my allocated three minutes, then thanked them for their time and offered to respond to any questions they might have for me. At that point, I thought I was doing pretty good. Nobody had yawned or excused himself to go to the bathroom and then the Honorable Ezra Busbee cleared his throat and cocked his head in my direction.

Congressman Busbee is a tall, thin, intense-looking man

whose jacket sleeves and pant legs are always a little too short, which makes him bear more than a passing resemblance to Ichabod Crane. In spite of this unfortunate image problem and his total lack of support outside of his own small district, he's been around long enough to sit on a number of powerful committees, including this one.

"I've got a question for you, *Joyce*," he said with a tight little smile like we had a first-name relationship going. "May I call you Joyce?"

I wanted to say, *Of course, if I can call you Ezra*, but I didn't. I needed his vote.

"Certainly," I said, with my own small smile.

"Well, *Joyce*." He held up his copy of the "Ten Things." "This is a very interesting document."

Was "interesting" good or bad?

"Thank you," I said.

"Can you do all these things?"

"Almost all," I said.

"Then would you call yourself a *free woman?*"

"Yes," I said. "I would."

"And that's what you're raising over there in . . . Idlewild, is it? *Free women?*"

He made it sound like I was running an illegal mink ranch. "Well, I wouldn't say *we're raising them*," I said. "Most of our core constituency is eighteen to twenty-two."

"And they already have babies?"

I kept my voice as neutral as possible. "Not all, but many of them do have children, yes."

He nodded and peered through his glasses at the list, reading through it again quickly. "And what's your definition of a free woman again?"

I think that for some men, using the word "free" and "woman" so close together seems such an obvious oxymoron that they assume it must be the setup for a funny story. Ezra struck me as that kind of guy.

"A free woman," I said, reminding myself to keep smiling too, "is one who can fully conceive and consciously execute all the moments of her life."

I could tell he had no idea what I was talking about.

"Look out, Ezra," chuckled the committee chairman, a jovial grandfather from a tiny town as far into northern Michigan as you can go without falling into Lake Superior. "I have it on good authority that Mrs. Mitchell here is something of a *women's libber*."

What century were they living in? The other members of the committee chuckled, but Ezra was not impressed. He waved the "Ten Things" in my face a bit more aggressively.

"Well, I don't know much about women's lib," he said, "but I can't see much point in spending people's hard-earned money giving sex education to unwed mothers. Isn't that a little like closin' the door after the cow's already out of the barn?"

Several members of the committee laughed. That's what I get for saying he could call me *Joyce*. Give these guys an inch and they'll take a mile.

"That's just a small part of what we do," I said.

"But you do it, right?"

"Yes."

The laughter had awakened the dozing reporter for *The Capital Daily* and her note taking inspired Ezra to pursue the question.

"And you think that's the role of government, do you, Joyce?"

Truth, I reminded myself. *Just tell him the truth.*

"Yes, I do," I said. "I think the role of government is to support and nurture a strong, self-reliant population, regardless of gender. Don't you?"

He looked at me and frowned. "I think I'm asking the questions here, Ms. Mitchell, not you. That's what I think."

I felt my face flush. "Excuse me?"

"In fact," he said, turning to the chairman. "I have a number of questions that I would like to ask Joyce about her training ground for so-called *free women* before we vote."

"I object to that characterization of our program!" I said.

"It is not your place to object," Ezra interrupted me.

"My place?"

"I move to table this application until we have time to study it more carefully and determine the full scope of Joyce's program goals. I'm tired of the taxpayers' money being wasted when all these girls need is for somebody to teach 'em how to keep their dresses down and just say *no!*"

"Mr. Chairman, I have a right to respond!" I said.

"If you're not a member of this committee, you have no rights in this room!" Ezra snapped.

Enough was enough. I stood up. "Then I don't belong here," I said, reaching for my coat.

"There is a motion to table on the floor!" The chairman was tapping his gavel for order. The reporter was scribbling enthusiastically now, happy for any kind of story at the end of a long, dull day.

"I second it," boomed a freshman legislator from Grand Rapids who had a pretty young female constituent watching his lackluster performance admiringly.

Before I could object any further, they had delayed action on our proposal pending my satisfactory answers to a list of questions that Ezra handed to the committee chairman, who accepted them, took another fast vote and adjourned the meeting for the day.

For a minute, I was too stunned to move as they all began to file out of the small room. I caught up with the chairman in the hallway, scurrying back to his office.

"Bob," I said, too frustrated for formalities. "You know it will take months for us to get back on the agenda if we get turned back now! What happened?"

He patted my shoulder without slowing down and handed me Ezra's list. "Don't take it personal, Joyce," he said and winked. "It's an election year, remember?"

Then I understood. Ezra wanted to use his opposition to us as a way of getting a little free campaign publicity. I looked at the list. The first question was "How many illegitimate babies have your followers brought into the world for somebody else to take care of?"

There were six or seven more, but that was enough for me. I crumpled the paper in my hand and just stood there for a minute. What now? I closed my eyes and took a deep breath. I had said I was a free woman, so what would a free woman do?

I walked over to the chairman, who had stopped to have a word with Ezra.

"Excuse me," I said, tossing the balled-up paper in his direction so he had to fumble to catch it. "I won't be needing those. I withdraw our application."

He looked at me, too surprised to say anything, which was fine with me. I turned to Ezra.

"Two things," I said to him. "There are no *illegitimate* babies; and from now on, *you can call me Ms. Mitchell.*"

When I passed a big trash can in the parking lot, I slowed down long enough to take out my last copy of that carefully crafted proposal and tossed it in. Whatever happens next, The Sewing Circus is going to stand or fall on our own reality. What's the point of fighting for the truth if you're not allowed to tell it?

FIVE

the weary traveler

THE ADVANTAGE OF FAITH in moments of crisis and transition is that when the rest of us find ourselves swimming in guilt, fear, confusion and second-guessing, the true believer simply goes with the flow. I'm not quite there yet, which is the advantage of having a friend who is also a minister. When I got back to Idlewild, I went by the church first.

It was already six-thirty, but I could see a light in Sister's office window. She was working late too, so I pulled into the parking lot and blew the horn. Her face appeared in the window immediately, smiling and waving for me to come inside. I knew she would. Ministers are pretty much obligated to welcome the weary traveler. They never know when the Christ child might show up.

Sister Judith is a minister, not a nun, but she likes to be called

Sister because it's a term of religious respect that doesn't carry with it what she calls "the undeniable scent of the patriarchy" like the word *reverend*. She's from San Francisco, and they take their feminism seriously out there. I tend to be a little less ideological, especially when it comes to what we call ourselves. I don't really care. I'm a lot more concerned about what we *do*.

It's like the ongoing debate about whether *African American* is more correct than the more generic *black*. I prefer *Negro* myself, but if you say *Negro* to a bunch of young people, they take it as an insult, which is counterproductive, so I usually stick with *African American*, although I still think it's unwieldy, but that's just me.

Same thing with women. The labels don't matter much to me—womanist, feminist, suffragette, even my committee's choice of the decidedly old-fashioned *women's libber*. There are infinite choices that are acceptable to me if they all mean *free*. I myself have tried to lobby for the more mythological and, I think, spiritually powerful term *Amazon*, but I can't get anybody around here to buy into that one. They claim it sounds too much like *Xena, Warrior Princess*. I don't care. I still like it.

"I was just thinking about you," Sister said, hugging me through our two overcoats. Fuel oil is expensive and Sister often economizes by turning the thermostat way down and keeping her coat on when she's working. But only when she's alone and never on Sunday morning. Most of our congregation is over sixty-five; old people will forgive you a lot, but not cold feet.

She opened her office door and ushered me quickly inside, where it was warmer by about fifteen degrees, thanks to a small space heater glowing in the corner next to her desk and her usual collection of brightly burning scented candles. Today, the small room had a decidedly tropical aroma.

"Want a cup of tea?" She reached for her thermos to share with me whatever fragrant herbal blend it held today.

"Don't you keep some unconsecrated wine around for these moments?" I said, collapsing on her office love seat, suddenly exhausted. Don't let people tell you begging strangers for money doesn't take it out of you. *It does.*

She raised her eyebrows. "Which moments?"

"Moments when nothing goes according to plan," I said, stretching my feet toward the heater.

"Oh, those," Sister said, handing me a cup of steaming tea that smelled like cinnamon and apples. "You've heard that old joke, right?"

"What old joke?"

"If you want to make God laugh, make plans."

I looked at her. "That is not only an *old* joke. That is a *minister* joke."

"Sorry," she said. "Drink your tea."

I took a long swallow and we just sat quietly for a minute. Sister's good at silence and after the day I just had, her peaceful presence was as soothing to me as all the reassuring words in the world. Sister is the best thing that's happened to Salem Baptist Church in a long time. When old Dr. Ross finally retired five years ago, we got a really awful guy from Chicago for about six months. After we got rid of him, we didn't even have any prospects. Then, out of the blue, the Baptist Board sent us a letter saying we're really lucky because they'd just been contacted by an outstanding young minister in California who's interested in coming to Idlewild. She could be there in a month, and oh, by the way, *did we care that she was a woman?*

That was Sister. Within a month, she and her husband, Bill, drove up in a U-Haul truck with the windows open and the radio blasting Al Green's "Let's Stay Together." We've been friends ever since.

I admit it was strange at first, having a close friend who was also an ordained minister. I kept waiting for her to be more "ministerial," whatever that means, but Sister acts just like any other fortyish female except that on Sunday mornings, she stands up in front of everybody and calls the spirits in. Over her desk, she has a quote from the Dalai Lama that says "Kindness is my religion." I like that. It doesn't leave you any *weaseling* room. Everybody knows kindness when they see it.

"So I take it things did not go well," she said, after giving me a chance to catch my breath.

"I withdrew the proposal."

"Withdrew it?" She looked as disappointed as I felt, but her voice was calm. "What happened?"

"Well, they had a few additional questions for me."

"Like what?"

"Oh, some basic stuff. What's a free woman? Are you sure we should be trying to raise them in captivity? How come they have so many *illegitimate* babies? Stuff like that."

"Well, *shoot!*"

Sister doesn't curse, so *shoot* is about as good as it gets. She poured me some more tea and I sipped it slowly. On days like this, sometimes the best you can hope for is a sympathetic shoulder to whine on until you have a chance to regroup. Sympathy is practically Sister's middle name and a little whining can be therapeutic as long as you don't make a habit out of it.

"I don't get it," she said. "Your proposal was great. What do they want?"

"You got me," I said. "I feel like I'm spending all my time pretending to do something they can understand so they'll give me money to do something they don't even care about. It's depressing."

Sister reached across her desk and patted my hand. "Do you think you can raise the money someplace else?"

"That's what I've been thinking about all the way home," I said. "The truth is, I don't even have any prospects, but I think it's time for us to find another way to support what we do. If we never cut loose from the state, we'll never know."

"Good for you," Sister smiled. "You know the Buddhists believe that sometimes when everything is in turmoil, it's because something wonderful is ready to be born and that thing is distracting you so it can have some privacy during the birthing process."

"And that's the best distraction it can come up with?" I said, picturing a creature in the last stages of labor, frantically roaming the halls of the state capital, looking for a quiet corner in which to deliver. "This magical thing couldn't settle for a nice, distracting double rainbow over Idlewild Lake?"

"You were indoors all day," Sister said gently. "You would have missed it anyway."

She was right. I hadn't seen the sky since this morning.

"You know what really gets me?" I said, draining my mug. "I spent the whole day begging a bunch of men for money to help some women. I thought you feminists had a revolution. *What happened?*"

"Feminism doesn't mean no men," Sister said calmly, refusing to take responsibility for the failures of the women's movement. "It means no *sexist* men."

"Six of one, half dozen of the other."

"Come on," she said, "can you really imagine a world without men?"

"Absolutely," I said. "It's a peaceful place full of fat, happy women and no football."

She hooted at that. Sister's laugh is one of the best things about her. She had no interest in discreet chuckling or giggling into her hand. Sister laughed *loud* like a little kid at a birthday party, when blowing out all the candles is still cause for major celebration.

"I *like* football," she said.

"Do you ever watch it without Bill?"

Sister was madly in love with her husband, an English teacher at the high school and a would-be poet. If he had liked watching professional bowling, she'd have been right there, but left to her own devices, she was more inclined toward old Hollywood movies and *CBS Sunday Morning*.

"You're working too hard," she said. "Close your eyes."

I did as I was told and heard her unwrapping what sounded like a large paper bag. She took my right hand and folded my fingers around something cool and smooth. "What is it?" I asked.

"Open your eyes."

I was holding a perfect mango. The thick, waxy outside skin was the color of a rosy tropical sunset.

"Isn't it beautiful?" Sister said proudly, like she'd grown it herself.

I couldn't have been more surprised if she'd handed me a purple orchid. Mangoes do not grow around here and, unfortunately, if we don't grow it, there isn't much demand. Bananas are about as exotic as we get.

"Where did you get a mango?" I said, turning it over in my hand, loving the shape and the weight of it.

"At the market." She smiled. "I've got a dozen."

She held open the bag excitedly and there they all were, each one more photogenic than the last. I wondered if Sister's candles were really scented today or if the mangoes were perfuming this cold air in self-defense.

"Buddy said they were a mistake," she said as if the idea of something so lovely ever being called a mistake was a thought hatched in the brain of a fool. The local market was a constant source of irritation to Sister and Bill, who had been spoiled by the abundance and variety in their old West Coast neighborhood, where a rich blend of ethnicities guaranteed an international sampling even if you weren't looking for it. A sushi taco would not have been out of the realm of possibility.

"They were in with his regular order of apples and sweet corn. He didn't even know what to charge me, so I got the whole batch for five dollars!"

She reached into the bag, took one out and tossed it gently in her hand. "I offered him one so he could taste it and he told me he thought he had tasted all the new stuff he needed to, but thanks anyway." She shook her head in disbelief. "He's in the food business! If he's not ready for mangoes, what about kiwi and kumquats and Asian pears and escarole and artichokes?"

Like I said, they pay a lot more attention to food variety in San Francisco than we do in Lake County, but she was right about two things: These were beautiful mangoes; and Buddy didn't have much imagination. He asked me to go to the movies a couple of times after Mitch died, but all he wanted to do was talk about how weird it was that his wife had died and Mitch had died, and now here we were together. Dead spouses didn't seem like the best foundation for a long-term relationship, so I didn't pursue it.

Sister pressed a mango into my other hand. "Take another one with you," she said. "I'm going to get Bill to use the rest to make us some of his world-famous mango margaritas tomorrow night."

We eat at each other's house so often we tease about automatically setting a place for drop-ins. Sometimes we do potluck. Sometimes we do something elaborate like Bill's special paella or my pasta from scratch, but most of all, it's a chance for us to catch up and let our hair down.

We've all managed to find our life's work in jobs that require a certain amount of public decorum. As a minister, a social worker and a high school English teacher, we're expected to assume as part of our public responsibilities, a quiet dignity, an unshakable reserve and a constant seriousness that can sometimes become oppressive. Left unchecked, they can lead to a certain self-righteousness that is counterproductive to the work that we do. Being together, just the three of us, helps us *keep it real.*

"I've never had a mango margarita," I said.

Sister looked surprised.

"Don't look at me like that," I said. "Where would I get one?"

She shook her head. "You have to get out more."

"I'll work on it," I said. "What should I bring tomorrow?"

"Just yourself," she said. "Around seven, and wear something *festive.*"

"What does that mean?"

"Nothing. I just thought you might want to give all that black a rest and come out with a little color."

"Black *is* a color," I said. She was echoing my sentiments exactly, but I wanted to be the one to say it first.

"Wear whatever you want," she said, giving me a good-bye hug. "And don't worry."

I hugged her back. "I won't."

I was lying, of course, but she knew it, so I don't think it really counts. Sometimes you have to give the correct answer even when you're not really feeling it yet so you can hear how it's going to sound when you finally get it together for real.

Before I headed home, I still had to go by The Sewing Circus to make sure Tomika had locked up. Tee's been working in the office with me for a couple of months and I hope one day she'll be able to function as a full-fledged office manager. Right now, she's still getting used to the responsibility. She's nineteen and this is the first real job she's ever had.

I laid the mangoes gently on the seat beside me, and as I pulled out of the parking lot, I realized I had been right about that tropical aroma in Sister's office—it wasn't the candles. Outside, it was starting to snow again, but in my beat-up old Chevy, there was just the slightest whiff of mango.

SIX

the tree baby

WHEN I WALKED INTO the tiny office we share at The Circus, Tomika was barely visible above the double page spread of last Sunday's *New York Times*. I try to get them all to read it, but Tomika's the only one who actually does. It usually takes her all week to get through the whole thing, but she doesn't seem to mind. She's spent most of her life getting all her information from television and the tabloids. Her mind is having an orgy of new ideas.

"Hey, Miz J!" she said before I could even get my coat off. "Listen to this." She cleared her throat. " 'Authorities confirm a healthy female baby was born in a treetop'—a *treetop, okay?*— 'during recent severe flooding in Mo-mo-mo . . . ' " She slowly sounded out the unfamiliar name. " 'Mozambique.' "

"What?"

"They even got a picture. Look at the *babymama*. How she make out?"

Tee thrust the paper in my direction and there the *babymama* was all right, a tiny, rain-soaked African woman, clutching her newborn in the Associated Press wire photo that would introduce her to the world.

"Jesus!"

"You got that right!" Tee was looking over my shoulder at the woman's shell-shocked face. The baby was nursing. "This girl just delivered a baby in a thunderstorm up in a tree and they both made it! That's what's killin' me. They made it back to dry land *and* got they picture in the paper! So, how was the trip to Lansing? Should I start lookin' for another job?"

Tee changed subjects effortlessly without even stopping for breath. Whatever else she could or couldn't do, the girl could *talk*.

"We all survived it," I said, hedging.

"So it was cool, right?"

"So far, so good." No point everybody worrying at the same time. "Where's Mavis?"

Tomika's four-year-old daughter is a true Sewing Circus baby. She's been coming here for day care most of her life.

"Nikki took her to McDonald's with Tiffany and Marquis. I wanted to finish the Week in Review. That means all I got left is Saturday for Arts and Leisure and half of that is gonna be movie ads."

Tomika even read the Business section. In one of my many fantasies of her future, she is a successful stockbroker managing The Circus portfolio with such skill that we have not only operating expenses but an endowment and a scholarship program. I haven't told her about all of this, of course. They don't dream as big for themselves yet as I do for them. They've still got some catching up to do.

I shuffled through the stack of mail she'd laid out neatly on my desk. Mostly bills. Tee was clipping the tree-baby story for her "Say what?" file.

"This kinda stuff really makes you think," she said, cutting around the picture carefully.

"About what?" I flipped past the water bill and tossed a flyer from the grocery store into the trash can.

She shrugged, still searching the face of the tree *babymama*. "I don't know. Just the fact of somebody *regular*, just livin' her life. She got a man. She gettin' ready to have a baby, and *BAM!* all of a sudden all hell breaks loose and she havin' the kid in a tree!"

Tee had stumbled upon the exquisitely random chaos that makes the universe the truly challenging place we know it to be, and she didn't appreciate it. I know the feeling.

"You don't think things could break down that tough around here ever, do you?"

"We don't have hurricanes," I said.

She looked at me and grinned. "You a trip, Miz J. You always look on the bright side, huh?"

They tried calling me a couple of things before they settled on Miz J. Mrs. Mitchell was way too formal. Joyce was way too informal, and Sister Mitchell was a generation or two removed from what they know. Miz J was a shortened version of Miss Joyce, which sort of evolved from so many of them having south-ern roots. People south of the Mason–Dixon line add Miss to your first name as a sign of affection and respect, so I liked it right off.

"I do my best," I said.

"Well, then I got one more for you," she said, flipping through the paper quickly, the cut pages flapping in the wind like torn flags, her eyes scanning for another noteworthy item she wanted to share.

It'd been a very long day, but Tee loves to talk about what she's reading and I'd have to be a whole lot sleepier than this to tell her I'm too tired to keep up.

"Here it is! Listen to this!" Her voice rose with righteous indignation. " 'California study shows a dramatic increase in reported cases of domestic violence on Super Bowl Sunday. Experts suspect that increased use of alcohol and heightened emotional reactions to the outcome of the game increase the risk for women during this hotly contested annual event.' "

She tossed the paper down with a contemptuous flick of her wrist and I added anchorwoman to my list of Tee's future career possibilities.

"Isn't that just typical? These guys get so excited they got to kick somebody's ass and they ain't even in the game! They sittin' at home, watchin' it and drinkin' a beer just like everybody else."

"Do you think it's true?" I said, deciding I could do the rest of the mail on Monday.

"I know it is," she said. "Somebody always comin' over in a hurry at halftime 'cause the men at they house lookin' around for somethin' to hit."

She shook her head, setting in motion the tiny, blond braids that hung down to the middle of her back. Tomika liked more hair than she could grow, so she bought what she needed and wove it in. The colors she chose had little to do with what nature had given her, so I learned to think of her extensions like ribbons. The color wasn't there to blend in. It was there to *celebrate*.

Before she started working here, she was known primarily for her elaborately structured hairstyles, her equally elaborate fingernails, and her lack of tolerance for any form of fantasy, subterfuge, or pretension. She saw a movie once where a major character was described as being "brutally honest" and from that point on that is how she was thought of and conducted herself. It can be exhausting, but I'm convinced she's on a lifelong path to seek the truth and what kind of mentor would I be to discourage such a quest.

"When Sonny was still livin' at home, Patrice went to watch the game with him at his mama house one time."

Tomika rolled her eyes and I understood why. Patrice O'Neal was one of our regulars and Sonny Lattimore was her man and the father of her son, Sylvester, Jr., known as *Lil' Sonny*. Handsome and heartless, the five Lattimore brothers—Junior, Sonny, T. J., Maleek, and Jarvis—were as mean as they were good-looking. Tall and slender without being skinny, they looked like Chuck Berry in his prime. They had high cheekbones and deep, dark eyes that turned to flat pools of poison if you crossed them. The oldest four had fathered half a dozen children by as many women. Jarvis, the youngest, was only fifteen, and still childless as far as anyone knew.

"I'm sure it was an unforgettable afternoon," I said.

"Awful!" Tomika gave a sympathetic shudder at the memory of her friend's ordeal. "They started arguin' right after the first down. They were drunk before the halftime show. By the end of the third quarter, one of 'em was threatenin' to go out to the car and get his gun, and just before the two-minute warnin', another one pushed Sheila into the refrigerator 'cause she was too slow bringin' him a beer."

Sheila was their only sister. They regarded her as their personal servant, and their mother, usually drunk and always hostile, did nothing to disabuse them of that notion. The youngest of Sheila's two sons was widely rumored to be her oldest brother's child, but she always denied it. Even when you didn't ask her.

"It don't make no sense." Tomika was indignant. "Don't no women even care about the Super Bowl. They only watchin' it 'cause they tryin' to get next to some guy who watchin' it, or they already did that, and now he think part of the deal is you gotta be bringin' beer and slingin' nachos while him and his boys watch it."

I remember trying to figure out a football game Mitch was watching on TV one Saturday afternoon years ago and suddenly realizing that the whole thing was still as confusing to me as the first contest my father tried to explain when I was about ten years old. I figured that was enough effort to understand a game I didn't even want to play, excused myself and never looked back. Life is short and football is not required.

"We ought to have an anti–Super Bowl party," Tomika said. "Let them have the day to themselves, period. Then, if they want to beat on somebody, at least it'll be a fair fight."

I looked at her. "That's a great idea."

"What?"

"What you just said. An anti–Super Bowl party."

She looked confused. "For real?"

"We could do it right here."

A look of confusion flickered across her face. "But we're not open on Sunday."

Having a great idea is one thing. Making it real is something else altogether. The social worker in me lives for these moments.

"We can be open anytime we want," I reminded her. "We voted on it, remember?" I'm big on participatory democracy. We vote on everything around here.

Tee was still a little skeptical, but I had piqued her interest. "I guess we could do *somethin'*," she said slowly. "Otherwise, I'ma have to hear everybody complainin' all week about how they hated watchin' it and which one of these fools hit somebody."

"We can get whatever we need tomorrow," I said.

"And I'll call everybody."

We sounded like one of those Judy Garland/Mickey Rooney movies where one looks at the other one about forty minutes into the movie and says, "Why don't we do our own show?" And the other one says, "We can hold auditions right here in the backyard!" And before you know it, they've run up some costumes, hired a band, and scheduled an opening night.

"Don't forget to tell Sheila," I said.

Tee snorted. "They ain't gonna let that girl out. Who gonna bring 'em a beer if she over here hangin' out wit us?"

She was probably right about that, but maybe we could sneak her out for a minute or two just to take a break.

"I gotta go, Miz J." Tee took her coat from the hook behind the door and slipped her arms in. It was almost Mavis's bedtime and Tee was big on bedtime stories ever since I told her that was how my mother taught me how to read. Tee wants to give that gift to Mavis. "But can I ask you something?"

"Sure." I handed her the scarf that had slipped from her sleeve to the floor.

She zipped her coat slowly and pulled on a pair of fur-lined red leather gloves, an extravagant gift from an out-of-town boyfriend who hid up here long enough to father Mavis and celebrate her first birthday, but not long enough to outwait the rival who shot him dead his first day back in the big city. The gloves were almost five years old now, but other than Mavis, they were all Tee had to remember him by, so they weren't going anywhere.

"It didn't go so good today in Lansing, did it?"

"It wasn't so bad," I said, sounding a little too cheery even to myself. "We'll figure it out."

She frowned at me and tossed her braids off her face impatiently. "How *we* gonna figure it out if *we* don't tell *me* what really went down?"

She had a point there. There was no reason not to tell her the truth. Withholding information isn't exactly like lying, but it's close enough.

"I'm sorry," I said, and I meant it. "I didn't want to worry you."

She snorted at that. "You the worrier, not me! What happened?"

"They didn't respect me or you or any of the work we're doing here," I said slowly, wanting to be clear, but not get hung up on the details. "So I withdrew our proposal."

Her eyes opened wide with surprise. She knew how hard I'd been working on it. "For real?"

I nodded.

She thought about that for a minute. "Because you didn't want them even considerin' us after what they said?"

"Exactly."

"It was that foul?"

"Pretty foul."

"So did you go off or did you just walk away?"

I smiled a little at the memory. "I went off a little and then I walked away."

"Did you cuss?"

I shook my head. "I was too righteous to cuss."

She grinned at me. "You know you can be righteous when you want to!"

I laughed, relieved she understood and didn't panic.

"I saw this comin'," she said.

"Saw what coming?"

"I knew they were gonna piss you off and I knew you were gonna tell 'em where to put they money and walk out."

"You're a psychic now?" I said.

She just shrugged. "No, but the way you were talkin' when you went to that grant class and those guys marked up your proposal with that red pen . . ."

I was surprised she remembered that, but she was absolutely right. That red pen had not endeared them to me. The last time somebody marked up something I had written in red ink was in high school and I didn't appreciate it then either. "How was I talking?"

"Like somebody whose last nerve was bein' worked on one time too many."

"So why didn't you warn me?"

"What was I gonna say? Miz J, *don't go down there askin' those white folks for no money!*" She shrugged again. "You had to try. We need the money, right?"

"Yeah, we do," I said. "I just hope I did the right thing."

She looked at me like she was surprised to have to remind me of something I should already know. "What do you always say when we're not sure about somethin'?"

I answered like a confident third grader about to win the spelling bee. "What would a free woman do?"

She grinned her approval. "So did you ask yourself that question?"

"Yes," I said, proud I had remembered one of the lessons I'm always so busy teaching. "I did."

"That's when you went off and walked out?"

I nodded.

"Well, then," Tee said, like the matter was settled. "It's all good!"

I laughed out loud because she was absolutely right. I had asked the required question, given myself an honest answer, and acted on it with finality and just the right amount of Amazonian indignation. What happens next is just that: what happens next. But Tee was right, for now, it's all good!

"How did you get so smart?" I said, hugging her at the door as she headed for home before Mavis was too sleepy for another few pages of *The Cat in the Hat.*

"I've been hanging around with you." She laughed. "How ya think?"

Which was, of course, the nicest thing anybody had said to me all day.

SEVEN

permanent shit list

I TRY NOT TO spend too much time being mad when things don't go according to plan. My personal experience is that things almost never go according to plan. Even a good plan. Accepting that as a fact of life instead of as evidence of the universe's personal grudge against me for unknown crimes saves me from having to waste a lot of time being angry, time which can then be spent solving the problems at hand.

Friday went by in a blur. I spent most of the day going over the books to see where I could cut corners instead of services and wondering how I could raise money for The Circus without pretending we are something we're not. Even though it was going to be tight for a while, I hadn't had any second thoughts about what happened at the committee. If you have any interest in maintaining your self-respect, there sometimes comes a moment where you just have to say *no*. This was one of those moments and, to tell the truth, I was sort of exhilarated by it.

Tee was busy calling everybody about the anti–Super Bowl party and it was clear this was an idea whose time had come. The response was overwhelming. I had never considered the use of football as an organizing tool for female empowerment, but maybe it was time to take a second look. Defiance is always one of the best emotions to tap into when you're asking powerless people to stand up for themselves. Turning our backs on football seemed made to order. Next year we ought to consciously program Monday nights during the regular season.

By six o'clock, we had confirmations from all of our regular members except Sheila Lattimore, whose mother had answered the phone when Tee called, said her daughter was busy on Sunday and hung up. I thought about stopping by there on my way to Sister's for dinner, but what's the point? Talking to Anita Lattimore is an exercise in futility. At forty, she's the mother of six and the grandmother of at least seven, maybe more. Ten years ago, when he was fifteen, Junior, her oldest, ended her years of violent abuse at the hands of his father by shooting him to death. The murder occurred in full view of the other Lattimore kids, who ranged in age from thirteen to five.

The court ruled it self-defense and allowed the family to stay together in the vain hope that, freed from the father's reign of terror, it could repair and rebuild itself. Unfortunately, Anita wasn't strong enough to do much besides get a job as a maid at the Motel 6 to keep a roof over their heads and minimal food on the table. She supplemented her income by turning tricks when the manager wasn't looking and becoming a willing partner in the many illegal get-rich-quick schemes that Junior dreamed up during his hours spent smoking dope, drinking beer and watching television on his mother's tattered living-room sofa.

Anita believed Junior had saved her life and for that she was his constant defender against any and all comers, including his siblings, his *babymamas* and whatever law enforcement and other agency officials found their way to her door. My appearing to ask that Sheila be allowed to join us for an anti–Super Bowl party would have been a fool's errand anyway. My relationship with Anita had deteriorated rapidly after I encouraged Patrice and Tiffany to file for child support from Sonny and T. J. Their mother's position was that since "those fast-ass girls" had "tricked" her boys into getting them pregnant in the first place, they had no business to expect money to start flowing now. When the family court did not agree, I earned a place on what she told me was her "permanent shit list." I didn't have *just dropped by to say hello* license at the Lattimore house anymore.

The truth is, at this moment, that's fine with me. I'm in no mood for a run-in with an angry matriarch. I'm in the mood for mango margaritas.

EIGHT

a con man's dream

I HEARD THE MUSIC as soon as I stepped out of the car. Something Latin. Bill and Sister were going to Havana with a group of ministers in August and their house had become a repository for all things Cuban. They were seasoned travelers who've spent at least two weeks out of the country every year since they met in graduate school. Bill says it's important to regularly remind yourself that the center of the world is not necessarily the piece of land where you happen to be standing.

Sister opened the door before I had a chance to knock, kissed my cold cheek and drew me quickly inside before the wind came in too. Bill, in baggy jeans and a big red sweater, was at the stereo programming a full evening of music in advance. I admire people who can use new technology effectively, but I still miss those old turntables with the plastic covers and the tone arm that could be set to repeat a single scratchy 45 forever. The day before we moved here from Detroit, I remember kissing Steven Robinson for three hours straight while the O'Jays sang "You are my sunshine" over and over until I thought I would surely die of desire right there in his parents' rec room.

"*Buenas noches,*" Sister said, smiling and taking my coat.

"*Buenas noches* to you." Never let it be said that I am not an international woman.

Sister was wearing a pair of billowy orange pants, a purple silk tunic and a pair of embroidered Chinese slippers. Her braids were tied at the nape of her neck with a bright strip of kente cloth, and delicate filigree hoops sparkled in her ears. She looked—there is no better word for it—*festive*. I felt like a strange black moth dropped into the middle of a butterfly's nest.

"Listen to these guys," Bill said, already shouting to be heard across the room and then turning up the volume another notch so we could fully appreciate the sublime harmonies of the Buena Vista Social Club, a group of legendary Cuban musicians, average age seventy-five.

My Spanish pretty much begins and ends with *buenas noches* but I recognize a broken heart when I hear one.

"He's been playing these guys nonstop," Sister said. "Turn it down a little, sweetie, would you?"

"They give me hope for old guys," Bill said, reluctantly returning the sound to a more conversational pitch.

"What's he saying?"

Bill closed his eyes, placed his hand over his heart dramatically and did the simultaneous translation.

"A broken shadow/without you, Only the twilight accompanies me now. Now your love is gone/there is no happiness for me."

The music ended on a note of perfect longing and Bill sighed with satisfaction and glided across the room to give me a welcome squeeze. Among his many talents, Bill is a world-class *hugger.*

"Where you been, girl? Are you brightening up some other parlors besides our own?"

"No chance," I said. "This is by far my favorite parlor for at least a couple of hundred miles."

Bill laughed. "Perfect answer, and deserving of a perfect margarita."

"Sit," Sister said, poking the logs in the fireplace as he disappeared into the kitchen and I sank into a cozy corner of her pillow-strewn sofa. Her earrings glowed in the firelight against the copper-colored smoothness of her cheek. Sister and Bill were about the same height and built sort of round. Not *fat.* Just *cozy.* Hugging either one of them always felt like home. "We've got a fourth coming."

She said it real casual, like we were entering a bridge tournament, but I was immediately on the alert. She denies it, but Sister is one of those people who is so happy with her partner, she wants to see the rest of the world, including me, paired off as quickly as possible.

She's tried to set me up a couple of times with people she thought might be good potential mates, each time with disastrous results.

"You never learn, do you?" I said.

"I don't know what you're talking about," she said.

"Who is he?"

"His name is Nate Anderson," she said. "He's the new vice principal up at the high school. He's only been here two weeks."

"He missed the whole first semester? Sounds like a dedicated educator, all right."

"It wasn't his fault," Sister said. "They didn't even offer him the job until after Thanksgiving."

That was typical. The schools around here seem to fling open their doors in the fall and hope for the best. Half the time they don't have enough teachers and the administrative turnover is ridiculous. I can't blame the ones who leave, though. There's never enough money and always too much work. Throw in some unmotivated students and uninvolved parents and what's not to love?

"He's living in a motel until he can find a house to rent."

"A house?"

She nodded. "That's what he told Bill."

"Think he'd be interested in the Smitherman place?"

"I'm sure he would," Sister said immediately. "That's a great idea."

The Smitherman twins, ancient, alabaster aristocrats, lived in a beautiful two-story house across the lake from my place, but they had a smaller house, on a smaller lake, that they rented out. I knew it was empty because the last tenant had been instructed to leave the key with me a couple of months ago when the end of his lease coincided with the twins' annual theater and museum trip to New York and Chicago. I still had it hanging on a hook in my kitchen. If he seemed personable, they'd probably be happy to have him move in right away.

"So what's he like?" I said.

"Seems like a nice guy. I met him the other day when I went to pick up Bill. He was in the gym lifting weights."

"Lifting weights?" When I was in high school, the vice principal was a white-haired old guy who specialized in calling your parents for the slightest infraction, a disciplinary method that earned him the nickname "the Tattler." The heaviest lifting he did was to take the Texas fifth of vodka out of the freezer to make himself a good, stiff drink at day's end.

"When's his wife coming?"

Sister looked startled by the question. "His wife?"

"He's married, right?"

Sister busied herself at the fireplace again. "He's divorced, I think."

"You *think?*" This evening was looking more and more like another ill-fated attempt to play Cupid.

"How old is he?"

Sister shrugged. "I don't know. Ask Bill."

Her husband reappeared as if on cue with a small tray of perfectly frosted margaritas. "Ask Bill what?"

"How old is your friend?"

"Nate?" Bill handed me a cold glass and frowned slightly like the question had never occured to him. "I don't know."

"What's your best guess?" I said. Bill is great on the big, cosmic questions, but the more mundane details like names, dates, ages and marital status tend to escape him.

"Somewhere between twenty-five and fifty."

Sister laughed and shook her head. "You're a big help!"

"You can ask him yourself as soon as he gets here," Bill said. "But for now—*cheers!*"

We clinked our glasses lightly and I took a long, cold swallow and sighed. Whatever the ingredients of Bill's special margaritas, he had done nothing to overpower the delicate flavor of the fruit.

"Well?" Bill was grinning at me like he knew exactly how wonderful this frozen concoction really was.

"As long as you can make something that tastes this good, you don't have to keep up with the details!" I said.

"Thank you!" Bill beamed. He responded to praise like that cartoon *Precious Pup*—glad all over.

"I'm going to do the salad before Nate gets here," Sister said, heading for the kitchen. "Tell Joyce about your new poem."

A week ago, Bill had told me he had decided to compose a cycle of love poems dedicated to Sister. It must be going well. When he was blocked, asking Bill about his writing was unwise.

The music had changed. More drums. More horns. Faster guitars. If I was a dancing woman, I'd have been tempted to make this one a ladies' choice, but I've always been too self-conscious to enjoy anything in public but the kind of slow grind that's only allowed after midnight in the darkest corners of a blue-light basement party where nobody sees and nobody cares. Bill wasn't that kind of friend and this definitely wasn't that kind of music. This music needed a hot night, a crowded dance floor and a lack of inhibition that only happens in my dreams.

"Bamboleo," Bill said, reading my mind and naming the group for me.

"They're great," I said. "Tell me about the poem."

"I thought you'd never ask." He sat down and took a slow breath, suddenly serious. "It's the epic saga of an ancient African warrior king who journeys through time and space to find himself marooned in twenty-first-century America until he can fight his way home."

I was confused. "I thought you were writing love poems."

"It is a love poem," he said brightly.

"Oh." None of what he had said sounded remotely like love to me.

"A love of destiny and history and a man's place in it. A love of the monumental battles between good and evil, right and wrong, through which every generation of males must test itself and put forward their own definition of manhood."

Oh, Lord! Even a perfect margarita doesn't require me to let this kind of stuff slide. "Where are the women?"

Bill smiled confidently like he had already considered this question. "The women are engaged elsewhere in battles of their own to which I, as a mere man, could not be expected to be privy."

I started sputtering immediately, not realizing he was teasing me until a timer dinged in the distance and he stood up, laughing.

"See there!" he said, heading for kitchen before Sister could start stirring things that were supposed to be left alone. "Just like a black woman! Always prepared to believe a brother is afraid to confront the real questions!"

"You wouldn't know a love poem if it hit you in the head," I called after him, laughing in spite of myself. Bill liked to tease me about almost everything, especially the mysterious dance that always ensues when men and women find themselves in the same house/same room/same bed. I was the perfect foil, passionate and gullible; a con man's dream.

The fire shifted and rearranged itself, dislodging one small, glowing log. I stood up to replace it among the others and caught sight of my sister's wedding picture on the mantel. That was a night when *everybody* danced. Bill was in charge of the music then too and he had something for everybody, including a late-night segment that sounded very close to what I was hearing right now. By that time, most of the kids were asleep and the oldsters had drifted away home. The rest of us were involved in a collective perfect moment and had sense enough to surrender and enjoy it.

I turned up the music a little, remembering, swaying in spite of myself. This is my night off, after all. These are my good friends and this music is *cookin'!* I swayed a little more. Was Ava's wedding really the last time I danced? *That was three years ago!* What's that Emma Goldman quote that makes such a great button: "If your revolution doesn't include dancing, I'm not interested"? She had a point there.

The vocalists on Bill's CD had kicked the beat up another notch. Their mission seemed to be to make you throw caution to the winds and *shake it.* Knowing Bill would take it as a compliment and not a sign of insanity, I cranked the music up another few notches and started dancing around all by myself. I shimmied around the couch. I grabbed my skirt and sashayed between the wingback chairs. I shook my shoulders in front of the poinsettia sitting on the coffee table, and the more I danced, the better I felt.

I positioned myself directly between Bill's giant floor speakers, closed my eyes and let that Cuban music take me where it wanted me to go. Suddenly, this *was* Havana. The air was soft and warm. The night was young and I was wearing the most amazing red dress. . . .

The tap on my shoulder almost scared me out of my wits. I jumped a foot in the air and turned to face a *gigantic* stranger. He had to be six seven or eight, deep mahogany brown, and thick around the chest and shoulders like somebody who keeps in shape and then some. His deep brown eyes were clear and curious and rimmed with eyelashes that were so long they would have been feminine without the strength of his nose and his big square chin. His great big head was completely bald and there was one small gold hoop in his left ear.

He was smiling a *don't worry, I'm not dangerous* smile, so I reached over to turn down the volume.

"I knocked," he rumbled pleasantly from somewhere way down in that great big chest. "I don't guess anybody heard it."

"You startled me," I said, wondering what it felt like to be that tall. I extended my hand and made a mental note to ask Sister if there was any particular reason why she had neglected to mention that, in addition to being huge, he was undeniably *fine*. Being religious does not make you blind, just like being a widow does not make you oblivious, especially when you've been drinking mango margaritas.

"I'm Joyce."

"Nate Anderson," he rumbled.

We shook hands, mine disappearing completely inside his giant paw, and he grinned at me like we already shared a secret. "Nice music."

"Thanks," I said, feeling suddenly sixteen for no good reason, except maybe the fact that I can't remember the last time I spent an evening with an attractive man who wasn't twice my age, or half of it, or married to my best friend. I wondered how long he'd been standing there.

"Are you a dancer?"

Among the five most flattering questions I can imagine being asked, "Are you a dancer?" is definitely at the top of the list.

I laughed. "No. I guess I was just feeling *festive*."

"Great," he said. "Festive is one of my favorites."

"What happened to the music?" Bill came out of the kitchen

and spotted Nate. "Hey, brother! Didn't hear you come in! Good thing I wasn't talking bad about you."

"Just walked in," Nate said, slipping gracefully out of his coat and handing it to Bill. "I was complimenting Joyce on the music."

Bill was delighted. "You into *timba brava?*"

"I grew up listening to it," Nate said. "My father liked everything about Cuba except Castro. He took the revolution *personal.*"

"Was he Cuban?"

Nate shook his head. "He was a Pullman porter, but he used to travel as a personal valet to some black gangsters who went down to Havana two or three times a year. Castro put an end to all that in '59. My father never forgave him."

Sister walked in from the kitchen wiping her hands on a dish towel. When she saw Nate, her face lit up in a warm smile.

"Just in time," she said. "Welcome!"

"Thank you," he said.

Sister turned to me. "Did you meet Joyce?"

"He caught me doing what I thought was a very private mambo," I said, looking at how tiny Sister looked standing beside him.

Bill was delighted. "You were dancing?"

"Good for you," said Sister quickly, heading Bill off at the pass before he could start teasing me again. "Why don't you get Nate something to drink?"

"Sure," Bill said, not through with me by a long shot. "You're not going to break out again while I'm out of the room, are you?"

"I'll try to restrain myself," I said.

Nate stood leaning easily against the mantel, smiling and looking big. I sat down on the couch wondering how many times he's been asked about the weather up there, and how long I could resist the temptation to inquire.

"Sit down, sit down," Sister said. "You have any trouble finding us?"

Nate shook his big head, which was perfectly shaped without any lumps, rolls or razor bumps, and claimed a space at the other end of the couch. I waited for the end I was sitting on to rise up like a teeter-totter.

"Not a bit," he said. "I've been finding my way around pretty good, so far. Once I figure out which roads dead-end at the lakes, I'll be fine."

That's the biggest frustration for newcomers. A street that begins in a dense grove of pine trees can open up into a sandy strip of beach with no warning.

"The only good thing about getting lost up here," I said as Bill returned with a frosted glass for Nate and a pitcher to refresh the rest of our drinks, "is that anybody you ask can probably tell you how to get where you're going."

"Men never get lost," Bill said. "Didn't anybody ever teach you that?"

"No," I said. "I must have been absent that day."

"How's the house hunting?" Sister sounded sympathetic.

Nate groaned. "I haven't had time to make much progress. I'm still at the Motel 6."

"All the way out on the highway?" I said.

He nodded. "I've been at the school until late every day, so I haven't really had time to look around."

"I know a place you might be interested in," I said. "It's lakefront. Is that okay?"

He smiled. "That's a trick question, right?"

"Why?"

"Given a chance, is there anybody who doesn't want to have water outside their front window?"

I wondered if he liked to swim, but I refused to allow myself to imagine how he'd look in a bathing suit. "If you're going to be at the school tomorrow, I can drop off the key and the directions. You can go over and take a look."

"I'll make it a point to be there," he said, looking relieved.

"Good," I said. "Around four-thirty or so?"

"Great!"

He was practically beaming. Sister was too, but I ignored her. I was just being *neighborly*.

"Well, there you go," Bill said. "The beauty of small-town living."

Nate nodded his agreement. "Absolutely!"

"So other than the Motel 6," I said, "how do you like it up here so far?"

"It's great," he said enthusiastically, clasping and unclasping his big hands. "I was really ready to get out of the city for a while."

"How long have you been teaching?"

I wondered how students reacted when they encountered him in the hallways of Baldwin High. It made me remember the scene in *The Green Mile* where Michael Clarke Duncan's character first enters the prison and the white guards behold this black behemoth in tattered overalls and immediately share one thought: *What the hell are we gonna do if this big Negro goes off?* Nate was that kind of big.

"Five years," he said. "I was a Detroit beat cop for six years before that, until it occurred to me that my time might be better spent trying to interpret these young brothers *before* I had to put the cuffs on them."

"Well, don't give up on those cuffs just yet," Bill said. "The semester's just getting started good."

"Stop being cynical," I said. "He just got here!"

"Thank you," Nate said. "If I wanted to be cynical, I could have stayed in Detroit."

"That's no challenge," Bill said. "It's easy being cynical in a place like Detroit. Up here, it takes a much greater effort."

Nate laughed, a sound not unlike the rumble of thunder. "But it's not *required*, right?"

"Not only is it not required," Sister said. "On this particular night, it's absolutely forbidden!"

"Amen!" I chimed in.

Bill turned to Nate with a rueful grin. "See what happens when you get two or more women together in one place? They start outlawing things!"

"Our dispositions improve dramatically when we're well fed," I said, feeling a little light-headed after two margaritas on an almost empty stomach and the unanticipated rush of adrenaline Nate's appearance had precipitated.

"Then I have only one more thing to say." Bill stood up and looked at his watch.

We all looked at him expectantly.

"Dinner is served!"

NINE

another kind of test

IF YOU COUNT THE mangoes, Nate was my second surprise in as many days. He was smart and funny and he had opinions without being overbearing. Conversation at dinner ranged from the plans for our anti–Super Bowl party to his stint as a Detroit cop, to my recent misadventures in the hallowed halls of government, to Bill's poem-in-progress and Sister's hope to do an Idlewild oral history before too many more of her members made their transitions and took their stories with them.

By the time we moved back into the living room with coffee and Sister's homemade apple pie, we were talking like old friends, and I had almost gotten used to the way he towered over the rest of us, even when we were sitting down.

"Aren't you afraid you'll get bored in a little town like this?" I said to Nate, taking the seat next to him on the couch.

"That's sort of the whole point, isn't it?" he said.

"Boredom?" Sister sounded surprised, curling up like a cat in her favorite chair.

"No," Nate said, watching Bill add another log to the fire. "The fact that it's a little town. You can still make a real difference in a place this size. That means a lot to me."

Bill sat down on the arm of Sister's chair. "Don't start romanticizing, brother. It ain't Detroit, but it ain't Nirvana either."

Nate smiled. "I don't know as much as you all do about Idlewild yet, but I can tell you this. The big cities are gone and most of the middle-size towns are already touch and go. If we can't figure out how to fix what's broke in a little bitty place like this, we might as well just throw in the towel."

"That's not an option," Sister said, always the optimist.

"It's never a conscious choice," Nate said slowly, looking into the fire and choosing his words carefully. "The jobs dry up and the businesses move elsewhere and the trash doesn't get collected anymore and the jails are too crowded and there's crack everywhere. . . ."

That sure sounded like Detroit. Last time I drove down with Sister, I stopped at a traffic light and every person that passed in front of my car had that gray, frantic, *too skinny to be alive much longer* look that is all the identification crackheads require.

"But it doesn't happen all on the same day." Nate was looking at me, and I looked right back. "It happens little by little and you accommodate it like that, little by little, until one day, you look up and you're living in a war zone."

He turned back to Sister. "When I was a cop we always dreaded Halloween because that's when the young brothers collectively lose their minds. They rob the trick-or-treaters. They do home invasions when people open their front doors to give out candy. They throw concrete blocks off the freeway overpasses, and they set lots of fires."

I knew he wasn't exaggerating. Seven years ago, I was there for a conference. You could look out the window of the hotel and see the flames. I remember the sound of sirens and the smell of smoke.

Bill draped an arm around the back of Sister's chair and frowned. "I thought all that stopped after the Million Man March."

That's what I had thought too. I remember pictures of black men in groups of three and four standing, unarmed, on the corners of their communities, keeping watch, keeping peace, doing what good men are supposed to do, keeping an eye on the others so they don't act a fool.

"Two years." Nate shook his head like he was still incredulous at how quickly things went back to normal, if burning down your own neighborhood can be classified as normal, even in Detroit. "That's as long as the brothers could sustain the effort. First year, they had patrols on every corner. Second year, they had less than half that many. By the third year, we were the only people on the street again. Just cops, and a few little kids whose parents didn't care that they were out trying to trick-or-treat on a battlefield."

Raising sane children in a place like that must be like learning how to swim in a whirlpool, I thought. Maybe it's not impossible, but close enough.

"I think," Bill said into the silence, "that every generation of men looks to test itself in battle. These young brothers didn't have an outside war, so they made up one in their backyard."

I never understood the idea of war as a manhood test. It requires and develops such a specific set of skills that the next question has to be how do you translate the things that make a great soldier into the things that women want and children need from that very same man once the war is over?

At this point, brothers usually remind me that the war is *not* over, and I can't argue with that, but I also know the most lethal campaign being waged by black men is not against white men. It's against the women they say they love and the children they don't make time to care for——and what kind of manhood test is that?

This line of reasoning was not going to do much for my disposition. Besides, Sister had said no worrying allowed tonight, so I turned to her for assistance.

"You think they'd be open to another kind of manhood test," I said, hoping she'd follow my lead. "A dance contest or something?"

She grinned at me like she knew exactly what I was doing. "How about karaoke?"

"Good one," I said. "Or bid whist."

"Double Dutch," she said, nodding. "Snow shoveling."

We were on a roll. Bill and Nate, unsure of the proper response to this sudden swerve toward frivolity, looked at each other uncertainly.

"Hula-Hoops," I said, looking at Nate. "Pie eating."

"I think," Bill said slowly, "this means it's time to change the subject."

Nate looked at me real hard and then he grinned a grin as big as he was and held out his plate to Sister. "Speak for yourself, man. I'm a pie-eatin' somethin' when I put my mind to it!"

We all laughed then, partly because it was funny, but partly because forgetting how to have a good time on Saturday night is as lethal as smoking crack. It just takes a little longer to kill you.

TEN

all i can do

"I LIKE HIM," SISTER said after we had all reluctantly decided it was time to say good night and Nate had headed back to the Motel 6.

"I liked him too."

Bill, as always the perfect combination of liberated partner and traditional husband, had gone outside to brush the snow off my windshield and warm up the car. The idea of staying inside his cozy kitchen while I scraped the back window would never have occurred to him. He saw me watching out the window and blew me a kiss. Bill loves an audience.

"I thought you might," Sister said.

She was holding my coat with a look of pure innocence, which didn't fool me for a second.

"Stop matchmaking. I'm old enough to be his mother."

"You are not!" she said. "He's forty if he's a day."

"He's thirty, *max*," I said, zipping up my coat. "Thanks for dinner. Next time, my place."

"Shall we invite Nate?"

"Sure," I said, remembering the low rumble of his laugh and wondering how much bigger he'd look in the confines of my tiny kitchen. "The more the merrier."

"Good," she said, beaming.

"You're incorrigible! Good night!" I laughed, slipping out fast to let in a minimum of cold air and to cut off any further conversation about Nate's romantic potential. I liked him, but I wasn't looking for a boyfriend. I had the best and I'm not greedy. Besides, Sister's wrong. I know plenty of fifteen-year-old mothers.

Bill was patiently scraping the ice from my back windshield.

"Want some help?" I said.

He shook his head, chipping away methodically at the last stubborn corner. "You're wrong, you know."

"About what?"

"About me not knowing any love poems."

"Oh, yeah?" I said, lobbing a soft snowball in his general direction. "Let's hear one."

"Poets don't work on demand," he said, dodging it easily. "You should know that."

The air was so cold and clear I wanted to drink it like water. "Then what good are they?"

That made him laugh. "Philistine!" he said, finishing up and stashing the scraper back in the trunk. "Okay! Here's one just for you."

He closed his eyes and touched his right temple lightly like he was receiving a transmission from Venus.

"A Poem for Joyce," he said, starting slowly, as all things associated with love are wont to do. "This woman/who cannot
surrender/without freedom/who will not surrender/without
peace . . ." He hesitated for a moment, searching for the right
words, finding them. "This woman is so brand new/It's all I can
do . . ." He opened his eyes triumphantly. "Just to love her."

"Show-off!" I said, kissing his cold cheek.

"Watch it." He pointed to Sister smiling in the window. "My
wife doesn't play that stuff."

"Your wife is a saint," I said, climbing into my car.

"That's what you think," Bill said, grinning as he slammed
the door behind me and took his back steps two at a time.

And just for a minute, I was jealous of their closeness; envious
of the fact that after they cleared the table and washed the
dishes, they were going to crawl into bed with each other to ward
off the chill. It's been so long since I've fallen asleep with someone's arms around me that I should be used to sleeping alone, but
I guess it's like getting older. No matter how many times you celebrate those postforty birthdays, you're never quite ready to *greet
that woman of a certain age* looking back at you from the bathroom mirror.

ELEVEN

better than that

"DID YOU KNOW I was named after a poet?" Nikki Solomon said as soon as I walked into The Circus the next morning. Tomika had opened up early and Mavis was watching a video of *The Lion King* in the community room until her friends arrived, which on Saturday, was usually about noon. When she saw me, she waved and pointed enthusiastically at the TV screen.

"Nala!" She smiled, her pleasure in the big-eyed female cub undiminished after more viewings than she or I could count. I waved back and threw her a kiss.

"Don't change the subject!" Tee said while I hung up my coat. "We ain't talkin' 'bout no poetry."

Nikki rolled her eyes and frowned. Tall and voluptuous with dark velvety skin and big smoky eyes, she was widely acknowledged to be the prettiest girl in Lake County, but this morning she looked edgy and tired.

"Ask her about her new job, Miz J." Tee sounded a little edgy herself.

"Can you just chill for a second"—Nikki looked annoyed—"and let me tell her my own news in my own way?"

That's not a good sign, I thought. "In my own way" means putting the best face on something that is probably a very bad move.

Nik's mother went to high school with me. Jasmine was a beautiful girl who grew up thinking that was all she needed to be. She moved to Detroit after we graduated and married a man who agreed with her, had Nikki and started eating. She gained a hundred pounds in one year, and her husband, taking that to mean their contract was null and void, divorced her, kissed his daughter good-bye and headed for the West Coast, leaving no forwarding address. Jasmine packed up, skipped out on her last month's rent and moved back here.

Nikki inherited her mother's good looks, and by the time she hit puberty, she was a real beauty. When Junior Lattimore spotted her in his sister's gym class, he demanded and got an introduction, swept her off her fourteen-year-old feet with his eighteen-and-a-half-year-old thuggish charm and the rest is history.

I tried to get the conversation back on a positive note.

"You found a job?" I knew she had been looking, but there aren't many jobs around for nineteen-year-old women with limited literacy and only the most cursory understanding of basic job skills. "Where?"

Nikki looked uncomfortable. She twisted the poetry book miserably in her hands, its diversionary potential useless in the face of Tomika's relentless demand for the truth—*the whole truth and nothing but the truth.*

"At that new place out by the interstate."

Tomika snorted rudely. The two of them had grown up together and they fought like friends but forgave like family.

"Which one?" I tried to picture which of the fast-food emporiums had decided to unleash the undeniably high-strung Nikki on their unsuspecting customers.

She didn't answer right away, casting one last look at Tomika, who rejected the unspoken plea for a little slack.

"Don't be lookin' at me all pitiful," Tee said. "You took the job, so *represent.*"

"It's a club," Nik said carefully.

"A nightclub?"

"Sort of, but it's open in the daytime, so I won't always have to be workin' late."

She offered this last with a hopeful look and I smiled encouragingly. "That's good, right?"

"Go on!" said Tomika.

"Go on *what?*" Nikki snapped at her. "I'm not talkin' fast enough for you?"

"You're not talkin' straight enough for me, how's that?"

"Maybe I should go out and come in again," I said.

"You ain't gotta do all that," Nikki said. "Tee just mad 'cause she don't think I should be dancin' and I don't see nothin' wrong with it, and besides, *it ain't her decision to make.*"

"Dancing?"

"*Strippin',* Miz J. She scared to say it, but that's what she gettin' ready to do for a livin'. Let these niggas watch her take her clothes off!"

"At least I'm gettin' paid for it!"

Tomika just looked at her. "I wouldn't be braggin' about no shit like that if I were you."

"But you *ain't* me, okay?"

"Hold it," I said, more sharply than I meant to. I turned to Nikki. "You're working at a strip club?"

"Yes, but it's strictly legit! They even got dressin' rooms and a bouncer."

A bouncer?

"And ain't nobody sellin' no drugs up in there either."

I wanted to say, *Girl, where is that community college application I gave you? Have you filled it out yet?* But I made myself ask the only relevant question first. "Do you want my opinion?"

She hesitated. "Will you be mad if I say no?"

I shook my head.

"Then *no!*"

"All right then," I said. "Good luck and be careful."

Tee looked at me like I had lost my mind, but I try to be real clear with myself and with them about this whole advice thing. I only give it when they want to hear it. Sometimes, it's hard for me to watch the things they do and not offer an opinion, but they're not children. I figure everybody has the right to figure out how they're going to pay their own rent.

"That's it?" Tomika sounded incredulous. "'Good luck and be careful'?"

"What would you suggest?"

"Tell her what you think!"

"What's the difference between that and giving advice?"

She looked completely exasperated with me. "Givin' advice is tellin' people what to do. Sayin' what you think is more of a *this is how I see it* kinda thing."

Nikki was watching us with interest, glad the focus was off of her, even temporarily.

"Show me," I said.

Tee looked at me, then turned to Nikki and flipped her braids over her shoulder. "Okay, here's the advice. *Quit!* Go tell them you quit and don't do no more stupid shit like that as long as you live!" She took a deep breath. "But here's what I think." Her voice was calm. "I think you deserve better than that, Nik. I really do. That's why you need to quit. Not because it's danger-ous or crazy or nothin' else except for the fact that you *better than that.*" She leaned over and hugged Nikki, who hugged her back, hard, then stepped away quickly and left the room without a word.

Neither one of us spoke for a minute and then I picked up the poetry book that had been left behind.

"Nikki Giovanni," I said, remembering when I gave this book to Jasmine back when we were both in high school, amazed she still had it and even more amazed it had taken her almost twenty years to share it with her daughter. "That's the poet she's named after."

Tomika, at the window, didn't say anything. She was watch-ing Nik get into her car and drive off toward the danger just like they always do in the horror movies; gripping the wheel, gritting her teeth and swearing she doesn't believe in ghosts.

TWELVE

busted

EVERYTHING WAS IN PLACE for the anti–Super Bowl party tomorrow. All I had to do now was drop off the keys I'd promised Nate and do my grocery shopping. Otherwise, dinner was looking like another round of leftovers and that wasn't going to get it.

I was looking forward to a night to myself. It was my intention to take a long hot bath, make a fire and see how much of *Booty Call* I could get through before I fell asleep. I've been trying to keep up with as many of the young actors as I can. My current interest was Vivica A. Fox. I admired her work in *Why Do Fools Fall in Love?*, especially her character's vulnerability even as the woman's life added harder and harder layers.

I liked her even more in *Set It Off,* especially when she gets angry at the timid girl in the gang after their first successful bank robbery. She denies her a share of the money but then comes back to apologize, saying "it's not you I'm mad at" with the perfect blend of rage and resignation.

I liked her in *Independence Day* too, and appreciated the dignity she maintained even when they made her do a scene backstage at the strip joint with her incredible body fully on display. So when I heard she had made a movie called *Booty Call,* I wondered why. I hoped taking a look at it might help me understand.

When I pulled up to Baldwin High School at four-thirty, the building was empty. All the team practices and Saturday activities were over, but Nate had told me he'd be lifting weights, so I headed for the gym. I graduated from this school and the halls are full of good memories. When we moved here, I was fifteen and about to start my sophomore year. I left behind a boyfriend who I had allowed to kiss me passionately whenever we could find a place to do so, which wasn't that often since neither of us could drive and my parents were not about me having company when they weren't home. I knew better than to even *think* about going to my boyfriend's house when his parents weren't there, since I was lovesick but not crazy.

The only time we broke the rule was right before my family left town and we were desperate to express what we regarded as undying love before my father's dreams ripped ours to shreds. We spent an endless, sweaty, nerve-racking afternoon trying to get as close to having sex as we could without removing a single article of clothing. A week later, I arrived a Baldwin High, lonely, heartbroken and convinced the best part of my life was over. Then I met Mitch and realized how wrong a person could be.

I opened the big double doors to the boys' gym and Tupac Shakur's voice brought me up short with its unique combination of rage and defiance and love and confusion and a sensuality so specifically black and male that he still stands alone, all these years after the tragedy of his death.

At the far end of the room, Nate was doing sit-ups on an incline bench with his hands behind his head. He was wearing black sweatpants and a sleeveless T-shirt that said PISTONS on the back and, even at this distance, gave me an unobstructed view of his huge arms and gigantic shoulders. From where I was standing, they looked to be sculpted of dark mahogany. Still unaware of my presence, he stood up and stretched to his full height. His massive size, plus the macho music and the smell of generations of young male bodies, bathed in sweat and ruled by raging hormones, joined forces to make me feel like a female interloper in an environment geared to another sensibility altogether.

That's when he turned around and saw me, waved and headed in my direction, stopping to turn down the boom box so Tupac was a whisper not a shout, and we could greet each other without shouting.

"Hey," he said, smiling, seeming to get bigger and bigger the closer he got until I realized I actually had to look up if I didn't want to spend our conversation gazing at his nipple line. "How long have you been here?"

"I just walked in," I said. "I didn't want to stop you. . . ."

Up close, he was so beautiful and alive that I wanted to touch his skin, stroke his shoulders, tug that earring in his ear. I could practically feel the heat coming off of him in waves. How old was he anyway? If I could establish once and for all that he was out of the range of age acceptability, maybe I could stop this involuntary lusting after him before it got completely out of hand.

"I was almost finished," he said, wiping the sweat off his

forehead with a massive forearm. "Takes a little longer to keep everything together once you get past forty."

Past forty? Well, that eliminates the *old enough to be his mother* defense. I was on my own, staring temptation in the face, or, more accurately, in the chest.

"Of course, you don't know anything about that," he said, endearing himself to me forever, even if he was teasing, maybe flirting just a little.

"Right," I said, laughing and handing him an envelope that contained the keys, the alarm codes and directions to the house. "That's everything."

"Great," he said. "Maybe I'll go by there on my way home tonight." He grimaced slightly.

"What's wrong?"

"Nothing," he shook his head ruefully. "I don't want to start thinking of the Motel 6 as home."

I nodded sympathetically. "I understand. It's kind of like thinking of McDonald's as dinner."

"Exactly!" He looked pleased that I understood.

"I think you'll like this house."

"Have you been in it?"

He still doesn't understand how small this town is.

"The owners are friends of mine."

"How tall are the ceilings?"

I shrugged, trying to remember. "Just regular, I guess. About like Sister and Bill's."

He looked relieved. "Good. I looked at a place when I first got here and I swear the ceiling was less than eight feet. I felt like it was resting on top of my head."

Here was my opening. He'd brought it up without any prompting from me, so a follow-up comment was not out of line.

"How tall are you?"

"Six eight."

Why did that make me blush? Maybe because he was standing there, sweating and looking so effortlessly sexy that my brain couldn't help going back to the question we would have had to ask each other if he had shown up when we were sixteen-year-old virgins without a clue: *If his feet are that big and his hands are that big, what about his ...?*

"I think you're the tallest person I've ever met," I said.

He grinned down at me. "How tall are you?"

"Five six," I said, adding half an inch in self-defense.

"Well, I'll make you a deal."

"What's that?" I was trying unsuccessfully not to look at his arms, his shoulders, the way his big, wide back tapered down so dramatically that he looked like the mustachioed strong man in the old circus cartoons.

"If you don't ask me 'how's the weather up there?' I promise not to call you 'shorty.' " Even without the biceps, his smile was worth the price of admission.

I laughed. "It's a deal, but I have to confess that the night I met you at Sister's, it was the first thing that popped into my mind."

He groaned.

"Sorry," I said, "but at least I managed to restrain myself."

"At least that's something, I guess," he said, still smiling that megawatt smile.

"The house lights are on a timer so you don't need to turn anything on or off when you leave," I said.

The Smitherman sisters weren't due back from New York for another week. In the meantime, I could handle the transaction and present his occupancy as a fait accompli when they returned.

"Thanks," he said, folding his arms across his chest. I wondered if he wore his earring when school was in session. He had it on now, and even in his workout clothes, it gave him the look of an exceptionally fit pirate.

"I'd better get going," I said, wondering how long it would take for me to get used to his size. More than two days, obviously. "Let me know what you think after you take a look at the house."

"I'll call you tomorrow," he said immediately.

The Motel 6 must really be working his nerves. I could picture his feet hanging off the end of the bed; the mirrors reflecting him only from the shoulders down.

"All right," I said, heading for the door. "I'll be at The Circus most of the day."

He fell in step beside me easily. For someone who had worked up a good sweat, he wasn't the least bit funky. When we got to the door, he reached to open it for me.

"Don't step out," I said, sounding maternal. "You'll catch cold."

"I'll be careful," he said, watching me like Gregory Hines keeping an appreciative eye on Loretta Devine in *Waiting to Exhale* as she goes home to make him a plate of fried chicken, collard greens, candied yams, a slice of ham and some cobbler. He watched me all the way down to the end of the hallway. How do I know that? Because when I turned around to check, he waved.

Busted! I thought, and I didn't even care.

THIRTEEN

first thought, best thought

THE SUPER BOWL STARTED at four, but we told everybody they were welcome anytime after noon, so I went over early to open up and turn on the heat. The pale sunlight was promising another cold January day, but no snow was predicted until tomorrow.

I didn't see the small bag hanging from The Circus doorknob until I reached for it to put my key in. It was a soft sack made of purple velvet and tied at the neck with a golden cord. *Sister's been by here.*

I took the bag inside and laid it on my desk, turned up the heat and flipped on the lights. The place had never looked better. At the far end of the community room, Tee had gathered all the toys in one big play area. On the low table we use for the kids, she put out our collection of puzzles, the communal coloring books

and a huge box of crayons. Picture books were arranged magazine style on a freshly painted rack and a trio of uniformly
chocolate-brown baby dolls sat in their tiny plastic high chairs
waiting for someone to give them their even tinier plastic bottles.

At the other end of the room, we had set up the VCR and
stacked sitting pillows nearby for easy access and comfortable
viewing. We watch a lot of movies around here. It's usually
pretty easy to spot somebody making a bad choice in the movies.
That's why we all holler when the terminally naïve teenage victim skips off to picnic in the woods. My hope is that if they can
recognize preventable foolishness on the screen, the lessons they
learn will carry over into their real lives.

Of course, I'd rather they got some of this information from
reading classics like *The Color Purple* and *I Know Why the
Caged Bird Sings*, but as my mother used to say, if wishes were
horses then beggars would ride. Once I told my mother she
should collect all her sayings and write them down and she said
writing books for black folks was like doing sleight of hand for
the blind. My father told her to stop being cynical, but she just
rolled her eyes. My mother was not what you would call "a race
woman."

Waiting to Exhale was the first movie I tried to get them to
analyze. All of our regulars were here that day: Tee, Nikki,
Tiffany Smith, Patrice O'Neal, Sherika Hill, Sheila Lattimore,
Deena Anderson and Regina Johnson. At first everybody said
what sets all the bad stuff in motion is when the philandering
husband informs his wife that he won't be taking her to the company Christmas party because his mistress doesn't want to be
alone and "she shouldn't have to be."

"Plus," Nikki had said, rolling her eyes, "to add insult to
injury, she's a *white* woman."

I agreed that was a pretty terrible moment, but I argued that things had gone bad long before he appeared in the mirror over his wife's shoulder wearing that beautiful tux and a look that said whatever the problem was, it was all her fault.

"When was it, then?" Patrice asked, sounding doubtful.

"I think her defining moment came when she started doing things for him that she didn't want to do," I said, "like postponing her plans to open her own business, continuing to make love after he started counting—"

"Puttin' her kids in a school where they were the only black ones," offered Deena, a devoted mother of twins.

"Not puttin' him out after she found out he was foolin' around," Regina added.

"So are you sayin' it's her fault?" Tee was still frowning.

"Not her *fault*," I said. "Her *choice*. She didn't have to stay with him if he didn't respect her."

They were quiet for a minute. The idea of leaving all that status, material wealth and male protection behind on principle would take some getting used to. *How many women ever got to live in a house like that?*

"Well, I know one thing," said Tiffany, cuddling Diamante, her six-week-old son by T.J., the Lattimore brother currently serving time for armed robbery, "Miss Girl sure messed homeboy's stuff up big time."

There was admiring laughter and a chorus of *amens* for the wronged wife's dramatic destruction of the contents of her husband's carefully organized closet.

"I like when she tossed that match in and set the whole mess on fire!" added Sherika, who didn't have any kids yet, but often had one of her younger sisters with her.

"A woman got ten years for that in Texas," I reminded them. My comment elicited a general groan.

"See there, Miz J." Tiffany spoke for the group. "You always takin' the fun out of stuff. In real life, Gregory Hines ain't necessarily gonna move in next door to Loretta Devine either, but let us have that, okay?"

I made a mental note to remember that today. It's important not to spend every waking moment teaching somebody something. You wear people out. Sometimes, it's better to just *let it be*. Besides, Gregory Hines has to live somewhere, right?

In the small kitchen, Tee had paper plates, plastic cups, a case of fruit juice boxes, trash bags and a mountain of Pampers. The floor had been swept, the bathrooms had been scrubbed and the only snow on the front steps had fallen after midnight. There was absolutely nothing else left to do, so I sat down to open Sister's bag of goodies.

The sack contained a fat white candle, two small blue bowls, a bottle of spring water, a red silk rose, two small onions, a packet of matches from a restaurant whose name was not written in English and a note.

Dear Joyce (it said in her trademark bright purple ink),
Once again, you and The Sewing Circus have pointed the way. I'm enclosing all necessary ingredients for one of my favorite anti–Super Bowl rituals.:

1. Burn the crackly brown skin of two onions;
2. Put out a bowl of clear water and a flower that blooms red;
3. Light a candle;

4. Invite the spirits;

5. Sing a love song.

Please complete all steps in order.

She underlined that, which was just like her. Give you a magic spell to perform and then direct you to complete all steps *in order* like it's the math portion of your SATs.

I crumbled up the onion skin in one bowl and emptied the water into the other one. I laid the rose at the base of the candle and struck a match, but what was I going to sing? I lit the onion skins to buy some time and watched them smoke and curl while I put another match to the fat candle and smelled the scent of spice and jasmine. I closed my eyes and invited all the spirits I could stand, *but what about the song?*

The only one that came immediately to mind was the Barney classic, "I love you, you love me." I was hoping for something a little more soulful, but first thought, best thought. It's the kids' hands-down favorite, plus it's a song even I can sing without worrying about hitting the high notes. I'd hate to mess up a perfectly good ritual trying to belt out an acceptable Dr. Feelgood.

I dipped my finger in the water for luck.

"I love you/you love me . . ."

I could hardly hear myself. I cleared my throat.

"We're a happy family . . ."

I sang it through twice, and you know what? By the end of the second time, I was starting to sing a little louder. By the third time, I didn't even feel silly anymore. By the time I finished a cycle of five, I felt so good I started to hit a chorus or two of "Dr. Feelgood" just for the hell of it, but I didn't want to press my luck. Barney is one thing. Aretha Franklin is something else altogether.

FOURTEEN

this denzel thing

THE LADIES' USHER BOARD had agreed to prepare a real Sunday supper for the party and three of our regulars, Sherika, Regina and Patrice, had been charged with delivering the precious cargo of baked chicken, candied yams, macaroni and cheese, collard greens, corn bread, sliced tomatoes and assorted desserts. They were all crammed into Regina's big old Pontiac, along with her two boys and Lil' Sonny.

Patrice climbed out carrying a large, foil-covered pan while Regina unbuckled the kids and handed them out to Sherika.

"Hey, Miz J!"

"Hey, Sheri!" I was pleased to see her. "I thought you'd be watching the game with Brian."

Her boyfriend was the captain of the high school football team and had headed for college in September on an athletic all those well-meaning layers of hand-knit wool. During last year's knitting craze, everybody was constantly making scarves, sweaters, mittens. We were drowning in afghans. Then suddenly it passed. Nobody was knitting anymore. But there was still the question of all those scarves.

"Why not Sam Jackson?" Deena was unable to resign herself to another showing of *Malcolm X*. "He's been married to the same woman since he was in college. Got a kid too."

Tomika stuffed Mavis's mittens into her jacket pocket. "You see *Pulp Fiction*?"

Deena sighed and retied the twins' matching pink ribbons. "That was a movie. We talkin' about real life."

Tomika looked pained. "I'm talkin' about the fact that movies always show you somethin' that's goin' on deep down inside the actor."

Deena looked skeptical. "Where'd you get that from?"

I was curious too. Had she been watching the Actors Studio sessions on cable?

"I saw this guy one time on TV. Blow!" Tomika put a Kleenex under Mavis's nose, and she obliged her mother with an enthusiastic *honk*. "He played one of the gangsters in that movie *Goodfellas* and he said you have to reach down inside and draw out that part of you that is the character, but that it has to be in there already or it won't work."

"So what are you sayin'?" Deena was trying to hold a wriggling twin on her lap long enough to tie her shoe. "You don't like Sam Jackson because you think deep down he's that crazy hit man who kept quotin' the Bible and blowin' people away?"

"I'm not sayin' he's ever done that for real," Tomika said calmly. "All I'm sayin' is, *it's in him*, or else he couldn't play it so good. Denzel ain't never played no part like that in his life. Plus, he won't kiss a white woman on-screen no matter how much money they throw at him."

"That's cool, but . . ." Deena knew she was going down for the third time. The best she could possibly hope for now was being allowed to decide between *The Hurricane* and *Remember the Titans*.

"Sam Jackson has still made some good movies."

Tomika tucked Mavis's shirt into her pants. "Sam Jackson always killin' somebody. You see *Shaft?*"

"He didn't kill nobody in *Eve's Bayou*," I said.

"That's right!" said Deena, emboldened by the presence of an ally.

I had watched that one on video not long ago. It felt like being in the middle of somebody else's dream. Mostly, I remember how beautiful those actresses managed to look while their worlds fell apart. That one with the dimples lost three husbands, and when the mysterious stranger showed up at her front door asking to be number four, she put on her pearls and rose to the occasion. *Amazing*. I've only lost one husband and the idea of taking another is inconceivable.

Tomika sniffed and smoothed the edges of her hair. "*Eve's Bayou* doesn't count."

"Why?"

"Because nobody saw it," Tomika said, like she was stating the painfully obvious.

"*I* saw it." I was unwilling to dismiss such a beautiful dreamscape just because it didn't crack the box office top ten. "I liked it."

Tee smiled at me like that was an amusing fact, but completely irrelevant. "Of course *you* liked it, Miz J. You like *foreign* movies too." And she smiled sweetly at me and Deena and herded the three little girls down to the play area, where the baby dolls were waiting patiently for their breakfast.

Deena sighed loudly. "Tee carryin' this Denzel thing too far. Look at this!"

She had a point. Tomika had brought six videos: *The Hurricane, Mo' Better Blues, Remember the Titans, The Pelican Brief, Devil in a Blue Dress,* and of course, *Malcolm X.* Not that Tee was political. She just liked that red zoot suit favored by the preconversion Malcolm when he first hooks up with West Indian Archie and becomes a *sho' nuff* gangster.

"Why don't you wait and see if anybody else brings anything?" I said, sitting down at my desk where someone had left a small crayon drawing of what looked like a blue duck wearing a bright red hat.

"They *know* better," Deena whined. "She gonna play what she want anyway."

I took a deep breath. This is the way they all tend to think:

1. Identify the problem (always someone else's fault);
2. Identify the cause of the problem (always external);
3. Resign yourself to finding no solution to it; and finally,
4. Restate the whole thing in a way that emphasizes both your powerlessness and the mysterious implacability of your perceived opponent.

The hardest thing for me to do was not to say, "Look, it's easy! Why don't you just bring some videos of your own and we'll show those. If you don't have any, why don't you get a Blockbuster card and get some? And while you're at it, why don't you rent a few movies you haven't seen before or follow one actress's career to plot her growth and development or track down some black classics from before you were born?"

The problem is, all of those are *choices,* and that is what they are not used to having. What they know how to do instead is blame, deny, deceive, distrust and abdicate. The only way to break the pattern is not to supply the options. So I didn't say anything, which she rightly took to mean I was waiting for her to figure it out.

She sighed and then brightened suddenly. "Can we vote on it?"

I nodded. "Sure we can."

I didn't ask her what exactly we'd be voting on in this particular case. The important thing was that she had figured out something to do besides sit there and complain. *One small step for Deena Anderson. One giant step for The Sewing Circus.*

FIFTEEN

count on it

I WAS IN THE process of giving myself permission to leave everything on my desk exactly where it was until tomorrow when the phone rang.

"Sewing Circus. This is Joyce."

"Joyce? Nate Anderson." He even rumbled on the phone. "How's the anti–Super Bowl party going?"

He had been really curious when I was talking about it at Sister's. I think he was a little surprised when I said no men were allowed. He didn't pursue it but I got the feeling that was less because he understood the reason for some activities to be all female just to keep the focus steady than a real inability to imagine any man choosing not to watch the Super Bowl.

"We've got a full house," I said. I could hear the television station vaguely in the background. He was probably holed up at the Motel 6, sitting in a little bitty Motel 6 chair, watching the game.

"Great," he said. "I won't keep you. I just wanted to let you know I went by the house and it's perfect. Where do I sign?"

I laughed, but I was definitely sympathetic. "You're not a big fan of motel living, are you?"

"Not really. Especially today. It's like watching the game in a dollhouse."

I felt sorry for him. "Well, the owners won't be back for a week, but I can vouch for you until then."

"Vouch for me?"

"Sure," I said. "It's partially furnished, as you saw, and the heat's still on. You can move in today if you want."

"Today?"

He sounded so hopeful, I laughed. "Right now if you want."

He wanted out of there so badly, he was afraid to believe me. "If you're kidding, tell me now."

"Don't worry," I said. "I'd never kid about the Motel 6."

He let his relief out in a long, relieved *whoosh*. "All right!"

Deena appeared in the doorway and, seeing me on the phone, whispered urgently. "She gettin' ready to pick the video!"

Her courage had failed her at the moment when the vote would have to be taken. Tee was never less than a passionate advocate for whatever point of view she held and Deena hadn't even figured out what question she was calling for yet. She definitely needed backup.

"You still want to vote?" I said.

She looked nervous but determined. "Yeah, but she gonna make it come out her way if it's just me askin'!"

"Is this a bad time?" Nate's voice in my ear rumbled apologetically.

"Hang on," I said, giving Deena the answer she wanted so she'd give me a minute to myself. "Go tell her you'd like to take a vote and I'll be right here for the discussion."

Deena looked relieved. "Can I tell her *you* want a vote?"

I gave her a *don't push it* look.

"Never mind. I'll tell her."

"Sorry," I said into Nate's patient silence.

"No problem," he said. "I just wanted to tell you how much I enjoyed spending some time with you the other night."

"Thanks," I said. "I enjoyed it too."

"Our conversation really helped me bring some things into focus about what I'm doing here," he said.

"I'll take that as a compliment," I said, pleased to have it.

"I meant it as one."

Deena was hovering in the hallway looking anxious.

"Listen, I've got to go," I said. "Call me if you have any problems at the house."

"Can I call you even if I don't have any problems?" His voice was as rich as a hot fudge sundae with a smile on top.

"Sure," I said. "That would be a nice change!"

"Good," he said. "Then count on it."

SIXTEEN

when junior started trippin'

"ALL RIGHT, Y'ALL," TEE WAS saying to the group as I took a seat on the couch next to Patrice. "What's it gonna be?"

"Whacha got?" Tiffany said. Her oldest son, Marquis, three, was asleep in the back with the other kids. She was rocking the baby, Diamante, against her shoulder.

"You know what she got." Sherika, teasing, provided the opening Deena needed.

"You might not know *what*, but we all know *who*."

Tee raised her eyebrows, feigning surprise.

Patrice groaned. "Oh, Lord! Not again!"

"What?"

"Nothing," Patrice said quickly. "I just, you know, Denzel is cool and everything, but he kinda, you know, boring sometimes."

"Boring?"

"What she tryin' to say is Denzel fine, but he won't let you see him really *get down,*" Tiffany said, shifting her now dozing boy from one shoulder to the other. "The only movie I can remember where he was even hittin' it a little bit was when he was cheatin' on Spike's sister in *Mo' Better Blues,* and even then, he wasn't that into it."

Sherika giggled. "That's cause Pauletta ain't havin' it!"

Pauletta Washington always got big props from the group for holding on to her husband in the midst of his rise to Hollywood stardom.

"What about the beginning of *Devil in a Blue Dress,*" Tee said, defensive but determined. "When that girl with the big titties keep tellin' him he's hittin' her spot?"

"That girl on TV now too."

Regina snorted. "Doin' what?"

"Playin' the black roommate on a all-white show."

I suddenly remembered a video I had watched a couple of months before this whole Denzel thing took hold. "What about *Mississippi Masala?*"

"I ain't interested in nothin' got *Mississippi* in the title," Tiffany said. "Those country Negroes ain't got nothin' I need."

"Oprah from Mississippi."

"Oprah from wherever she wanna be from," Sherika said, echoing their jointly held belief that money buys not only happiness but world citizenship.

"Denzel is the star," I said, bringing them back to the subject at hand.

Tomika looked suspicious. "How come I never heard of it?"

I shrugged. I knew exactly why. "It was directed by a woman too."

"A sister?"

"An Indian." That was why.

Tiffany laughed. "What's Denzel playin'? A cowboy?"

"Not that kind of Indian," I said. "She's from India."

"What she doin' directin' a black movie?"

"There's Indians in it too."

"That must be where the *masala* comes in," said Regina, rolling her eyes. "Whatever *that* is!"

"It's an Indian stew," I said. "Like gumbo."

Regina made a face. "I don't like gumbo. Too much weird stuff in it."

"So what's Denzel doin'?" Sherika said. "Cookin'?"

"He falls in love with an Indian woman whose parents disapprove," I said.

"He has sex with her?" Tiffany demanded, suddenly indignant.

I nodded and Tee gave her braids an energetic shake.

"Well, that's why I haven't seen it. The *last* picture I want in my mind is Denzel rollin' around with some chick in a sari."

"You just mad 'cause he ain't rollin' around with you." Tiffany was teasing, but Tee didn't have a chance to affirm or deny because Nikki Solomon burst through the door and slammed it hard behind her.

"Who chasin' you, girl?" Regina said, only half kidding.

"Nobody, I hope," Nikki said, glancing out the window while she pulled off her coat.

"You wake up this chile, you gonna have me chasin' you," Tiffany said, gliding off quickly to a quieter corner.

Nikki was too busy pacing to apologize. I walked over to the back window and looked out, but I didn't see anybody.

"Calm down," I said. "Are you okay?"

"I'm just tired of it, that's all!" Her voice was shaking with anger or fear, I couldn't tell which one yet.

"What happened?"

"They mean anyway, but when they drinkin', the shit is just ridiculous!"

We knew immediately she meant the Lattimore brothers.

"Where's Sheila?"

Nikki had arrived alone.

"I went by the house to pick up the kids like she asked me to and that's when Junior started trippin' about me startin' to work at the club on Monday. He said he didn't want no niggas looking at his woman but him, *period*."

Tee resisted a golden opportunity to say *I told you so* and Nik went on.

"I told him if he was payin' his woman's rent maybe he'd get a vote in the shit, but since he *ain't*, he *don't*."

Tiffany, listening from a few feet away, shook her head. "You the one trippin'! What'd he say?"

"He didn't say nothin'! I was the one talkin', so then I told him he wasn't my man no more, and if he brought his sorry ass up in my place of employment, I'd have them great big bouncers throw him out the back door with the rest of the trash!"

Patrice gasped. "You said that to *Junior?*"

"Junior can kiss my ass!"

Tomika joined me at the window. "Do you think he followed you?" She sounded as worried as I felt. Even among a group as volatile as the Lattimore brothers, Junior held a special place. He was the one *they* thought was crazy.

Nikki shook her head. "Not unless it's halftime." She was still pacing. "He just mad 'cause I finally quit his ass."

Junior and Nik, who turned nineteen on Christmas day, had

been together five years. She'd been threatening to quit him for three.

"They always think 'cause they your first, they 'spose to be your only," Patrice said softly.

"Well, he better think again," Nikki said, then looked at Tee and giggled.

"What?"

"He couldn't believe I said that shit!"

Tomika grinned in spite of herself. She had been trying to get Nikki to break up with Junior forever. "I can't believe it either!"

They all laughed at that, delighted by her defiance, but I was wondering if Junior was really going to let it slide and how we were going to deal with it if he didn't.

SEVENTEEN

war song

I TALKED MYSELF OUT of calling the police immediately by giving Junior a half hour in which to simmer and fume and then decide not to retaliate. I don't remember exactly how I came up with thirty minutes as the danger zone, but the specificity of it somehow reassured me. I didn't want to be the woman who cried wolf if this was more drama than danger.

I also decided reluctantly against calling Sheila since it might further irritate her brothers. I left the group going over the details of Nikki's close encounter and went back to the office, where I could watch out the window without making everybody more nervous than they already were.

We have agitated boyfriends cruise up here every once in a while looking for somebody who has moved out or moved on.

Most of the time I can defuse the situation by looking stern and talking tough. None of the Lattimore brothers have ever been here except Maleek, who sometimes drops off his sister or picks up his nephews. It's kind of ironic in a way since we have at least two, maybe three, of their children here every day. Participatory fatherhood is a concept the brothers have yet to embrace fully.

After the first fifteen minutes went by uneventfully, I started to relax a little, which was a mistake, because that's when Junior Lattimore's beat-up old Buick pulled into the yard, going way too fast, and rocked to a stop. Maleek was driving, Jarvis was in the backseat with Sheila's boys and Junior was riding shotgun. I wondered how drunk he was. I didn't have to wonder for long. When he opened the passenger door and got out, he could hardly stand up straight.

"*Nikki!*" he bellowed. "Get your ass out here!"

My heart sank. So much for the thirty-minute window. "Tell Nik to stay out of sight," I said, pulling on my coat. "I'll handle it."

When I stepped out on the back porch, Junior looked at me like I was the last person he expected to see. I've known him since he was a kid, and I was counting on that connection, however tenuous, to help me convince him to go home and cool off.

"Hey, Junior," I said pleasantly. "You come over to drop off the kids?"

He mumbled something I couldn't hear, but Maleek and Jarvis both laughed.

"I couldn't hear you," I said. "What did you say?"

He frowned drunkenly at me, anger twisting his handsome face. "I didn't say nothin' to you. I'm lookin' for Nikki."

"She doesn't want to see you right now, Junior."

His eyes narrowed. "She want these kids, though, right?"

"They know me," I said. "I'll take full responsibility." I waved at Sheila's boys sitting big-eyed and silent in the backseat. "Hey, Duane. Hey, Daryl."

"Knowin' you ain't the question," Junior growled. "Sheila told me Nikki 'spose to get 'em and she they mama, so Nikki who I need to see, otherwise I can take the little niggas back home right now."

"You don't have to do that—" I said, but Junior cut me off and took a staggering step in my direction.

"Didn't I tell you we didn't have nothin' to talk about?"

Nikki was out the door and off the porch before I could stop her. Things were going from bad to worse at an amazingly fast clip.

"What the hell do you think you're doin'?" Nikki stopped a foot away from Junior. Duane and Daryl scrambled to the back window and looked imploringly at her, hoping she could rescue them.

Junior's lip curled in what probably passed for a seductive smile in the Lattimore family.

"Came to see you, baby," he said, his voice a drunken slur.

"Let 'em out."

Junior nodded at Jarvis, who opened the car door and pushed his nephews out into the snowy yard. They were hatless, coatless and shivering. They hesitated for a minute, unsure of their role in this adult drama and not wanting to make the wrong move and piss off their uncle.

"Go on inside," Nikki snapped, and they bounded up the stairs to me. I hustled them quickly inside where Deena was waiting by the door.

"Call the police," I said. "And tell them to get somebody over here *now!*"

"Go home, Junior." Nikki was still standing too close to him for my comfort, but she sounded unafraid.

"Thanks for dropping off the boys," I said, moving to stand beside her. "I'll make sure they get home safely."

He ignored me, all his attention on Nikki. "Who gonna make sure you get home safely, sweet thing?"

Nikki narrowed her eyes. "That's none of your business anymore, is it?" Her voice was hard.

"Let's go inside, Nik," I said, but as she turned toward me, Junior grabbed her arm and snatched her back hard.

"What the fuck you say?"

"Hey!" My voice sounded high and thin. "Stop it!"

I tried to get between them. I was holding Nikki around the waist, and every time Junior pulled her, he dragged me along too. Through the car window, I could see Jarvis and Maleek laughing. Why hadn't I called for help immediately? *If anything happens to this girl, I will never—*

"Freeze!" a voice shouted behind me.

I turned toward it, and there was Tomika standing alone on the porch step with an angry-looking snub-nosed revolver in her hand. She was holding it out in front and steadying her wrist with her other hand like a pro. Huddled at the back door, Sherika, Patrice and Tiffany stood watching. I didn't even know Tee owned a gun.

"Back off, Junior," she said. "Right now!"

"Or what?" He sneered. "You gonna shoot me?"

"I'm gonna do the best I can."

"What if you miss?"

Tomika didn't blink. "I won't."

"Come on, man," Jarvis was whining out of the car's back window. "These bitches crazy. Let's go before they call the cops."

That must have been the magic word because Junior suddenly released Nikki's arm like holding on to her was the last thing on his mind. I pulled her back up on the porch.

Junior glared but didn't make a move in our direction. "Fuck you, Nik. You ain't got the only pussy in town."

I kept my arm tightly around her shoulders, hoping she wouldn't answer him. Tomika had spoken for us. No other response was required. Maleek pulled out almost before Junior had slammed the door behind him. Tee was still pointing her pistol at the spot where he had been standing. She slowly lowered it to her side.

"You okay?" I whispered.

She nodded and looked at Nik. "You okay?"

Nikki managed a small smile. "Since when you start carryin' a gun?"

Patrice and Tiffany looked at Sherika and they all burst out laughing. *What was so funny?*

"Tell her," Tiffany said, "so she won't think we all gone crazy!"

Tomika grinned at me. "It's a toy."

"A toy?"

"I took it off Duane last week. He said his uncle Jarvis gave it to him."

Tee handed me the gun. Up close, you could easily see it wasn't real, but it had looked real enough a minute ago to convince Junior to get back in his car and go home. I couldn't believe this was a *toy*.

Nikki picked it up and turned it over in her hand like she couldn't believe it either. "Well," she said finally, "then I guess it's a good thing Jarvis didn't get out the car. He might have wanted it back!"

We all laughed. At that point, I guess we were a little hysterical. By the time one of Idlewild's finest pulled up a few minutes later, we had calmed down enough to make our statements. By the time he left, it was snowing again, the kids were waking up from their naps and the telling and retelling of Tomika's brave improvisation had become our little tribe's first war song.

Somebody produced a pocket camera and suggested we record the moment for posterity.

"Should we hold up the gun?" Tiffany said, a now wide-awake Diamante gurgling happily against her shoulder.

"No," I said quickly. "Let's hold up the baby."

So that's what we did.

EIGHTEEN

the designated man

I THOUGHT IT WOULD be a good idea for Tee and Nikki to stay the night at my house in case Junior was still feeling crazy. Nik said she'd bunk with her mother until things settled down a little, but Tomika immediately took me up on my invitation.

I told her to put Mavis to bed while I made us some chamomile tea. When I came back in the living room, she was already curled up on one end of the sofa. I handed her a cup. She took a long swallow and sighed.

I joined her on the couch and we tucked one of the world-famous Circus afghans around our feet and sat for a long, quiet moment.

"Were you scared?" I said finally, really wanting to know.

Tee considered the question. "I was too mad to be scared. Either The Circus is our place or it ain't, right?"

I nodded. "You know how I felt out there?"

"How?"

I held my cup with both hands and the warmth was as comforting as a pair of slippers that have been sitting beside the fireplace. "*Helpless.* I don't know what would have happened if you hadn't done what you did."

"You'd have thought of something." She smiled with a lot more confidence in my abilities than I felt at that particular moment.

"Maybe," I said, "but I didn't have to. You handled it. I owe you one."

She grinned. "One what?"

I grinned back. "One absolutely unexpected moment of creative *sister strength* when you truly need it."

She laughed softly. "That sounds pretty valuable, Miz J. Maybe I should get it in writing."

"Don't worry. I won't forget."

We clicked our mugs to seal the deal and then just sipped our tea in silence for a minute or two. It was one of those good silences where you feel like everything is already clear, so there's no reason to muck it up with a lot of chatter. I refilled our cups and Tomika chuckled softly.

"What?"

She pointed at the bag of videos she'd picked up on our way out. "They been fussin' at me about these videos all day and we never even got to 'em."

"Can I ask you something?"

"Sure."

"What is it about Denzel?"

She laughed softly. "Well, a couple of months ago, I went to this revival in Big Rapids with my cousin Jan. The preacher came all the way from Chicago and he kept sayin' that to be a good Christian, all you gotta remember to ask yourself is *What would Jesus do?* That made sense to me. It's like our free woman thing, plus it's easy to remember. Once you read the Ten Commandments, what he would or wouldn't do is pretty clear, so I started thinkin' about what if we had somethin' like that about *guys.*"

"What guys?"

She leaned forward, eager to make me understand. "The guys we . . . you know . . ."

Boyfriends? Babydaddies?

"Lovers?"

"Right!"

"A lot of them are truly sorry, but since they all we see, we 'bout to forget what a good man even look like, much less how one 'spose to act."

She's right about that. Most of these girls have never had a relationship with a man who didn't abuse them.

"That's when Denzel popped into my mind, right there in the middle of the revival."

"Why?"

"Because he put out a lot of movies where he act like a man is *'spose* to act. He take care of his family. He look out for his friends. He always got a job and he ain't never hit no woman or abused no kid."

She sipped her tea, her braids falling on either side of her face like a veil. "I was still with Jimmy back then."

Jimmy was her ex live-in, a pretty boy with a bad attitude and no visible means of support.

"That's why I was sittin' up there in the first place, prayin' over his ass, because of course, he was actin' a fool, shovin' me around, tellin' Mavis he was gonna whip her, takin' money out of my purse when I'm sleep. So I thought to myself, if Denzel was your man, *what would he do?* Just thinkin' about it, about how different it would be, made me start cryin' so hard my cousin thought I was gettin' saved."

"Maybe you were," I said.

"I don't know about that, but I know I went home and told Jimmy he was going to have to make other living arrangements."

"Is that when he moved out?"

"That's when I *put* him out." She set her cup down. Chamomile tea was the last thing on her mind. "Miz J, you only need to see one do *right* to see all the others are *wrong*. I found me one in the movies and I'ma watch him as hard as I can. I'm tired of wastin' my time lookin' at niggas who don't know how to treat a woman no better than they know how to be a man." She took a deep breath. "Maybe this way I'll recognize him when *my* Denzel show up."

It was such a perfect response to such a terrible problem that I just sat there. In the absence of flesh-and-blood examples of the real thing, Denzel had become the designated man, a good brother, whose behavior could be observed and codified. *What would Denzel do?* Easy to remember; easy to understand. I wondered if we'd have to get his permission to put it on a button, a poster, a billboard over Times Square!

"Mama!" Mavis was rubbing her eyes sleepily in the doorway. "I woke up!"

"Come here, baby," Tomika said to her daughter, who staggered over sleepily, fell into the safe haven of her mother's arms and went immediately back to sleep. Tomika adjusted the afghan.

"You know what?" I said, excited by the possibilities for the application of Denzel theory. "I think you just had another big idea."

She shook her head and grinned at me. "I hope this one don't make me hafta *really* shoot Junior Lattimore."

"No way," I said. "I don't believe in guns."

She looked exactly like she would have if I had said *I don't believe in gravity*. "You know soon's he find out what happened, he gonna hafta try and beat my ass or somethin'," she said matter-of-factly. "He can't be no punk."

I had been thinking the same thing myself. "Maybe he won't find out."

"Nik gonna tell him."

That hadn't occurred to me. One of the others maybe, accidentally, but not Nikki. "Why?"

She shrugged and Mavis mewed softly like a newborn kitten. Tee rubbed her back in slow circles. "First time he make her mad once she stop bein' scared, she gonna throw it in his face."

"But they broke up."

"Yeah, well, all I'm sayin' is, I know he's gonna act a fool and I'ma be ready when he does."

"What do you mean?"

She kissed the top of her daughter's head and looked at me. "I don't know yet."

Mavis nestled closer to her mother's breast and smiled in her sleep: peaceful. What kind of woman would she grow up to be if we could make sure she always felt that loved, that protected, that safe? I don't know, but I damn sure intended to find out.

"The truth is, Miz J"—Tomika's voice trembled just a little— "I was sorta hopin' you'd help me figure that out."

I reached over and took her hand. "All right," I said. "I will."

part

two

NINETEEN

time is money

I HAD JUST STARTED pumping my gas when Anita Lattimore pulled up to the pump in a bright purple Impala. The car had definitely seen better days, but as each of her sons came of age, they continued to adorn and personalize it until they saved or stole enough to buy vehicles of their own. At that point, the family car returned to their mother's primary custody, but the distinguishing decorative touches remained; red crushed velvet seating, now liberally pocked with dope-seed holes and cigarette burns; faux gold rims, minus two of the original set; a vanity plate reading BORN BAD; and, of course, the flat purple perpetually peeling paint job.

Seated next to her in the front seat was a woman probably ten years younger, but already showing the ravages of too many bad drugs, too much mean sex and a steady diet of barbecue potato chips, fried pork rinds and Pepsi-Cola. The passenger was talking animatedly on a tiny cell phone, but Anita leaned across her, opened the door, stuffed some money into her hand and pushed her out into the cold afternoon to pump the gas.

The woman, dressed in a red miniskirt and a short fake fur jacket did not appreciate the division of labor. "Why I always gotta pump the damn gas?" she said, shivering and trying in vain to pull her skirt down over a little more of her thighs.

"One, because you ain't got no damn car. Two, because you ain't got no damn money," Anita snarled through the open door. "And three, because you can always walk your broke ass home if you don't like it."

Anita slammed the door, leaving her friend outside, and lit a cigarette. The woman, having no other options, sighed deeply and set about her task while resuming her phone conversation at the same decibel level she'd used speaking to Anita.

"You there? Yeah, girl, I already told the muthafucka all that shit. He a lyin' ass if he say I didn't. When he first stepped to me last time they came through, I said we do head and hand jobs only. No fuckin'. I ain't 'bout no AIDS and Nita ain't either."

I wondered if she would censor her conversation a little, or at least lower her voice, if I had been a young person who presumably had not been exposed to the full vile possibilities of her mother tongue, or an older one who might hope that one of the privileges of age would include the right to pretend people don't really talk like that except in the cable movies they avoid as assiduously as they do the playgrounds where the young men congregate to play basketball and see who can talk the loudest or the nastiest, or both.

Probably not. I don't think she was even conscious of me being there. Between pumping gas, rolling her eyes at Anita through the windshield and making it clear that whoever they were discussing on the phone had been fully apprised of the rules of whatever exchange had occurred, she was fully engaged in her own moment.

"Damn right," she said, watching the meter carefully so she wouldn't go over the amount of the crumpled bills Anita had shoved into her hand. "Plus that shit take too long. Niggas wanna be up in the pussy for two, three hours!"

Two or three hours? What kind of men were these?

The woman cackled at the response I couldn't hear and replaced the pump. Five dollars on the nose. Her laugh had a raspy, desperate quality that held no hint of real amusement. "You got that right! I *know* it's good, *but time is money!*"

As she headed inside to pay, I saw Anita looking at me through the window with an expression of pure malice. I wondered what part of what happened yesterday had reached her ears via Junior's lying lips. I waved to her, knowing I wouldn't have to wait long to find out.

She rolled down her window in a series of jerky, indignant motions and spit the words in my direction. "You ain't gotta be wavin' at me like ain't nothin' gone down between us," she said. "My boy tole me everythin' and I tole him he oughta get a lawyer and file charges against that lil' bitch and all the rest of y'all, too, for lettin' her do it."

I assumed she meant Tee, but it could have been Nikki, for whom Anita had a special dislike since she was Junior's long-time girlfriend. Some mothers have a difficult time sharing their sons.

"He was wrong," I said. "He put his hands on one of our members."

"One of your *members?*" Anita snorted with contempt.

"Nikki Solomon been fuckin' my boy since before she got her period. Now all of a sudden she need y'all to run him off her?"

My first impulse was to argue the facts with her, then clarify the legal implications, then point out her role in all this as his mother who should have raised him better, but that was exactly what she wanted me to do so she could get out of the car and we could stand toe-to-toe, trading insults, charges and counter-charges until we got tired or somebody called the sheriff to come break up the brawl. But there was no satisfaction for me in that kind of standoff and no protection for Nikki or Tee. I wasn't required to spend a nanosecond engaged in this dispute, especially since her backup was headed our way, still shouting into her cell phone and, I'm sure, armed with an arsenal of curses she had hardly begun to showcase and which I truly didn't need to carry around in my head for the rest of the day.

I said nothing, swiped my credit card at the pump and waited for my receipt.

Anita narrowed her angry eyes. "Oh, you ain't got nothin' to say now, right? You just all about business and shit." She laughed, a barking, phlegmy, smoker's laugh as mirthless as her girl-friend's cackle. "Aw-iight. Take your tight ass on, then. Save that shit for when the sheriff come."

"The sheriff's already talked to me," I said, opening my car door and unable to resist a small parting shot. "I hear he's look-ing for you. Didn't he call your job yet?"

She looked surprised, and her friend stopped talking long enough to wait for the response. Their overtime at the motel where they were working included a lot of activity that didn't bear scrutiny.

"What he wanna talk to me for?" Anita said, immediately wary.

"I don't know," I said. "Maybe you should ask him when he calls."

Before they could decide whether or not I was bluffing, I pulled out. In the rearview mirror, I could see them pull out behind me and turn toward town. At the very least, I figured that would give Anita food for thought before she got too self-righteous about her sorry son. I'd had enough of Junior Lattimore already and the day was just getting started good.

TWENTY

so far, so good

NIKKI'S MOTHER DOESN'T WANT her to file a formal complaint. She's convinced that would make Junior even madder and we should just "leave well enough alone." I spent all afternoon trying to convince her otherwise, but I should have saved my breath. Jasmine had never been bothered by Nik's relationship with Junior. A Sunday afternoon skirmish where no bones were broken seemed a minor inconvenience.

Finally, she got tired of listening to me. "Listen, Joyce, I know you tryin' to help, but Nik been with Junior since they was both kids. She know to handle him."

"Has he abused her before?"

"*Abused* her? He ain't abused her. They might have a little tussle every now and then like everybody else, but he ain't never *ripped her up* or nothin' like that."

These distinctions are important. It's like the Eskimos having so many different words for snow. People always name carefully what they have to come up against to survive. An avalanche and flurries are both snow, but one will kill you and the other one won't.

I hung up the phone and considered my options. If Nikki didn't file a complaint, the most we could hope for was that the sheriff would go by the house and *talk* to Junior, which people had been doing since he started kindergarten with no visible positive effect. Without Nik's cooperation, there was nothing else we could do but hope things died down of their own accord.

Tee had to leave early to take Mavis to the doctor to see about a cold that kept hanging on, so I was busy answering calls from everybody wanting an update on the news. Even Sister checked in to be sure I didn't need her to come over and chase out the evil spirits or the infidels, whoever was acting the biggest fool at the time of her arrival.

It was after five when Deena stuck her head in the door. She was already in her coat and boots.

"Sheila runnin' late, but everybody else been picked up and I gotta go, so I'ma drop off Daryl and Duane on my way. Anything else you need me to do?"

She had been assuming more and more responsibility for our day-care program. She was a natural teacher with infinite patience and a good sense of humor. Once her twins were in school full-time, I was going to encourage her to go for a degree in elementary education. She had gathered all four kids at the back door, stuffed into their jackets, ready to go.

"Go on," I said. "Tell Sheila to call me, will you?"

Deena shook her head. "She ain't gonna do that. She too embarrassed about what happened yesterday."

"Tell her it's not her fault. She can't control Junior."

"I tole her. She still embarrassed."

"Okay," I said. "Maybe I'll go by there later."

"Better take Tee wit you if you do!" She was only half joking. Deena had been proud of Tee yesterday. Having survived an abusive father and several rough boyfriends, she admired a woman who didn't back down. "See you in the mornin'!"

I stepped out into the hallway and waved at the kids who stood in a row waving back as if they were awaiting the arrival of a train that was running late. Deena shooed them out, strapped them into their car seats and headed off. I was alone for the first time today. I took a deep breath and closed my eyes for a minute. My brain couldn't decide whether to focus on Junior or his mother or Jasmine or Nik or Tee or . . .

I opened my eyes and decided I had done enough for one day. I walked into the community room and looked out the big picture window. The sun sets early up here this time of year and the gray sky over the lake was promising more snow. There's a stark beauty to these woods in winter that the summer people never see, and I pulled up a chair and sat there for a minute to admire it. I think Alice Walker was right about recognizing God in a field of purple flowers. I feel the same way about sunsets.

I took a long, slow breath.

Breathing in, I know that I am breathing in. . . .

Breathing out, I know that I am breathing out. . . .

I felt the tensions of the last couple of days begin to leave my body immediately. *Why haven't I been meditating?* I knew why. It always makes me feel so much better that I immediately stop doing it. *Well,* my warped reasoning goes at that moment, *why should I waste twenty minutes a day to encourage clarity, sanity and peace in my life? Surely that time is better spent running around in circles like a chicken with my head cut off!*

Breathing in, I know that I am breathing in....

A flock of ducks winged in over the lake, swooped down low for a quick look and headed away again, their honking audible and urgent. These are the moments when missing Mitch becomes a sharp pain instead of a dull ache. The moments when the impulse to turn to him, knowing that he's seeing and feeling exactly what I'm seeing and feeling, is so strong it's actually made me weak at the knees a time or two. Good thing I'm already sitting down.

Breathing out, I smile....

And I did. I was still smiling when Nate pulled up and rang the front doorbell a few minutes later.

TWENTY-ONE

the nearest starfish

"GOOD AFTERNOON," HE SAID when I opened the door, stomping the snow off his big brown boots and stepping inside. In an environment scaled to kids and largely frequented by women, his huge, undeniably male presence seemed even more so.

"I've been trying to call, but either your phone is on the fritz or you've had a hell of a busy day."

"Option two," I said, surprised to see him. "But I think it's winding down. Come on in."

"Good," he said. "I just wanted to bring you this letter of intent."

He handed me a white business envelope with MS. JOYCE MITCHELL neatly typed on the outside.

"Letter of intent to do what?"

That didn't sound right when it came out, but before he could answer, the phone rang in my office.

"Make yourself comfortable," I said. "I'll be right back."

"Take your time." He slipped off his coat and looked around. The chocolate babydolls regarded him from their high chairs with the unflappable sweetness that is their trademark and he looked at them with benign *bigness* like Gulliver first encountering the tiny people of Lilliput.

I hurried back to my office and dropped the envelope on my desk. "Hello?"

It was Johnny Tyler from the sheriff's department asking if Nikki had decided to come down and swear out a complaint or not.

"Not today," I said.

On the other end of the phone, Johnny reminded me gently that time is of the essence in harassment cases.

"If the perpetrator has an opportunity to feel his own power, the victim may be putting herself at increased risk by waiting."

I decided it wasn't necessary to mention that I was the one who told him that. Sometimes your ego will tell you it's important to get the credit for assisting in somebody else's growth and development, but it's not. What's important is that Johnny now had a new piece of information he could use.

"How about I call you in the morning," I said. "And we'll try to come down then?"

"Around nine-thirty?"

The last thing Nikki had said to me was *forget it*, so I was not optimistic about us showing up anywhere by nine-thirty.

"We'll be there soon as we can get there," I said. *That was true*. Tomorrow morning. Next weekend. Next month. Like the Jamaicans say: *soon come*.

When I walked back into the community room, Nate was standing in front of the original framed copy of the "Ten Things Every Free Woman Should Know."

"Can you do all these things?" he said, unconsciously echoing Ezra Busbee.

"Almost all," I said. "I'm still a little shaky on self-defense."

He nodded, still looking at the list thoughtfully. "Did you ever try to come up with a list like this for men?"

"No," I said, realizing the top of my head didn't even reach his shoulder. "Did you?"

He smiled. "No, but somebody ought to. Pretty much the only advice I remember being given as a youngblood was, and I quote, 'Don't be a punk; don't be a pimp; and don't take no shit off no white boys.'"

"What about women?"

"You don't want to know," he said, shaking his big smooth head. I wondered how often he shaved it. "But what I was thinking was that it might make The Circus more appealing to those guys at the state legislature if you had a program for the guys too."

At Sister's, I had told the tale of my latest foray into the world of public funding. I liked that he had clearly been listening, even though I didn't particularly like where I thought he was going.

"What kind of program?"

"You know," he said. "The same kind of thing. 'Ten Things Every Free Man Should Know.'"

I was disappointed. He clearly hadn't understood a word I'd said the other night. The problem wasn't that some people might think we didn't want to be around men. The problem was if men didn't collectively change their evil ways, we wouldn't have much reason to. Suddenly, I felt overwhelmed by the necessity to explain; to always *explain*. He was a smart man. Why didn't he know?

"That's not my job," I said. "I work with young *women*."

He turned away from the "Ten Things" and looked down at me. "Can I ask you a personal question?"

"Sure," I said.

"Are you a separatist?"

"A *separatist?*" I was a little confused. There are some sixties radicals who live up here who might still consider themselves black separatists, but there were so few white people around here on a day-to-day basis, the whole question seemed sort of rhetorical to me. "What kind of separatist?"

He shrugged his big shoulders and the brown sweater he was wearing rippled right with him. He was without a doubt the best built *past-forty*-year-old man I'd ever seen.

"You know, women over *here*. Men over *there*."

"A gender separatist?"

He nodded. "I guess that's what you would call it."

He looked so serious and the question was so unexpected, I almost laughed out loud. He must have taken a few women's studies courses when he went to graduate school. No way he was going to pick up an idea like "gender separatist" on the streets of downtown Detroit.

"No," I said gently. "I think it's fine for men and women to be together."

He looked genuinely relieved.

"But," I added quickly, "I don't think anybody's teaching them how to do it right. If two people are going to build a real family, each one has to bring a whole person to the bargain."

I tried to look him in the eye without tilting my head backward like a first-time tourist at the Eiffel Tower. It wasn't possible. I considered stepping up on a nearby kiddie chair just to even things up, but I figured that would only emphasize the physical differences between us even more.

"That's what we do at The Circus," I said. "Try to help the young women who come here figure out how to be whole human beings. Once they figure that out, all the other stuff is more likely to fall into line."

It must have made sense to him so far because he rewarded me with a smile and one more question. "Can't we work on it together?"

I wasn't sure if he meant our respective genders or the two of us, so I tried to forge an answer that would fit both possibilities.

"Eventually we can, sure," I said, "but at first, there's so much baggage on both sides, it usually helps to let the girls talk to each other alone until they get the basics down."

"How long does that take?"

Now it was my turn to smile. "As long as it takes."

"You're a patient woman."

"You ever hear the story about the kid with the starfish?"

He shook his big head again. "No."

"Sit down," I said, offering him a chair and taking one myself. "Okay. There was a big storm at the beach, and when the weather cleared, the ocean had washed up hundreds, maybe thousands, of starfish, who were surely now doomed in the heat of the noonday sunshine. A father took his young son out to see the strange spectacle, and as soon as he explained to the boy what was happening, the kid immediately picked up the nearest starfish and carried it down to the ocean. Then he came back and got another one and did the same thing."

Nate was watching me like the kids do at storytime usually

do, but he wasn't fooling anybody. He was a lot of things, but a kid was nowhere among them.

" 'Hold on, son,' said the father. 'There's too many. What you're doing won't make any difference.' The kid looked down the beach at all those living creatures and then back up at his father. 'But, Daddy,' said the kid, picking up another starfish. . . .' "

When I said the story's punch line, Nate said it right with me.

" 'It'll make a difference to this one!' "

He laughed and I laughed with him. "I thought you said you'd never heard it!"

"I never heard you tell it," he said, charming as hell.

"So now that I've told it," I said, "the question is, do you believe it?"

"Yeah," he said slowly. "Yeah, I do. That's why I'm here."

I nodded, glad I hadn't misread him. "Me too."

We were sitting there grinning at each other the way you always do when you bump up against a creature of like mind when you least expect it, when I heard the back door open and turned to see Sheila Lattimore standing there, shivering. She was wearing a thin coat, no hat and no gloves. She looked cold and miserable.

"I'm late," she said, like that explained her belated and bedraggled entrance.

I went over quickly and pulled her inside. Her hands felt like ice. She wasn't wearing boots either, and snow was packed around her shoes.

"Did your car break down?"

"N-n-o," she said through chattering teeth. "I w-w-walked over here."

"From your house?" That was a good four or five miles. "Why?"

But I knew why. The only thing that would make her walk all the way over here in this kind of weather was Junior. "I had to pick up the b-b-boys," she said, her eyes searching for them.

"Deena said she'd drop them off at your house. Didn't she call you?"

"She might have." I could hardly hear her voice. "They wouldn'ta tole me no way." Her face looked swollen, and the bruise on her cheek was new.

"What happened to your face?"

Her hand flew to the spot like she might still be able to cover it. "I f-f-fell. Comin' over here. There was ice on the road."

Nate walked up beside me holding his overcoat and draped it around Sheila's shoulders.

"This is Nate Anderson," I said. "He's a friend."

She nodded, totally dwarfed by that great big coat. She looked like the tree *babymama*, lost and amazed.

"You the new vice principal at the school?" He nodded and she pulled his coat around her a little tighter, her eyes round and childlike. The coat reached almost to her ankles. "My brother said you was real big."

"Who's your brother?"

"Jarvis Lattimore."

A flicker crossed Nate's face, but he just nodded. "Yes. He's in my first-period tutorial."

Sheila looked pleased, but I could see her teeth chattering.

"Look," I said, "why don't you go in the barter closet and see if you can find some dry socks and a sweater. I'll make us some tea."

More than a few times we've been a temporary shelter for some woman with an angry man at home and a backseat full of scared kids. Sometimes they stay a couple of days. One time Patrice stayed a week, just before Sonny went into the service. So we keep a "barter" closet full of clothes and even some shoes, where you take what you need and give what you can. Everything seems to even out in the end.

Sheila turned to Nate. "I'll bring your coat right back to you," she whispered.

"Take your time," he said, following me into the kitchen, where I filled the kettle and turned it up high.

"I'm sorry," I said. "We had some unexpected excitement around here yesterday and I think this is part of the aftermath."

"What happened?"

I tried to think of the most efficient way to tell him the facts without going into too much detail, otherwise we'd be standing here until midnight.

"Her brother Junior came by here yesterday, grabbed his ex-girlfriend by the arm and tried to drag her off."

"Why?"

"She had just quit him because he objected to her new job."

"He doesn't want her to work?"

"He doesn't want her to be a stripper."

"Oh."

The kettle was hissing on its way to a whistle. I took down the pot and dropped in three bags of peppermint tea.

"So what happened?"

"My assistant, Tomika, ran him off with a toy gun before the police got here."

Nate raised his eyebrows as the kettle whistled readiness. I turned it off and poured the steaming water into the teapot, inhaling the peppermint. That should warm Sheila up a little.

"A *toy* gun?"

I nodded.

"Did he know it was a toy?"

"No."

Nate kept his voice neutral, but I could hear the concern in it. "Probably better if you don't tell him."

"I couldn't agree more," I said, grabbing three mugs out of the cupboard and trying to sound confident about the way we were handling things. "Our lips are collectively sealed."

"No tea for me," Nate said as I arranged the cups on the tray with a honey bear and a couple of spoons. "She doesn't need to be worrying about talking in front of a stranger."

He was probably right about that, but I was sorry we hadn't had a chance to finish our conversation.

"Are you planning to drive her home?"

"Of course."

"Do you want me to follow you?"

I was a little confused. "Why?"

"This guy sounds like he might be trouble." He sounded really concerned. "I thought you might want some backup."

The thought hadn't occured to me. If I waited around for backup I'd never get anything done.

"No thanks," I said, figuring that the presence of a gigantic male stranger might not sit too well with the Lattimore brothers or their mother. What I needed to do was talk to Sheila again about moving out. She wanted desperately to do it, but her family wasn't about to surrender their slave without a fight. Literally. So far, Sheila hadn't had the heart to take them on. Maybe this time she would.

"But thanks for asking," I said, looking at Nate. "I appreciate it."

He opened his mouth to say something else, but Sheila padded into the kitchen wearing a pair of huge gray sweats, some red wool socks and a baggy sweater that reached almost to her knees. She was carrying Nate's coat.

She handed it to him and managed a shy smile. "Thank you."

"You're welcome," he said.

I handed the tray to Sheila. "Why don't you take this, and I'll be there in a second."

"Sure," she said. She turned for a last look at Nate. "Nice to meet you."

"My pleasure," he said, and did a little formal bow like a Japanese businessman respecting his own tradition even in a Savile Row suit.

He had parked out back, and I walked him to the door.

"Thanks for coming by," I said.

"Hey!" he said suddenly. "What about my letter of intent?"

My confusion must have been evident. I had forgotten he came here to hand me a letter. What had I done with it?

"About the house," he said. "I just wanted to make sure there was something written down between us since I'm never going back to the Motel 6 and evicting me could get ugly."

"We do things a little more informally up here than they do in the city," I said, holding out my hand. "A handshake will do fine."

"Done!" He shook my hand and we made his residency at the Smitherman place official. I wondered how long his fingers were, but I felt like it would be inappropriate to measure, palm to palm, like you do when you're a kid and all measures of who's the biggest are acceptable. In this case, the answer was truly obvious. His hand dwarfed my own.

"Sure you don't want me to go with you when you take her home?"

"I'm fine," I said. "Don't worry."

He smiled. "Once a cop, always a cop, I guess."

I smiled back. "Thanks for coming by."

"May I consider this conversation *to be continued?*"

"Absolutely."

"Good," he said, opening the door and stepping out into the cold. "I'll look forward to it."

"Me too."

I watched him get into that big black car and glide off into the evening and realized *I already was.*

TWENTY-TWO

here we go again

A HALF HOUR LATER Sheila and I had finished our tea and she had given me a pretty good sense of what was going on at the Lattimore house.

"They really mad about what happened."

"Who?"

She shrugged. "My brothers, my mama. All of 'em."

"They should be mad—at *Junior*."

"He say it was between him and Nik, and Tee didn't have no business to get in it at all."

"Is that what you think?"

She pulled the shapeless sweater tighter around her thin shoulders. "He was drunk," she said, like that explained everything.

"But what do you *think?*"

I wondered what plan of action the Lattimore brothers were capable of concocting, sitting around with the curtains drawn in the middle of the day, the TV light flickering on their handsome faces like the frames of an old-time silent movie.

"Junior mean, Miz J. He always been like that. Just mean as a snake, even as a kid, but he family, you know? He always gonna be my big brother and blood is blood, right?"

Right. "Did Junior hit you?"

She shook her head.

"Then who?"

"My mama."

"Why?" Was the whole family insane?

Sheila shrugged. "I told you they all mad about what happened."

"Mad at you?"

"Just mad."

"You know we've got plenty of sleeping bags if you and the kids want to camp out here for tonight."

"Nah. That'd just make 'em even madder."

"Oh." I didn't know what else to suggest.

We looked at each other and then she tried to smile in a way I guess she thought was reassuring and stood up.

"I guess I better start back."

I stood up too. "I'll drive you."

She hesitated.

"Sheila," I said, as gently as I could. "I'm not going to let you walk home in the dark in a foot of snow."

"Okay." She glanced out the window. She didn't hardly want to walk back those long, cold, solitary miles if she didn't have to. "I guess it'll be okay."

"I won't come in."

"Can you let me off at the corner?"

I wanted to say *no way*, but she was already so freaked out, I agreed.

"All right," I said. "But you call me if you need me to come and pick you and the kids up later."

"I will," she said, stuffing her feet into a pair of barter closet boots that were a couple of sizes too big, but fleece-lined and dry. With the big red socks they almost fit and Sheila smiled for the first time tonight.

When we got close, I let her off at the corner like I promised I would and that's when I realized Nate was following me. I thought I had seen his car after we left The Circus, but I figured it was just a coincidence. This is a very small town and the path to almost anywhere takes you across the path to almost everywhere else, but after a couple of turns down the decidedly non-major roads that lead to the Lattimore house, I saw him again.

If the trees hadn't been so bare, I might have missed him. He is an ex-cop, after all. He knows how to follow you without being seen if he wants to. But I grew up here. I know shortcuts he has yet to discover and two quick turns put me back on the main road right behind him. I pulled up close at the first stop sign and tapped the horn. His startled eyes in the rearview mirror were all the proof I needed.

When he turned in at the gas station like he'd been headed there all the time, I did too.

"Hello, again," I said, remembering that old Marvelettes song about the hunter getting captured by the game. "Were you following me?"

His smile was sheepish and surprised. "Will it do me any good to deny it?"

"Not a bit."

"Then I'll come clean. Yes, I was following you."

"Why?"

"I had some concerns about your safety."

He had some concerns? "Would those be the same concerns you mentioned to me earlier?"

"Those would be the ones," he said. "Were you really going to get gas? I can pump it for you while we talk."

"No, thanks," I said, not sure exactly how I felt about this, but pretty sure it was in the general neighborhood of uncomfortable. "I told you I'd be fine."

He was still smiling. "Like I said before, I thought you might need some backup."

I was *definitely* uncomfortable, but I just looked at him. We weren't even really friends yet (were we?) and I was already correcting him like he had agreed to the ground rules. Well, too bad. Here we go again.

"That's lovely," I said, "but you can't trick me into it. I'm a smart woman. If I need to be protected from something, you can tell me. Then we can discuss whether or not I agree, how I've handled the situation in the past and whether or not I'm open to that kind of help from you. Then I will decide to accept or decline your offer of assistance."

He was looking at me like I was crazy, but these kinds of discussions are always so fraught with misunderstanding, it's important to be clear, and when you're clear, you always run the risk of sounding doctrinaire and inflexible. I tried to soften it a little. "But I appreciate the impetus."

"The impetus?"

I nodded. "The fact that you wanted to help."

"You're serious, aren't you?"

I hate that question. It's like when the guy at the liquor store counter looks at your driver's license photo, squints and says, "This you?" because he doesn't recognize you without your glasses/bangs/dreadlocks/crow's-feet. What are you going to say? *Nah, man. That ain't me. I was just kidding around.*

"Of course, I'm serious," I said. "I don't like to have anybody making decisions about me but me."

"Even for your own protection?"

"*Especially* for my own protection." If that doesn't confuse him, nothing will. I tried to keep my face neutral and waited.

"Then I apologize," he said after a minute when I couldn't tell what he was thinking. "And I stand corrected."

"Do you have any idea what I'm talking about?"

He shook his head in a way that could only be described as rueful. "No. I can't truthfully say that I do."

Good, I thought. Admitting confusion is always an important first step, especially for those self-confident brothers who seem to have a deep faith in their own infallibility coded into their DNA.

"Well, I'd like to stay and explain it to you," I said, "but I've gotta go." I smiled at him as I climbed back into my car. "To be continued, remember?"

"Right," he said, looking more confused than ever. "Good deal."

To be continued was right. Something told me that me and big Nate had a whole lot of talking to do before we finally saw eye to eye, but I'm up for the challenge. If I can make him understand the basics, maybe we can actually be friends.

TWENTY-THREE

the last thing
on my mind

THE GOOD THING ABOUT having the house to myself is that everything stays exactly where I put it. The bad thing is that tonight that includes the breakfast dishes. I filled the dishpan with hot soapy water while I sliced up some fresh vegetables and put on a pot of brown rice. Bill says I eat so much rice and drink so much tea I must have been Chinese in one of my most recent past lives. That's highly possible, but I have no memory of past lives, ancient or otherwise. If I could pick, I'd probably choose this one all over again, even though being black and female in a place that doesn't bring a whole lot of love to either group is probably not the most luxe life I could come up with.

On the other hand, I've been well loved and truly blessed with friends and family and even a social house cat or two, and here I am tonight standing at the sink in my own cozy little house, smelling my dinner on the stove and wondering how to fit a great big beautiful stranger into what I think is already a pretty full life.

Sister would tell me to relax and go with the flow, which is, of course, exactly what I should do, but I can't help trying to define a place for him in my mind as educator, optimist, neighbor, friend, before that little voice in there that hasn't been allowed out for so long defines things for me in terms that would let him know beyond a shadow of a doubt that being a separatist is the last thing on my mind.

TWENTY-FOUR

best of all
possible worlds

MAVIS WAS FEELING FINE again, so Tee came in early. By the time I got there, she had settled Mavis in the community room with a new coloring book and Tee herself was scribbling furiously on a legal pad. Her desk was already covered with crumpled yellow sheets she had rejected.

"Good morning," I said. "What're you working on so hard?"

"I had another idea," she said without looking up. "I think it's better than the first one."

I was still in awe of the perfection of her anti–Super Bowl inspiration and her Denzel theory. I couldn't wait. *Three's the charm.*

"What is it?" I said, hanging my coat in the closet.

"Hold on a second," she said. "Get your tea, and I'll be ready to brief you."

"To brief me?" She sounded like a presidential press secretary. The surprise in my voice made her look up, grinning.

"I been watchin' *The West Wing*, okay?"

I laughed. "You keep having big ideas, that's where you're going to end up."

She shook her head. "Not me. I'd be slappin' people regular if they leaked my stuff after I told 'em not to."

She bent back over the pad and I examined her hair. Today's braids were still blond, but gathered on top for an overall waterfall effect. She had pulled them so tightly that her already almond-shaped eyes suddenly had a pronounced slant. It wasn't unattractive so much as unexpected.

I went to the kitchen and poured myself a cup of peppermint tea, complimented Mavis on her ability to stay within the lines of her new Barney activity book and made a mental note to schedule an appointment with the new kindergarten teacher at the public school. Three of our Circus babies will be starting there in the fall and I want her to know I have high expectations for their continued growth and good nature.

Most of the teachers I've worked with have been at the high school level, but now the babies are growing up and I'm meeting a whole new group. What I always do is tell them what I know about the kids, about their family situations, and offer assistance in keeping the mother active and involved. I've never had a teacher who was less than grateful. As overworked as most of them are, any help is like an unexpected blessing.

When Deena arrived with the twins and Marquis in tow, I headed back to Tee, who was waiting for me in the office, her eyes shining with excitement.

"Okay," she said, "here's the deal."

I sat down, took a swallow of tea and prepared to listen.

"We need to have a film festival."

"A film festival?"

She nodded and thrust a clipping at me from last Sunday's *New York Times*. "They got a million of 'em goin' in New York all the time. Movies I ain't never heard of."

She pointed to an announcement of a series dedicated to the work of Japanese director Akira Kurosawa, one of my favorites.

"That's because you won't watch anything but American movies," I couldn't resist pointing out.

Tee looked annoyed. "That's not the point, Miz J. The point is, they chargin' people money to see old movies and they gettin' it too. Sellin' out the place."

She handed me another clipping that included a photograph of an intense-looking group of young people listening to a discussion of the French New Wave.

"And they not just foreign movies either," she said. "They had one where they only showed Spike Lee movies and he came there himself to talk about what he had in mind when he made 'em."

The clipping showed Spike fielding questions from a packed house after a showing of *Malcolm X*.

"They should have gotten Denzel," I said, just teasing, but Tee nodded enthusiastically.

"Now you feelin' me!" She beamed. "That's exactly what I'm talkin' about!"

"Getting Denzel?"

"Havin' a film festival!"

"A Denzel Washington film festival?" I immediately wondered about the possibility of an even stronger anti-Denzel backlash, but Tee was one step ahead of me.

She shook her head and grinned. "They'd never let me get away with that," she said, "but it don't hafta be him for the first

one. It's a lot of movies people like to see, especially if we do it
like we do when it's just a few of us here."

"How's that?"

She shrugged, tugging at a few braids to loosen them, round-
ing out her eyes just a little. "You know, how you always ask us a
bunch of trick questions so we end up seeing some stuff we
never would have got just talkin' about it regular."

"They're not trick questions," I said. "They're to make you
think."

"Whatever," Tee said. "The point is, if we have a festival, we
can make it somethin' special by gettin' people who come talk
about it afterward."

Our marathon postmovie discussions are legendary around
here. We don't really schedule them. It's just that some films
raise a lot of questions worthy of exploring. I try to guide things
in a way that helps us draw some useful conclusions, but I'm also
trying to give them the pleasure that comes with a free exchange
of ideas.

After we watched *Set It Off* one night, the conversation
touched on the problems of bank robbery as a career option, the
challenge of keeping your friends when you are trying to move
up in the world, whether or not lesbians can really be in love the
same way heterosexuals are in love, the easy availability of guns
from people like Black Sam and the constant problem of inflexible bosses like Luther of the self-monikered janitorial service
where the women worked between heists.

By spending a minimum of time on questions like whether or
not a fine, educated brother-with-bank like Blair Underwood
would ever have hit on a girl from the projects who wandered
into the bank even if she was fine, and if that was *really* Jada
Pinkett Smith's round brown behind in that nude shot, we were

able to keep the discussion moving and not get bogged down in the gossip zone.

Tee obviously enjoyed these discussions as much as I did, but the idea of expanding them to a more general audience took me by surprise. *Could it work?*

"We'll announce a whole series," Tee said. "A coupla weekends, maybe tie it to Black History Month if we hurry up, and don't charge too much, maybe two dollars, just so they get used to the idea of payin' *somethin'* and almost everybody got two dollars. . . ."

"You want to charge admission?"

Tee looked at me real serious. "Look, Miz J, we need to raise some money, right?"

I nodded.

"And you tole those guys in Lansing to take a hike, right?"

"Right." Even though I hadn't figured out how to replace that money, I still wasn't sorry.

"So where we gonna get it from?" Tee spread her arms as wide as her smile. "From us! Look at this!"

She snatched up the legal pad she'd been working on, and shoved it across the desk in my direction. "We can get a hundred people in here if we set the chairs up close together in the big room, and if we charge everybody two dollars, we can clear a coupla hundred bucks a night."

Tee was on a roll. This idea had real possibilities. Two hundred dollars wouldn't be near enough, of course, but every little bit helps. Even better, it would get everybody involved, which was the only way we were going to survive over the long haul. This was, in fact, a best-of-all-possible-worlds idea. It was entertaining, it had real use and educational value *and* it generated income.

I looked at Tee's careful calculations and then at her, perched expectantly on the corner of the desk. "You've done it again," I said. "I think this can really work."

Tee glowed. "Of course it can."

My brain instantly began to organize things. What films should we show? Who should lead the discussion? What about child care? Should we pop popcorn and sell soft drinks? But before I had a chance to start asking questions, Tee hopped off the desk and held up her hand. Her fingernails, as always, were brightly painted in a shade to match her lipstick. She was wearing a pair of tight pants and an equally fitted sweater. No one who saw her buying makeup at the mall, a favorite outing, would guess what kind of creative mind is nestled under all those golden braids. Her protective coloration was so complete that if it had been conscious, I would have called it a disguise. But it wasn't. It was just Tee, *keepin' it real.*

"So I just thought this last night, okay? I just tole you all I know, and so far, it sounds good, right?"

"It sounds real good," I said. "I can't wait."

"Well, you gonna have to," she said. "Because I gotta think about it some more before you start askin' me questions."

She knew me too well. "What makes you think I was going to start asking questions?"

She rolled her eyes as if to say *puh-leez.* "Weren't you?"

In response to a direct question, I'm not allowed to lie, so I laughed and confessed.

"Okay, just a few," I said. "It's such a great idea and I just wanted to know how——"

"Stop!" she said. "You tryin' to sneak one in, but I know you, Miz J, and I'm not goin' for it. You got work to do. So do I. As soon as I figure some more stuff out, I'll tell you."

"That's fair," I said.

"Good." She sat down and something flickered across her expression like a small cloud in a perfectly blue sky. "Now I got one more thing to tell you."

I shifted into neutral. "What's that?"

"Junior been callin' me."

"Here?"

She shook her head. "At home. He don't say nothin' and he don't leave no message and he callin' from a street phone so no number show up on the caller I.D., but I know it's him."

"Can you hear anything in the background?"

"Naw, not really. It ain't nothin', I guess. He just call and hang up, call and hang up."

"How many times does he call?"

She looked at me without any change of expression. "He call a lot."

My heart sank. "How many times would you say?"

She looked at me and her chin trembled slightly. "Last night, he call for a hour. Every time I pick it up, he just click off, but he did it for a hour."

"Why did you keep answering?"

Her eyes flashed. "So he'd know I wadn't scared! It's my phone at my house. When it ring, I'ma answer it."

"Do you want to call the sheriff?"

"What's he gonna do? Nothin'." She shook her head. "Naw. I don't need to call nobody. I just wanted you to know so if anything go down, you'll know who did it."

That really sent a chill through me. What did she think was going to happen? "I think you should come and bring Mavis and stay with me a couple of nights. You know I've got plenty of room."

"So do I," she said. "I worked hard to get my place fixed up just the way we like it."

Tee rented a tiny, barely winterized cottage not far from The Circus. Once her last boyfriend had moved out, Tee began the slow process of transforming the place. She painted the inside, put up a swing set for Mavis and considered planting flowers until she realized gardening is hell on a serious manicure, even with gloves on. She settled for three pink flamingos in the yard instead and a huge metal daisy whose petals rotate with the wind. Tee loved her house and dreamed of buying it. For Junior to run her out was unthinkable, and I had to respect that.

"All right," I said. "Tell me if he keeps calling, okay?"

"I will," she said, picking up her legal pad. "Now if you don't mind, Miz J, I got work to do."

TWENTY-FIVE

getting better
all the time

I HADN'T HEARD FROM Nate since our exchange at the gas station the day before, but when I got home, his voice was the first one on my answering machine. It was so deep, I had to adjust the volume to bring up the rumble.

"Joyce?" he said, sounding like I imagine Barry White sounds when he just wakes up in the morning. "It's Nate. Just wanted to say—"

He stopped abruptly and there was a long pause, followed by what sounded like a low chuckle or not too distant thunder. This man even laughed large.

"What do I want to say? I guess just that you made me consider some things the other night, standing by the side of the road—" Another pause. "And I don't think, no! I *know* I wouldn't have thought about them at all if you hadn't pulled my coat, so—"

Pause. "So, thanks. I guess that's what I wanted to say. Thanks for taking the time, you know, and not just assuming I'm a macho fool who can't . . . who can't deal with a woman as a full equal."

Another pause. I was right. He was definitely a product of some prolonged exchanges with some serious women who had taken time with him. If all women's studies classes ever do is get a man or two to hesitate, however briefly, like Nate was doing, before deciding they automatically know more/better/best, just on the basis of *maleness*, those programs will be worth all the struggles it took to get them.

"So thanks," he finished up quickly. "And I hope we can do some work together and maybe even be . . . friends."

I ran the message back a couple of times to check the tone of voice, study the nuances and duration of each pause. It was beautiful. A readmission of his initial confusion, an offering of his gratitude to me for providing new and useful information, all topped off with an offer to be friends. *This guy was good.*

The only other message was from the Smitherman twins.

"Hello, dear." Geneva's sweet contralto voice greeted me with just the barest tremble of age. "We're back! Thank you so much for looking after everything and how wonderful to know you've rented the house already." I had left them a note and a copy of Nate's letter of intent. "Our trip truly wore us out, so we're turning in early, so you don't need to call tonight, but come by and see us in the morning on your way in. We've missed you!"

"And bring some sugar," Lynette called quickly just before the click.

I wrote myself a note so I wouldn't forget and propped it against the sugar bowl. I had missed them too, plus their timing couldn't have been better. It gave me a reason to call Nate. Somebody had to introduce him to his landladies, right?

TWENTY-SIX

same woods, same water

THE SMITHERMAN TWINS HAVE been here so long nobody can remember when they weren't, beautiful and brilliant, elegantly ensconced in their large lakefront house, tending their garden and each other with equal delicacy and care. Their father was a gangster who made a fortune during Prohibition and ran several successful speakeasies in Detroit over the years. He also operated a legendary Idlewild club that was famous for its Creole food and spacious dance floor. Labor Day weekend, you couldn't get a table unless Mr. Smitherman knew you, or Mrs. Smitherman thought you might be a good catch for one of her daughters, who, to her constant annoyance, seemed completely uninterested in anybody's company but their own.

At seventy plus, they were still each other's best friend. They spent four or five months a year traveling, including their annual

sojourn to New York and Chicago, which allowed them to
indulge a shared passion for theater and fine dining. It also
afforded them an opportunity to catch up with a tiny circle of
very old friends with similar shadowy backgrounds. All were
equally independent and equally ancient women who sometimes
pulled up at the Smithermans' in their chauffeur-driven limos
for a surprise overnighter on their way to Miami for the season
or Atlanta to see their grandchildren.

It was a rarefied and exclusive little club, these pampered
daughters of men whose fortunes had been made so long ago
nobody was alive who remembered the specifics. They never
used the word *gangster*, and in front of them, neither did anybody else. I always thought of Mr. Smitherman as a businessman. When my dad decided to move here, it was Mr.
Smitherman's old club site that he bought to renovate and
reopen as his own. After I had so much death in my family, the
twins made it their business to keep me from going off the deep
end, which is right where I was headed. Survivor guilt can be
terminal if you let it. I can't begin to tell you how many nights
they insisted I stay in one of their big empty bedrooms so they
could feed me dinner and tuck me in and assure me that *yes*, I
was allowed to live through it.

"Nobody ever died of a broken heart," Lynette would
say, although in those days I thought my chances were about
fifty/fifty.

"You can't afford to go yet," Geneva would remind me, kissing me good night like I was her child instead of her friend.
"You still have work to do."

When they're in town, I usually see them every couple of
days. Since their house is directly across the lake from mine, in
good weather, I can watch them do their t'ai chi on the deck, but

today they were inside by the fire, drinking strong coffee and listening to Dinah Washington singing "Unforgettable." Even at eight o'clock the first morning after their arrival, they were up and fully dressed in good wool skirts and cardigan sweater sets. They looked like teachers, although neither one had ever held a full-time job. Their parents allowed them to go to college, but working for a living was out of the question.

"Well, aren't you a sight for sore eyes!" Geneva, the oldest twin by ten minutes, greeted me with a smile, drawing me inside to her sister. "Look who's here, Nettie."

Lynette Smitherman was sitting on their old Victorian sofa with a giant scrapbook open on her lap and an art deco footstool at her feet. Their furniture was all from another era, but not necessarily the same one.

"Thank goodness," she said, throwing up her hands in exasperation. "Maybe you can recognize some of these Negroes!"

"Which Negroes are those?" I said, slipping off my coat and going to look.

"We're trying to get organized." Geneva chuckled at her sister's well-known impatience and sat back down beside her. "Our first task is to get the old scrapbooks in some kind of order." She gestured vaguely at a huge stack of photograph albums on the floor beside them. "Some of these belonged to mother, so you know how long ago that was!"

"How many have you got?"

"Too many!" Lynette said. "We haven't even been back a good twenty-four hours and now, just because she couldn't recognize some people we haven't seen in forty years, Gen thinks we've got to turn this place into the Library of Congress and start labeling everything in sight."

"Welcome back," I said, sitting down on her other side and looking at the pages she was perusing with not only her own bifocals, but a huge magnifying glass whose ivory handle was elaborately carved into the shape of an elephant. Their house was filled with exotic mementos of their travels. I knew, for example, that this elephant had come all the way from a teeming marketplace in the middle of central Ceylon.

Lynette was using the glass to examine two large photographs on facing pages, both from some long-ago formal event being held at what was probably the Lot Owner's Club House. Both pictures were carefully posed with smiling women in satin gowns seated in a semicircle on folding chairs while their tuxedo-clad husbands stood behind them, looking as handsome as they ever would—and knowing it.

"We had a little reunion this trip," Geneva said. "Dolly Barthwell passed and we wanted to have a little toast for her."

"Champagne," Lynette said, turning another page. "Dolly would only drink champagne."

Geneva nodded. "So a couple of people brought their scrapbooks, and when we started going through them, we realized we couldn't remember everybody's name anymore."

Lynette harrumphed at that. "Which is no great tragedy," she said. "I didn't remember most of their names back then either!"

"But I did," Geneva said gently. "And I want to again. What good is a photograph if you can't remember who's in it?"

"Anybody in here look familiar to you?" Lynette turned toward me.

"I'm sorry," I said. "I think this was before my time."

They looked startled, and then they laughed softly together.

"What?"

"Nothing, dear," Geneva said. "It's just that sometimes we forget how old we are."

"These photographs ought to remind us," Lynette grumbled.

"If you stop complaining," Geneva said. "I'll make you a fresh pot of coffee."

Lynette's eyes lit up. "Done! I'll be quiet as a mouse."

"How about you, dear?" Gen said to me. "Will you join us for a cup?"

"Thank you," I said, remembering the small packet of sugar in my coat pocket and handing it over. I'm primarily a tea drinker, but the Smitherman sisters only drink black coffee with lots of sugar. They told me once that when they were little girls, their father kept very late hours, and their mother was determined to be up and awake whenever he came home, no matter what the hour, so she drank a lot of coffee. It was years later that they realized she was always afraid he wouldn't come home at all. For them, the smell conjures up memories of their mother and father talking softly about the day just passed while most of their friends' parents were just getting up to make the five o'clock shift at General Motors or Ford.

"Here's one I'll bet you recognize," she said, and I looked over into my father's smiling face.

I recognized the photograph. My mother took it, and I have the framed original on my mantel at home. It was the opening of Daddy's club, and all his friends were there, wearing new tuxedos. They would never again be quite as certain that they were the men they wanted to be, but that night you couldn't tell them they weren't royalty. My father gave them that for one small moment, and they loved him for it until the day he died.

"Alonzo Harris," I said, pointing at each one in turn. "Mer-

shall Graham, Cunningham Beardon, Charlie Jones, Oscar Hand
and Daddy."

Lynette nodded. "That was an impressive group of men gathered at your father's place. They looked like kings."

I remember that night so well. The place was packed. The
band was hired all the way from Detroit. Everybody was dressed
to the nines and Mitch kissed me for the first time while my parents were busy greeting their other guests.

"You think we'll ever have a time like that again?" I said.
"When this really feels like a paradise for colored people?"

Lynette shook her head firmly. "You can get rid of that idea,
dear. It's never going to be that way again. Not like it was."

"Why not?" I said. "The same things that drew people here
before are still here. Same woods, same water."

"Negroes are different now," Lynette said. "We used to *want*
to be with our own kind. We needed that fellowship, that cama-
raderie, that mirror of what we really were, no matter what we
had to pretend to be out there trying to make a living wage."

She pointed to the photograph of another group in tuxedos.
"In real life, you know what these men did for a living?" Her
slender finger touched each face gently. "This one was a janitor
in a high school. This one worked at the Ford assembly plant for
forty years. This one was a superstar at the post office, just like
your dad."

In the photograph, they looked like heads of state, business-
men, educators, leaders; their best selves shone through like new
money.

"And what happened?" She closed the scrapbook with a snap
and looked at me. "Why did people stop coming here?"

This was a familiar topic in Idlewild, especially among the
oldsters, and I was sorry I had introduced it. I wanted to tell

them about Nate, not rehash our theories about what happened to paradise.

"I'll tell you what happened." Lynette was getting increasingly agitated and there were small spots of color on each of her ivory-colored cheeks. "They decided they'd rather be with white folks instead of each other. *Self-hatred*, pure and simple! That's all it is!"

"Hush, Nettie," Geneva said, coming in with the coffee on a small silver tray. "It's too early in the morning for you to be that cynical."

"What's the time of day got to do with it?" Lynette shot back. "You think anything's going to change between now and noon?"

"Yes," Geneva said, handing her sister one steaming mug and me another. "Your disposition."

She slid the scrapbook away from Nettie and placed it back on the stack nearby. "Take a break so Joyce can tell us about our new tenant."

Lynette was only too happy to comply. She took a long swallow of coffee that was still too hot for me to do anything but sip and nodded approvingly. "Best idea you've had all morning. I had almost forgotten about him."

"What's he like?" Geneva said. "He wrote a lovely letter."

"He's the new vice principal at the high school," I said. "Just got here from Detroit when a slot opened up. I met him at Sister's house last week. He seems really nice, loves his work and . . ."

I stopped myself. Was telling them how big he was appropriate? What difference did it really make? Besides, mentioning it might make them focus there when they otherwise might not even notice, although the chances of that were pretty slim. He was taller than everybody else around here by at least a foot.

"What is it, dear?" Geneva said gently. "What's wrong?"

Lynette frowned slightly. "Don't you like him?"

"Yes, yes, I do," I reassured them quickly. "I like him very much—so do Sister and Bill. He's just very . . . *tall*."

Their faces were immediately full of surprise and curiosity. "How tall?" They said in unison.

"Pretty tall," I said. "He's six foot eight."

"Oh, my goodness!" Geneva said with a gentle chuckle. "That's tall all right."

"And he's kind of big too," I said. "He lifts weights."

They exchanged a glance. "You didn't rent our place to a bodybuilder, did you, dear?"

"No," I said, laughing at what a mess I was making of a simple introduction. "I just didn't want you to be startled when you meet him. Sister didn't warn me, and when I turned around and saw him, I'm sure I was visibly surprised."

"I can't wait to see him," Lynette said, sipping her coffee. "I haven't seen anybody that tall since we met Wilt Chamberlain."

"You met Wilt Chamberlain?" I was amazed sometimes at the names they dropped into casual conversation.

Geneva nodded, smiling. "Nettie was so fresh. She followed the man around all night."

"I wasn't being fresh. I had never been close to another human being anywhere near that size. It was mysterious to me and, actually, quite wonderful."

"You weren't one of his twenty thousand, were you?" I said, teasing her about Chamberlain's legendary sexual prowess.

Lynette just lifted her finely chiseled chin and sniffed regally. "I've never been one of twenty thousand *anything*."

"I stand corrected," I said, laughing again and reaching for my coat. "I've got to go. Welcome home! I missed you two."

"We missed you too, dear," they said, walking with me to the door. "Bring Mr. Anderson by to see us soon, all right?"

"Of course," I said. "Just don't tell him I already warned you about how tall he is. It might make him self-conscious."

"Our lips are sealed," said Geneva, but Lynette just smiled.

TWENTY-SEVEN

for us, by us

I STOPPED BY THE bank to ask about a second mortgage and they took an hour to turn me down because they didn't want to hurt my feelings. I crossed another possibility off my list of potential money sources and reminded myself to ask Sister to tell me again how long this mysterious thing that's keeping up so many distractions might take to get itself born. In the meantime, I'm determined to take one day at a time.

When I got to The Circus, Tee was working on the festival.

"Got a minute?" she said as soon as I walked in.

"Sure," I said. "Got a plan?"

"Here's what I got so far," she said. "We'll do all four weekends in February."

"That's only a couple of weeks from now," I said, always the worrier.

"Right," said Tee with the confidence of a sleepwalker. "And it's Black History Month, so everybody lookin' for somethin' black to do anyway. We'll do Friday night, Saturday night and a Sunday matinee. Two dollars a show or five dollars for a weekend pass."

"A weekend pass? I like that."

Tee smiled like a proud mother whose kid had just finished her first solo at the Christmas concert without a hitch. "That was Deena's idea. She said that makes it sound like a bargain."

Deena, with two toddlers, was an expert at bargains, real and imagined.

"You told Deena already?"

Tee nodded. "Of course. Who you think gonna deal with all them kids they gonna bring wit 'em? And I called everybody to see what they thought and everybody down wit it."

There was no denying that Tee was covering all the bases. "Go on."

She consulted her legal pad. "We're gonna feature four actresses who starred in at least three black movies each."

"What do you mean by *black movies?*" I said, not wanting to make any assumptions. Will Smith, for example, is a black actor, but *The Legend of Bagger Vance* is not a black movie.

"I mean movies made *by us, for us,*" Tee said. "Some of these girls got Hollywood stuff goin' on too, but I don't want to see Miss Vivica A. Fox in *Batman.* I wanna see her in *Set It Off.*"

I couldn't even remember which *Batman* she was in. All I remembered was that feathered costume and I think Arnold Schwarzenegger was in there freezing people or something. Suddenly, I remembered my most recently viewed video. "You showing *Booty Call?*"

"Be serious," Tee said. "Everybody got a right to take a rent-payin' gig every now and then, but we ain't showin' *Woo* either, okay?"

Tee was a generous spirit, but her critical faculties were still intact.

"We gonna start with Halle Berry 'cause she producin' now too, so she need her props. Then we gonna do Miz Nia Long, Miz Jada Pinkett Smith and Miz Viv."

"My girls," I said, pleased she had picked four of my own favorites to feature. "Did you pick the movies too?"

"Of course." Tee flipped to another page on the legal pad. "I got three for each. Ready?"

"I'm ready."

Tee cleared her throat and read out her list slowly.

"For Halle Berry, we got to open with *Introducing Dorothy Dandridge* because she kicked ass."

I couldn't have agreed more. We had all been moved by the film and by Berry's long journey to get it done. I had been amazed that for so many of our regulars, this was the first time they had ever heard Dandridge's name.

"We also got *Strictly Business* 'cause that's her first starring role, and *Boomerang* 'cause I want to hear you dog Robin Givens."

"I don't dog people!" I protested, but if I did, Robin Givens might be one I'd pick. On the other hand, she's been through a lot already, being married to Mike and all. The fact that every-body made it out alive was pure luck. She probably doesn't need me to rub her nose in it.

Tee ignored me. "For Nia Long, we've got *Friday* 'cause she stand up to that big crazy nigga when he beats her sister, and 'cause Chris Tucker cute as he wanna be in that movie, even though he stay high. Then we got *Love Jones* and *The Best Man.*" She frowned. "You see it yet?"

I shook my head. She's been telling me to see *The Best Man* ever since it came out, but I can never find it at the video store and I missed it at the movies.

Tee reached into her purse and pulled out a Blockbuster bag. "You gettin' to be a lost cause, Miz J. You got *Booty Call* and ain't seen *The Best Man*. What's up with that?"

I accepted the bag without trying to defend myself.

"You'll like it," she said, going back to her list. "For Miz Jada we got *Jason's Lyric*, 'cause it's real romantic, *Low Down Dirty Shame* 'cause it's funny and that Spike Lee movie didn't none of us go see where they paint their face black."

Bamboozled didn't get a huge response from our core audience. They didn't know anything about the tradition of theatrical blackface, and the tap-dancing genius that made Savion Glover the darling of New York hasn't really penetrated the heartland yet. I liked it a lot and I know it will make them think and talk, plus it's funny as hell. That was a good choice.

"We close out with Miz Vivica in *Soul Food*, which also got Nia Long, *Set It Off*, which also got Jada, and *Why Do Fools Fall in Love?* which got more Halle Berry, so the last week, we kinda bring 'em all back together for the finale." Tee sat back and looked at me with a smile of pure satisfaction. "So, whattya think?"

There were a few I would have added, like *What's Love Got to Do with It?* because Angela Bassett is so fierce from start to finish, and Whoopi Goldberg's first concert movie because it's too good not to, and because most of our crowd have only seen her in *How Stella Got Her Groove Back*, not her best work, although her death scene was beautifully underplayed.

I even wanted to put in a good word for *Bulworth* and *Losing Isaiah* because of the presence of hardworking Halle Berry, and

I wrestled with a fast lobbying effort on behalf of *Made in America* because of the great scenes between Whoopi and Nia Long as her daughter, plus the sweetness of pre–*Independence Day* Will Smith, but race plays such a central role in all three, and once you start down that road, race is all you talk about. Tee was right. These movies needed to be *for us, by us.*

"I think we better figure out how to get some more chairs," I said.

"I'll take care of that," she said briskly. "You just need to get your questions together."

"My questions?"

She grinned at me. "We gotta have you talk your talk at the end, otherwise what's the point? We could watch 'em at home if you ain't gonna do your thing."

"What exactly is *my thing?*"

"You know what I mean! The way you always can see how every little thing fits together so at the end we got some kind of better understandin' of how it relate to us. So you gotta see all the movies and get some questions together so people will stay on point and not just be talkin' out the side of they neck."

I understood what she was saying and it made perfect sense. "Sort of an outline?"

She frowned at the word, which probably conjured up too many uncompleted term papers. I tried again.

"Questions," I said. "Some questions to get us started in the right direction."

"There you go!" she said. "That's what I need!"

"No problem," I said. "I'll get right on it. Anything else?"

"I know this one is like supposed to be open to the public and all, but how about we don't invite any guys?"

"Why?"

She put down her legal pad and looked at me. "Because when *they* come—"

The way she said *they* sounded like some alien life-form, known for bogarting into places where they aren't welcome.

"—it changes the whole vibe."

She was right about that. Dropping a few men into almost any group of women results in an immediate reshifting of priorities and alliances. Truth often falls by the wayside as hormones invariably rage.

"If it's a public event, I don't know if we can legally keep them, out," I said.

Tee just rolled her eyes and flipped her beaded braids over her shoulders. "All we gotta do is say it's *for women only*. Ain't no guys gonna try to crash an all-girl party!"

"You're in charge," I said. "Why don't you ask the others and then decide?"

"Okay." She made a note and then grinned at me. "I like the sound of that, you know? Bein' in charge?"

"Don't let it go to your head!"

"Too late," she said. "I'm just gettin' started good."

"That's what I'm afraid of." I laughed, only half teasing. Tee was off and running. All I could do now was get on board or get out of the way.

TWENTY-EIGHT

just friends

WHEN I CALLED NATE to set up a time for me to introduce him to Lynette and Geneva, he told me Anita Lattimore had just turned up at the principal's office because her son Jarvis had been suspended for a week after he got caught smoking dope in the boys' locker room. Anita took issue with the decision to interrupt her boy's education, although Jarvis was not known around Baldwin High School for his academic prowess.

The principal, a small, perpetually exhausted man whose good intentions had long since been overpowered by the day-to-day realities of American public education, called Nate for backup when Anita threatened to *whip his ass* unless her son was allowed back in class by tomorrow morning.

"What did you tell her?" I said.

"I told her that issuing terroristic threats was against the law and if she didn't want to go to jail she better find another way to express her displeasure."

"Did that work?" If I knew Anita, all that did was add fuel to the fire.

Nate's rumbling chuckle told me I was right.

"Well, she offered to whip *my* ass as soon as she got through whippin' Bernie's, so I don't know how much help I was."

"Congratulations."

"On what?"

"You are now an official resident of Idlewild," I said. "You've had your first official run-in with a Lattimore."

"I'd hate to think that's all that's required," he said.

"It's not. You're also required to meet the Smitherman twins, which we can take care of Thursday, if you're free."

"I'll be done here by five-thirty. Is that too late?"

"That's perfect," I said. "Why don't you come by my house first and we'll ride over together?"

Even as I said it, and he agreed, I hoped the offer sounded properly neutral. Just one friend introducing another friend to two more. Nothing wrong with that, so why did it make me feel the slightest flutter of butterflies? Maybe Sister's right. I need to get out more.

TWENTY-NINE

acting up

SISTER AND I TRY to get together a couple of times a month to practice what she calls our *other song*, the one, she says, we only sing when there's just women around the campfire. Once I pointed out to her that in the world beyond the Bay Area, we call those so gathered *girlfriends*. She assured me that in San Francisco, calling someone your *girlfriend* is an entirely different proposition.

Sister had been part of a group of women in California who met together for ten years. They'd been through births, deaths, marriages, divorces, spiritual awakenings and a range of commitments and partnerships across a dizzying landscape of races, classes, genders and sexual orientations. Anything discussed in the group had been discussed thoroughly and openly with full appreciation of the fact that the personal is always political. Tonight we were at her house, winding down and talking about friendship.

"Do you think it's possible for a man and a woman to be friends?" I asked.

"Sure I do," Sister said. "In my old group, we even came up with the four possible ways those friendships can evolve."

I smiled. *Of course they had.* "Only four?"

"When you're speaking of heterosexuals, and I assume we are, there are only four." She held up her fingers to count them off. "One, there's acknowledged sexual attraction on both sides and it's only a matter of time before friends become lovers, unless there is an honorable reason why they shouldn't, such as fragile health or a serious prior commitment. Two, there's sexual attraction on one side only, which, unless handled carefully, can result in complicated fantasies, unrequited longings, serious bouts of denial and ultimately a busted friendship and a broken heart. Three, there is no sexual attraction present on either side, in which case the friendship will quickly run its course since in most cases the only reason people cross the great gender divide is if there are sexual possibilities present on the other side. Otherwise, you're probably going to have more fun going out with your girlfriends or hangin' with the homeboys."

I laughed. "You're dating yourself! What's number four?"

"That's when there's sexual attraction on both sides, but the parties have, for whatever reasons, been unwilling or unable to express it, so they sublimate all that energy into shared work experiences that keep them in close contact until they figure out how to get together."

"Very impressive," I said. "And thorough."

Bill pulled up in the yard and tapped the horn. Sister waved through the window. He was doing a workshop in creative writing for boys only at the high school and their first meeting was tonight. I had teased him that he was just jealous of how much fun we had at our women-only gatherings, which he cheerfully admitted, so I rewarded his honesty by promising to wait for his return before heading home.

"Thank you," Sister said, accepting my compliment on her friendship discourse. Then she said, real casual, "Any of them sound familiar?"

"Not right offhand," I said, echoing her breezy tone. "But I'll keep you posted."

"Keep you posted on what?" Bill said, entering on cue.

Sister kissed his cold cheek. "We've been discussing the possibility of friendship between men and women."

"Heterosexuals?" he said, hanging up his coat and blowing on his hands to warm them.

"Yes," I said.

"Forget it," he said. "The man is lying."

"What man?"

"Any man who says he just wants to be a woman's friend is either lying or gay."

I laughed. "You're crazy!"

"Don't laugh. I'm from San Francisco. I know about these things."

"*We're* friends," I said.

"Yes, but I'm madly in love." Bill encircled Sister's waist with his arm. "And therefore, *safe*."

"And if you weren't madly in love?"

He grinned at me. "You'd be in a world of trouble."

Sister swatted him and we all laughed. Bill is a big flirt, but that's all he is. He says it's because he's still madly in love after all these years. Sister says it's because he'll never get to heaven if he breaks her heart, which sounds more like a threat coming from her than it ever did coming sweetly out of Dionne Warwick's mouth back when she was too busy making Burt Bacharach sound good to tap into her psychic powers.

"How was the workshop?" I said. "Anybody show up?"

"Unfortunately, yes."

"Unfortunately? I thought you were worried that nobody would come."

"That was before the five of them actually arrived."

"Five of them? That's great!" Sister said. "What happened?"

"They're in high school, right? They're sixteen, seventeen years old. Their hormones are raging. I figure I'll tap into that energy and ask them to write a paragraph about love."

"Since when did hormones have anything to do with love?" I said.

"*Now* you tell me," Bill groaned. "When I asked them to share what they'd written, the first two were so pornographic I told them we were out of time and sent them home."

Sister patted his hand sympathetically. "I'm sorry, sweetie. Maybe you can help them find a better way to express what they're feeling."

Bill shook his head sadly. "The problem is, I don't think I even want them to express what they're feeling."

"Sure you do," I said. "Silence equals death, remember?"

"That's an AIDS education slogan," Bill reminded me, like I didn't already know it.

"True," I said. "But not knowing the difference between love and pornography can kill you almost as fast as HIV."

"Don't let the people at ACT UP hear you say that," Bill chided me.

"They already know it." Sister smiled. "Why do you think they're acting up?"

THIRTY

nasty stuff

"I THINK WE SHOULD invite them," Tee said the next day as we shared some lunch during the peaceful oasis that is naptime. She said it as if we were in the middle of a conversation. I knew her well enough to know that simply meant she had been engaged in a lively internal dialogue that had now opened up enough to consider any opinion I might like to offer.

I spent the morning poring over funding guidelines from every foundation in the Midwest, but nothing looked very promising. I was ready for a break. "Invite who?"

"We're gonna show their movies, right? We're gonna—how did you say it?"

"We're going to place their work in context."

"Right! And we're gonna talk about it, so why not invite them to come and talk about it too?"

I briefly considered the effect the arrival of Halle Berry, Nia Long, Vivica A. Fox, and Jada Pinkett Smith would have on Idlewild, but I drew a blank. It had been a long time since any black stars ventured into the Great North Woods. They were rarer than winter mangoes around here.

"You mean invite the actresses?"

"Exactly," she said. "We want to draw a crowd, right?"

"Well, sure," I said, not wanting to discourage her, but figuring our chances of even getting them to respond to a request were between slim and none. "But I think we can do that on our own."

She looked at me like I must not be listening. "You think on our best day, we can draw as big a crowd as any one of them can just by passin' through?"

She was probably right, but before we could discuss it any further, Nikki appeared in the doorway looking miserable.

"What's wrong?" Tee said.

Nik was immediately defensive. "Why you think somethin' always gotta be wrong?"

Tee was unimpressed. " 'Cause I been knowin' you since third grade and the only time you look like that is when there's somethin' wrong."

Nikki looked at me, but we both knew Tee was right.

"So?"

She sat down in the chair next to my desk, but she didn't look at either one of us and her voice was so low I could hardly hear her. "Junior puttin' stuff in my mailbox."

Nikki lived alone in a tiny trailer at the end of an ugly dirt road.

"What kind of stuff?"

The possibilities were unlimited and probably all unpleasant.

"Nasty stuff."

Tee frowned. "What you mean *nasty stuff?*"

This kind of call-and-response was getting us noplace fast. "Be specific," I said.

She looked at me and sighed, clearly hating having to have this conversation at all. "Condoms."

"Condoms?" Tee and I sounded like the backup singers on a broken record.

"*Used* condoms," she whispered, averting her eyes.

I didn't know what to say to that, but Tee did. "How you know it's Junior?"

Nik's head shot up. "What you tryin' to say?"

Tee didn't blink. "I'm sayin' the kind of job you got, it might be one of your fans."

Nikki looked like Tee had slapped her, but she took a deep breath and her voice was calm. "You right, Tee. It might be any of them niggas, but I think it's Junior. What you think?"

I was still trying to get my mind around what kind of man leaves used condoms in his ex-girlfriend's mailbox. Even for a Lattimore, that was pretty gross. "I think it's Junior too," I said, before Tee could respond. "Did you clean out the mailbox?"

She shuddered. "Yeah. I poured bleach in it."

"Good," I said. "I'm worried about you being alone so far off the main road."

She shook her head. "Tell me about it."

"Can you move back in with your mother for a couple of more days?"

Nikki had taken temporary refuge with Jasmine after the face-off with Junior, but they saw too much of themselves in each other's faces and they argued continually. It had be a bigger crisis than this one for Nik to consider voluntarily placing herself in the path of her mother's disappointment. A mailbox full of male madness was close, but she still hesitated.

"Your mama will kill you quicker than a house full of Lattimores," Tee said with a sigh that meant she knew what she had to do. "You better come and stay with me."

Gratitude and relief flooded Nikki's face and I wondered if she'd hoped this would happen. Tee was more like her big sister, bailing Nik out of one scrape or another all their lives. The only thing that ever got in the way of their friendship was Nik's willingness to pretend and Tee's inability to do so.

"You serious?"

"I'm always serious," Tee said. "But you gotta promise me somethin'."

Nikki hesitated. "I can't quit my job, Tee. I gotta eat."

Tomika shook her head. "I'm talkin' about Junior. I don't want that mess around my daughter."

"That's all over," Nikki said, sounding so confident I believed her. "If I'm lyin', you can kick me out."

"If you lyin', I'ma kick your ass," Tee said, grabbing her keys. "Let's go get your stuff."

"I'll tell Mavis you'll be right back," I said.

Tee laughed. "That girl ain't gonna be awake for another hour. She is the queen of naptime."

"I'm not gonna forget this," Nikki said, heading for the door.

"I'm not gonna let you." Tee winked at me and laughed. "Believe that!"

Once they headed out, I realized this was the first quiet minute I'd had since I got here that morning. This is one of my favorite times of the day. Since Deena got the kids on a schedule, naptime is sacred. Some of the older ones, her girls included, don't really take long naps anymore, but they are all required to lie down for at least a half hour. After that, they're allowed to get up and play quietly until the others wake up and rejoin them.

I peeked in on the nap room, where the only sound was the regular breathing of sleeping babies, then crossed the hall to the community room. In front of the far window, Deena's twins sat on either side of their mother, quietly feeding their dolls like beautiful bookends while Marquis and Lil' Sonny, who considered naps an unnecessary break in the business of their day, shared a coloring book. Deena's nose was buried in a college catalog I'd been trying to get her to look at. Her daughters saw me watching and waved. I waved back and they rewarded me with identical smiles.

And you know what? Sometimes, at moments like this, when every single thing seems to be in transition at the exact same time, if it wasn't for two little brown girls with pink ribbons in their hair feeding two little brown babydolls, I don't know what I'd do.

THIRTY-ONE

a candle for nettie

I LEFT TEE TO close up so I could meet Nate at the appointed hour and officially present him to the Smithermans. I had already decided that I'd be ready to go when he arrived. This visit was really about business and I didn't want to confuse the issue by inviting him in for a glass of wine or anything.

At precisely five-thirty, Nate's car rolled into my yard and stopped. The weather and the things we use to fight it up here are hard on our cars and most of us forgo style for reliability, but if an exhausted American car was the third thing necessary for citizenship in our town, Nate was out of luck. He drove a spotless Lincoln Town Car that was as big and black and graceful as he was. When he stepped out into the yard, the car, relieved of his weight, rose slightly.

I reached for my coat but couldn't turn away from the window as he walked around the car and came toward my front door. The sight of him simply walking up the front steps produced such a strong sexual shiver in me that I shocked myself. What was going on? I am no blushing virgin or desperate widow. I've been doing fine by myself, and there was no reason for my hormones to go adolescent on me now.

I remember this feeling well. Mitch and I started having sex the night he asked me to marry him and I said I would. We were both virgins, but once we figured out the basics, we found in each other not only a soul mate but an enthusiastic sexual partner with no expectations except tenderness and truth. Our intimacy enriched and delighted us in the good times, and in the bad ones, it helped us stay as close as we needed to stay if we were going to survive.

After he died, my body missed him as much as my mind did, and as specifically. I didn't miss having sex. I missed having sex with Mitch. The idea that I could ever make love with another man had never occurred to me until now, all in a rush, and I didn't know whether to lean into it and see what would happen or run as fast as I could in the opposite direction. One thing was for sure, I couldn't keep fluttering like this every time I heard his voice or laid eyes on him. Fluttering is not my style.

I grabbed my coat and my purse and opened the door. Nate was standing so close to it that my forward motion literally bounced me off his chest. His arm shot out to steady me and I grabbed it.

"Careful!"

"Sorry!" I was off to a great start.

"I thought you saw me," he said apologetically, stepping back to give me some staggering space.

Of course I saw you, I thought. *How could I possibly miss you?*

"No harm done," I said. "I was trying to save you getting out in this cold."

"Can't save me there," he said. "My dad would never forgive me if I didn't offer you my arm on these steps."

He crooked his elbow and offered me an arm that looked big enough to swing on. I resisted the temptation, pulled the door shut behind me and accepted that arm with what I hoped was enough ladylike grace to erase the memory of our bump at the door. Whether it did or not, he didn't mention it on the short ride around the lake to the Smithermans'.

"They're looking forward to meeting you," I said, realizing he was wearing a suit and tie instead of his usual turtleneck. Probably his father's advice.

"Good," he said. "The feeling's mutual."

"They might invite us to stay for dinner, but you shouldn't feel obligated."

"I've got nothing but time," he said, turning into the long driveway up to their house. "The evening is in your hands."

An appealing notion, but unfortunately nowhere near the truth. When we rang their doorbell, Geneva opened the door looking so grief-stricken that I immediately thought the worst. *Where was Lynette?*

"What's wrong?" I said.

"Oh, my dear," she said. "We've just had some awful news."

Thank god she said "we." It wasn't her sister.

Gen's eye suddenly fell on Nate standing behind me, and she started just a little.

"It's Nate Anderson," I said quickly. Whatever happened, our visit was the last thing on her mind.

"Mr. Anderson," she said, and her eyes were sparkling with tears. "Forgive me. I'm not myself. Come in, come in."

We followed her into the small parlor where the photo albums they'd been working on the other day were still scattered around on the floor. She didn't sit, or ask us to, so the three of us stood in the center of the room. From upstairs, I could hear the sound of breaking glass. Nate looked at me, but I was as confused as he was.

"Is that Nettie?" I whispered.

Geneva nodded miserably. "She's beside herself. Absolutely mad with sorrow."

"What happened?"

She looked at Nate and hesitated. He spoke up instantly, his voice a reservoir of reassurance and calm.

"If you need to speak privately, I can wait—"

She didn't let him finish the sentence before she laid a delicate hand on that same tree-trunk arm I'd imagined swinging from and shook her head.

"No, no! What am I thinking? This is no time for secrets. That kind of thinking has already been the cause of enough suffering!"

Nate stayed where he was, and I put my arm around Geneva's shoulders. From upstairs we could hear the sound of someone sobbing, then more shattered glass.

"Tell me what's going on," I said. "Maybe we can help."

She shook her head sadly at me like of all people I should know that there are situations where offers of help are completely beside the point.

"No one can help," she said. "My Nettie's heart is broken and there is nothing anyone can do." She reached into her pocket, took out a tiny white lace handkerchief, blew her nose delicately, took a long, shuddering breath and turned to Nate.

"Mr. Anderson, you have walked into our lives on the day the man my sister has loved from afar for fifty years died in the arms of his wife. His actions almost cost my Nettie her sanity and her spirit when she was twenty-five and now he is trying her resolve one more time by dying before she could stop loving him."

There was another loud crash from upstairs, followed by silence. Geneva cocked her head, listening for her sister's tears.

"I've known this day would come, but forewarned is not always forearmed."

More breaking glass. Geneva shook her head sadly. "She's breaking the crystal. He always sent . . . crystal. She doesn't want it anymore."

Nate and I looked at each other. Neither one of us knew what to say.

"Under the circumstances, Mr. Anderson," Geneva said softly, "I think we might pick another evening to welcome you to our little town."

"Of course," said Nate as we headed for the door. "I'm very sorry for your sister's loss."

At the door, I hugged Geneva tightly. She looked at us standing there so concerned and managed a small smile.

"Don't worry," she said. "Nobody ever dies of a broken heart. They just think they will."

"I remember when you told me that," I said.

She nodded. "And you didn't believe me any more than she does, but I was right, wasn't I?"

"Yes," I said, hugging her again.

She patted Nate's arm like he was a beloved nephew and looked at me again. "Do something for me, will you, dear?"

"Of course."

"Light a candle for Nettie." Then she was gone, headed

upstairs to sweep up the broken glass and patch up her sister's broken heart.

I didn't invite Nate in when he dropped me off. The passionate energy at the Smitherman house had stunned us into silence during the short ride home, and I knew we both needed to digest what we had just seen and heard. Nettie's grief was almost too much for her to bear. As witnesses to it, I thought we owed her the respect our silence showed.

Nate walked me to the door. "Do you believe in signs?" he said.

It was a strange question, but it had been a strange evening. "Yes."

"Do you think that was one?"

I nodded slowly. "Yes."

"Good or bad?"

I stepped back and looked up into his face. "Too soon to tell."

"I think it was good," he said so softly his voice sounded like a caress. "Because it makes you remember that life is short and the worst thing you can be left with at the end of it is regrets about what you didn't do."

And I believe that too, although I hadn't had nerve enough to say it, so I did what I'd been wanting to do since I first saw him at Sister's. I stepped up and put my arms around his neck and I kissed him. Softly at first, but when he started kissing me back, so gently, with such urgent sweetness, all my restraint flew out the window and what I intended to be a friendly sort of smooch became instead the restatement of a promise that had been made between us that first night at Sister's when he saw me dancing. He wrapped those great big arms around me and I leaned into his mouth like he could drink me like a mango mar-

garita and it felt so good and it's been so long and then I thought
about Mitch. I opened my eyes and he might as well have been
standing right there beside us. I dropped my arms immediately
and slid down his chest back to my own two feet.

"What's wrong?" he said, releasing me slowly until I was
standing loosely in the circle of his arms, but no longer touching
him. *Sweet Mitch. What was I doing?*

I took a deep breath, but I didn't know what to say. We weren't
kids, but I felt like one. Mitch is the only man I've ever had.

"Tell me, baby," Nate crooned. "You can tell me."

What is it about being called *baby* that makes you want to tell
your secrets even when you didn't know you had any?

"I don't know," I whispered. "I'm just . . . I don't know."

"It's okay," he said gently. "You don't have to explain anything to me."

"Thanks," I said, stepping back, fumbling for my keys. I
needed a minute to myself to sort some things out. I looked at
him standing there, watching me, waiting for me to say something that made sense. "Why don't you call me this weekend?"

He looked relieved. "All right."

I smiled up at him, trying to collect myself. "All right. Good
night."

"Good night." And he was gone.

I let myself in and sat down at the kitchen table without taking off my coat. In matters of the heart, Bill says haste makes
waste, and I'm sure that's especially true when you're standing in
the moonlight and a woman whose house you can see from yours
thinks she'll never survive until morning and why is it that the
only real antidote to a broken heart is hair of the dog that bit you
and more of the same and love love love love love. . . .

I took off my coat, lit a candle for Nettie and called Sister.

THIRTY-TWO

stages

I TOLD MYSELF I was calling to tell her about Nettie's broken heart, but I knew that wasn't the only reason. Sister heard it in my voice. After we had exhausted the topic at hand, she listened to the sudden silence from my end and then stepped into it fearlessly.

"So, Nettie is in her big sister's capable hands. What's the matter with you?"

There was no point in hedging. I had called her to have this conversation, but I still wasn't sure how to begin. We had never talked much about sex. When your most recent experiences are five years old, your stories get a little stale. Plus, I think it's inappropriate to bring up the dead in that context, even if your best friend is a minister and used to speaking to and of the spirits on a regular basis.

"I kissed Nate."

Sister chuckled. "So are you calling me for advice or absolution?"

"Don't make fun of me," I said. "It was very weird."

"Did you like it?"

Why did the question make me feel so guilty? "At first, everything was fine, but when I opened my eyes, Mitch might as well have been standing right beside us, watching his wife making out on his back porch!"

"Calm down," Sister said. "Let's think it through."

Thinking it through was Sister's specialty. That meant at the end of this call, we would have clarified the question and arrived at an answer that led to action, since Sister says confession without closure is just whining.

"Okay," Sister said. "What was weird? The kiss itself or the fact of it?"

"The fact of it?"

"Did you want to kiss him?"

"Yes." *Oh, yes!*

"Did you initiate the contact?"

"Yes. Right after we came from Nettie's."

"Can I ask you a personal question?"

Weren't all of these personal questions? "Sure."

"Was Mitch the only lover you ever had?"

"Yes."

"Weren't you ever curious?"

"Sure, but all the stuff I was curious about, Mitch was curious about too."

"I don't mean about *stuff*. I mean about *people*."

"Sexually curious?"

Sister laughed. "Don't sound so shocked. Didn't you ever have fantasies?"

"Not that I can think of," I said.

"That's probably why you feel so guilty," she said. "This is all new for you."

Tears popped into my eyes. "I feel like I just betrayed my husband in such a terrible way," I whispered, hoping I wasn't going to cry. Sister could always tell.

"Relax, sweetie," Sister said very gently. "This isn't that complicated. It's just the last vestiges of survivor guilt. It's perfectly understandable. How long has it been since Mitch passed?"

"Five years." It seemed like yesterday and it seemed like forever. I felt a tear roll down my cheek.

"Okay, then you have to take this in stages."

"Take what in stages?"

"The decision to have sex again."

I was still trying not to feel guity about a kiss and she was already throwing us in bed together. I had a brief longing for the bad old days when any pastor worth his salt (they were all *he* back then) would have settled my dilemma by reminding me that the devil finds work for idle hands and steering me toward greater involvement with the Ladies Christian Missionary Society. I was still floundering around, trying to confess, and Sister was already in full strategic planning mode!

"Do you ever fantasize when you masturbate?" she said as I scurried to catch up.

"Sometimes. . . ."

"Is it always Mitch?"

"Always." Why did saying that out loud make me want to cry again?

"Well, next time," Sister said calmly as if we were talking about what to plant in our gardens, "see if you can substitute somebody else's face. Then, once you have a chance to see the fantasy of you making love with somebody else, it won't be so weird for the real you to consider the same thing."

See what I mean? If you can articulate the question, Sister can articulate the answer.

"Whose face should I substitute?"

"That's up to you," she said. "Movie stars and pro athletes are always good since you can be sure you're not going to run into them on Main Street and have to make pleasant conversation after you've seen them naked in your daydreams."

That made sense. Plus, I didn't think fantasizing about Buddy at the grocery store was going to be a step in the right direction.

"You're brilliant," I said. "That's so practical."

"You should try it tonight, sweetie, since the sexual energy is already present."

"Tonight?" I blushed.

"Tonight," she said firmly. "And buy some condoms."

That really confused me. I know AIDS has changed everything, but condoms for self-pleasuring?

"Not for the masturbation," Sister said. "For the next phase. This is the twenty-first century, sweetie. You don't have to pretend not to plan ahead."

"Yes, ma'am," I said. "Any other advice?"

"Be yourself," she said. "And don't forget to breathe."

THIRTY-THREE

sexual healing

SISTER WAS RIGHT ABOUT the energy. The memory of how good it felt to be in Nate's arms was fresh in my mind. I went upstairs and ran myself a bath, dropped in some sweet lavender oil and a handful of scented salts, lit the candles, sank gratefully into the steaming tub and closed my eyes. I ran my hands over my body lightly and tried to conjure up an object of desire.

Who could I use? Sister had suggested sports figures, but none of them really appeal to me except Tiger Woods, and since I am old enough to be his mother, he doesn't count. I used to like that wrestling guy who calls himself The Rock, but once he showed up at the Republican convention, he was no longer an option. As far as movie stars go, I considered Denzel, but figured Tee and Pauletta had that covered, so I rejected him as a serious possibility.

I added more hot water and, ignoring Sister's advice, considered the men in town between the ages of thirty and fifty. There were a few who I found reasonably attractive, even kind of sexy, but when I tried to put them in the fantasies where Mitch had always been, they just looked uncomfortable.

The water was getting cold and I finally decided the spirits of sexual healing must have slipped out while I was on the phone and I'd have to try another time. No problem. I'm old enough to know that sometimes the magic works and sometimes it doesn't.

THIRTY-FOUR

a trick question

OUR REGULAR WEDNESDAY DISCUSSIONS always start with a question. This week, the news had been full of a story about a case of date rape, or self-interested second-guessing, depending on whether you believe the defense or the prosecution. The crime was disturbing enough, involving as it did a junior-prom date gone bad, but the accompanying analysis was even worse. Filled with smirks and suggestive comments, it was clear that there wasn't even any general agreement on what crime, if any, had been committed. I figured that was as good a place to start as any.

"Okay," I said, "how many of you ever had sex with a man when you didn't want to?"

A general nervous laugh.

"Is this a trick question, Miz J?" Tiffany spoke for the group.

More laughter; still nervous. These are the nights we reserve for the things everybody would rather not talk about but really needs to. That night, we were Nikki, Deena, Patrice, Sheila, Tiffany and Sherika. Tee was home nursing Mavis through one more cold. Nikki hadn't been around much lately, and I was glad to see her.

"Anybody who hasn't done it?"

Sherika Hill raised her hand immediately, but Nikki was having none of it. *"Puh-leez!"*

"Please what?"

Nikki rolled her eyes. "You mean to tell me every time Brian want it, you want it too?"

Sherika couldn't decide if she wanted to be hurt or angry. She looked at me. "It's different when you love somebody. Then sometimes you do it when they wanna do it just 'cause you love 'em. That's not what you talkin' about, right?"

"Is there a word for what you think I'm talking about?"

Sheila Lattimore spoke up first. "Rape."

"There you go!" Sherika felt vindicated. "Brian ain't no rapist."

"That's 'cause you give it up whenever he want it," Nikki said, suddenly the voice of the cynical pragmatist.

"It ain't the same thing, Nik," Patrice said. "For rape, they have to hurt you."

"Hurt you how?" I said. Specifics are important. Some of these women don't think they've been hurt until they bleed.

"You know." Patrice shrugged, looking around for corroboration. "Black your eye; bust your lip; rip you up."

When she said this last one—*rip you up*—her hand made a vague gesture in the direction of her crotch and there were several nods of agreement. I wondered how much sexual violence they had collectively endured without knowing what to call it.

"Okay," I said. "What if he doesn't actually do those things but *threatens* to do them?"

"Threatens how?"

"By telling you what he'll do if you don't have sex with him."

They laughed nervously.

"Don't they all do that?" Nikki said.

"No," I said, speaking up quickly for all the ones who stand with us and for us as naturally as breathing. "They don't all do that."

"They don't always be hittin' you, but they don't think you ever 'spose to say no," Patrice said softly as if I hadn't spoken. "They think once they hit it, it belong to 'em."

"That's why they always be askin' you *What's my name? Say my name!*" Tiffany said. "It gets on my nerves. Sometimes I got another thought goin' good and here they come with *What's my name?* If I'm thinkin' D'Angelo, I don't want to be required to holler out *Tyrone!*"

Wednesday wasn't about final conclusions. It was all about exploration. That's what drives Sister crazy whenever she comes to these sessions. She wants to tell them the answers. I just want to help them recognize some other questions.

"Can a husband rape his wife?" I said at the end of their laughter.

The idea caught them by surprise.

"I don't think so." Regina sounded skeptical. "They 'spose to be havin' sex anyway, so what's the problem?"

"When?" I said.

"When what?"

"When are they supposed to be having sex?"

Regina looked confused. "*Whenever*. They married, right?"

Did I tell you how much I love confusion? You never look for the truth until it dawns on you that you don't already have it. "What if he wants to and she doesn't?"

"Then it depends," Sherika said eagerly, glad we were back to something she understood, "on the terms of their relationship."

"Damn right." Tiffany spoke right up. "If he tradin' a house, a car, a credit card, a cell phone and money in the bank, then I'm givin' up plenty of booty! If he ain't tradin' nothin' but his own broke ass and a bag of chips, he better *get up, get out and get some-thin'* before he start tryin' to talk up on some sex around me!"

"What if they're both just regular, hardworking people?" I said quickly before we could get sidetracked into the endless fantasies of what the invisible lover must bring to qualify for milady's hand. "Should she have to have sex just because her husband wants her to?"

I looked at Sherika, who had no idea yet that love doesn't eliminate contradictions. It intensifies them until they are resolved or fatal. She didn't know what to say.

"Nobody should *have* to," Nikki said into the waiting silence. "Everybody got a right to say no."

Nobody said anything for a minute and then Tiffany grinned at me. "I knew this was a trick question."

"They're all trick questions until you answer them," I said, glad we had come to a conclusion that was easy to remember and easy to pass on. *Everybody got a right to say no* is right up there with *no hitting* as a basic understanding required of a truly free woman. After all, if your peace and your body can both be invaded, how free can you really claim to be?

THIRTY-FIVE

bad memories

NIKKI HUNG AROUND AS the last of the group gathered their babies and their belongings.

"How's it going?" I said in what I hoped was a sufficiently neutral tone to let her take the conversation anyplace she needed it to go.

"Do you really believe that?" she said.

"Believe what?"

"That it's rape anytime you don't want it and they sorta force the issue."

Sorta force the issue. "Yes."

"Even if they not actually hittin' you?"

I looked at her. "If they're not forcing you and you don't want to do it, why would you?"

She shrugged. "I don't know. Lots of reasons."

"Any of them good ones?"

Deena was shooing her twins out the door since she was riding with Tiffany, who didn't like to be kept waiting even if you did bring your fair share of the gas money. She closed the door behind them, leaving me and Nik alone. I headed toward the kitchen.

"Want some tea?"

She shook her head. "I gotta go to work and tea makes me look bloated, but I was just wonderin'. . . ."

I put the kettle on and waited.

"I was just thinkin' that me and Junior went together for five years and I bet there wadn't ten times in all those years when I really *wanted* to do it."

"Why did you?"

This was the moment they usually want to avoid at all costs, the moment when you have to remember *why* you did what was probably some breathtakingly self-destructive stuff—and did it repeatedly. She looked at me and her lip trembled slightly like a frightened five-year-old caught with her hand in the cookie jar.

"When I turned sixteen, he took me out to celebrate my birthday and then we went back to my house but he was too drunk by then and I didn't wanna do it with him like that, so I said no." She hesitated, not sure how or what to tell, even three years later. "And he . . . he hurt me, Miz J. He hurt me real bad, so I never said no to him again 'bout nothin', till I quit him."

Nik shook her head like she was trying to chase away the bad memories. "Can I ask you somethin'?"

"You can ask me anything. You know that."

"You think he was rapin' me all those times?" she said softly.

"What do you think?"

She nodded slowly. "I think he was."

I put my arms around her shoulders and we stood there together. "I think so too."

She didn't say anything for a minute, then she looked at me with a shaky smile. "I gotta go to work."

"I know."

I wanted to tell her to take the night off, but I didn't. I hugged her again and waved as she pulled slowly out of the driveway. Sometimes the contradictions in their lives are so intense they seem manufactured for teaching life lessons, but it's hard to keep up with what you're supposed to be learning in that terrible moment between defiance and despair when all your energy is going into figuring out why it took so long to name the thing that's driving you crazy. At those moments, the best I can do is keep quiet and say a little prayer, which is what I did.

THIRTY-SIX

the best man

I'M CONFUSED. I JUST finished watching *The Best Man*, and I enjoyed parts of it a lot. I loved how pretty they all looked and how they all had jobs and ambitions and futures to discuss as well as sex lives. I love Nia Long's character, and I am in awe of her amazing ability to walk around on those impossibly high heels and never once wince. I loved the way she took charge in the control booth at work *and* at home when her wounded ex-almost-lover Taye Diggs comes crawling in for some comforting when he had promised a night of passion. I also loved that he was a writer and his partner had her own business and that how to tell the truth to people you love was a big concern for almost all of them.

On the other hand, I couldn't figure out how I felt about the groom at all. Is he a violent, spoiled, sexist, potentially abusive *asshole,* or is he a big, fine, passionate *thang,* capable of great love, real spirituality, fidelity, fatherhood and a productive life beyond the gridiron? Is "her pussy curves to my dick" really a compliment? And how can he tell, since it's a known fact that a vagina can snugly accommodate everything from a junior tampon to a baby's head (not to mention all manner of things in between), and never curve to anything other than its own sweet self?

I also need to know whether the light-skinned guy is a seeker of/speaker of truth or a sneering snob who betrays his friends, disrespects women and resents his father's legacy even as it finances his very comfortable lifestyle. And is there no redeeming quality in the light-skinned woman? No moment of self-doubt or compassion or humanity? Is she always a mean, controlling, materialistic bitch? And just because they deserve each other should we really cheer when they wake up together?

And how about the benign depiction of stag party strippers, including an Audre Lorde–quoting college student whose wide-eyed innocence is at odds with her part-time profession, but comes through so clearly to our dreadlocked young idealist that he invites her to the white wedding, therefore washing her clean of the sins of her past and preparing a place for her in the middle-class realm to which she seems to rightly belong?

Whew! Good thing Sister will be here soon. Once I start thinking like this, I can't stop until I've picked the bones clean and driven myself and everybody within earshot crazy. Sister helps me focus on the big picture.

"Thank goodness," I said when she arrived a few minutes later. "I was working myself into a frenzy over *The Best Man.*"

"A good frenzy or a bad frenzy?" Sister said, trying to get the facts before being required to offer an opinion.

I thought for a minute. "A little bit of both."

"A mixed frenzy?" She hung up her coat on its usual hook. "Sounds serious."

"You've seen it, right?"

Sister nodded. "Of course. I saw it at the theater the first weekend, like we were supposed to."

"Sue me," I said, having already apologized profusely for this crime against the race generally and *The Tom Joyner Morning Show* specifically. I know a solid black audience can give a black movie a chance for a decent opening weekend up against even the likes of Bruce and Jim and Julia and the Toms—Cruise and Hanks. I applaud Sister and Bill for regularly driving a half hour to the closest cineplex to support whichever young African American filmmaker is competing at the box office on any Friday night, but the truth is, no matter how much they badger me, I'm probably not going to see *Belly* on its opening night. If it scared Magic Johnson, that's good enough for me.

But *The Best Man* didn't seem to scare anybody except me, Sister included. "Did you like it?"

"I did," she said. "I had some problems with the groom being so violent, though."

"Exactly!" How can I not love this woman? "None of the reviews I saw even mentioned it!"

"Maybe they didn't notice it," Sister said, sitting down at the kitchen table.

I poured us each a glass of wine. "How could they not notice?"

Sister took a sip of her wine and nodded her approval. "Is this Ava's good Chianti we're drinking?"

I nodded. "Don't worry. I have permission."

"Good." Sister enjoyed red wine. She sipped it slowly while she considered her response to my question. "I believe," she said slowly, "that in many instances where people, usually men, have been assumed to be taking a less than enlightened position on one issue or another, that's not the case at all. They are either uninformed or misinformed and not conscious at all of the other questions that might be raised in regard to the same scenario."

Sister believes that the beginning of wisdom is to call all things by their proper names, so she's a fiend for the conscious use of language. It'll make you nuts until you realize how useful and necessary it is. When she first got here, she went down to the Lake County newspaper and asked to talk to the editor. When he reluctantly came out to see what she wanted, she told him she thought it would be helpful in news stories about a rash of assaults on young women walking alone to say "a man raped a woman on Baldwin Road," rather than the more generic "a woman was raped."

"By *whom?*" Sister told him. "That's the real question. If we don't identify the danger for them as specifically as we can, how are we going to protect our daughters from it?"

The editor, whose own daughter had just turned fifteen, said he'd think about it, and the very next day, he made the change.

"You see," Sister said, reminding me of this small but significant victory for clarity. "He just hadn't asked the right question."

"Which means?"

"Which means the key to your festival being more than just a bunch of screenings is making sure you ask the right questions."

"That's just what Tee said."

Sister reached into her purse and pulled out a small, handwritten but neatly numbered list. "I know. When you told me Tee had given you this assignment, I thought you might be open to some assistance, especially since I know you've been a little preoccupied."

I had told her I wasn't expecting to hear from Nate until this weekend, but she couldn't help signifying. I raised my eyebrows. It's hard to pull off self-righteous with a woman who's been advising you on masturbation, but I gave it my best shot.

"Preoccupied with what?"

She went for innocence, equally hard to pull off for the same reason. "Concern for Nettie Smitherman, for one thing."

"Have you seen her?"

Sister nodded. "She's really embarrassed that you and Nate were at the house when she was breaking the unicorns."

"That's what she was breaking? Why?"

Nettie had the most beautiful collection of crystal unicorns. When I admired them, she just said she had a friend who liked to send them as gifts.

"Her lover sent them," Sister said.

"No!" I felt like I was reading my mother's diary. "I didn't even know she had a lover until Gen told me."

"Do you know why he sent the unicorns?"

I shook my head, fascinated. "Why?"

"Because she met him at a play. He had gotten tickets, but his wife didn't like the theater and wanted to go shopping instead. They had a big fight, which was a regular thing for them, and suddenly he realized they were totally and completely wrong for each other and would never make each other happy for even one day. Fortunately, they were still childless, so he decided to ask her for a divorce."

Sister took a sip of her wine. "Feeling better for having reached a difficult decision, he went to the theater alone and was seated next to Nettie, who had also come alone because Geneva didn't care for Tennessee Williams. The play was *The Glass Menagerie*."

Sister and I shared a fondness for the plays of Tennessee Williams, who we claimed as a black writer due to our having read somewhere that he was probably an octoroon, and with family ties in New Orleans, probably a quadroon. We loved the women he wrote about in all their fevered-white-girl glory, and Laura, the fragile, damaged daughter in *Glass Menagerie* was no exception. Her loving care of her fragile unicorns while she awaits the nonexistent gentleman callers her once beautiful mother thinks are every young girl's birthright, is an unforgettable image that carries throughout the play.

"Nettie reminded him of Laura?"

Sister shook her head. "I didn't get the feeling that she reminded him of anybody. I think the point was the shared moment, the meeting of two souls with a shared destiny."

I laughed. "Now you sound like a romance novel."

"Those are *her* words," Sister protested. "She said they talked all through intermission, whispered nonstop during Act Two and, by the end of the play, acknowledged that they intended to spend their lives together, left the theater, rented a room and spent the afternoon making mad, passionate love."

"When did she tell you all this?"

"Yesterday when I went by to see her. She wanted me to tell you the story so you would understand her behavior the other night. She also said she hopes you'll tell Nate that she doesn't usually act that way."

"Of course I will," I said. "Go on!"

"Well, this is when it turns tragic."

"So fast? What happened?"

Sister took another sip of wine. "Her lover's wife fainted in

Bloomingdale's. When they took her to the hospital, the doctors discovered she was three months pregnant with their first child."

"So he couldn't leave her?"

"Never did, but every year, on the anniversary of the day they met, a package would arrive from wherever he was, and it would be another unicorn."

"For fifty years?"

Sister nodded. "Amazing, isn't it? She said he was the only man she ever loved and she always thought they'd live long enough to find a way to honorably be together, but they didn't; and the idea that she had wasted her life waiting for him was more than she could bear."

"What did you tell her?"

"I told her she needed a project to give her something else to focus on instead of her regrets and suggested that she talk to you about helping Tee with the film festival."

That was such a bold idea that I just sat there for a minute contemplating the possible outcomes of a project that combined the energies of two of the most formidable women I know. The mind boggled at the perfection of it.

"That's a great idea," I said.

"I thought it was pretty inspired," Sister said.

"Did Nettie agree?"

"She likes the idea, but she's not sure she'd be much help."

"I'll call and convince her."

"Let Tee convince her," Sister said gently.

That hadn't occurred to me. "How can she do that?"

Sister grinned. "By being Tee, of course. Now do you want to hear these questions or not?"

"You know I do," I said. I love working with Sister because there's no clear line of demarcation between our work and the lives we're living. It's all one cloth, which is the whole trick—to sync up who you are with what you do.

"Okay," said Sister, smoothing out her list, her eyes scanning it quickly. "These are mostly why and why-not questions. That usually helps get things going."

"Absolutely," I said, happy to have something tangible to hand Tee in the morning along with the name of her first senior volunteer.

Sister adjusted her glasses and cleared her throat. " 'Do I believe this character exists in the real world? Do I like her? Does she have a partner?' " Sister looked up. "I'm assuming for this first round, we'll be talking mostly about heterosexuals, but I didn't say, 'Does she have a man?' because I think we should be inclusive."

"I agree."

"Okay. 'How does she treat her kids? What does she want? When do things go wrong? What could she have done differently? What lesson does she learn and what lesson can she teach me?' And, last but not least, 'Is she happy?' " She put the paper down on the table and looked at me. "That's it."

"I like them all," I said. "In fact, when I give them to Tee, I'm going to claim I made them up all by myself."

Sister laughed. "That was Bill's contribution about her being happy."

"That's because he's a poet," I said.

"No," she said, still grinning. "That's because he's happy."

THIRTY-SEVEN

a gentleman caller

ON FRIDAY AFTERNOON, THE official beginning of the weekend, Nate called and invited me to dinner at Dot's, our local soul food place. As a vegetarian, I know it's cheating, since Dot thinks cooking vegetables without fatback is sacrilege, but all the herbs in the world can't match one small sliver of ham for flavoring collard greens correctly—and every now and then, I gotta have it.

"Sounds good," I said.

"Great. I'll pick you up around six-thirty."

Pick me up? "At home?"

"I can pick you up at The Circus if you're working late."

"I can meet you there," I said. That kiss was floating in my mind like a red balloon and I wasn't quite ready to return to the scene of the crime.

"I told you about my father already, right?"

"Your father?"

"About how he wouldn't understand if I pulled up at your house and blew the horn?"

That father was why I was required to take Nate's arm going down the same back steps I've been navigating without assistance since I was fifteen. So his father wouldn't think he didn't know how to treat a lady.

"He doesn't want me to meet you at the restaurant either?" I said.

"He figures since I invited you, I'm supposed to pick you up."

"What if I had invited you?"

"Then you can pick me up," he said. "Under one condition."

"What's that?"

"You get a bigger car."

I laughed. How could I resist? A man who can make you laugh is worth his weight in gold. And this was a very big man.

"All right," I said, glad he hadn't said anything about the other night. I didn't particularly want to explain throwing myself into his arms like he was the last lifeboat on the *Titanic*. "Six-thirty is fine."

"Listen, Joyce," he said. "Do you have a second?"

"Sure," I said. "What's up?"

"About the other night . . ."

Busted! I tried to head him off at the pass; keep it light.

"It was pretty wild, wasn't it?" I interrupted him with an unconvincing laugh. "Probably all that passion Nettie was flinging into the atmosphere."

To his credit, he ignored that. "That night brought up a lot of memories for me," he said, "most of them bad."

What did that mean?

"When my wife left me, I didn't break any glass, but I pretty well trashed my record collection. Every other song had been *our song* for at least a minute, so I just made a clean sweep."

I tried to imagine Nate stomping around, flinging his records against the wall, but I couldn't imagine it. I was still trying to picture Nettie and her unicorns.

"I tried everything I knew how to do with that woman, and it was never enough, no matter what I did. I just couldn't figure her out."

His voice still held the pain and confusion he must have gone through then, and I felt sorry for him. I don't have any memories of bad love. Being left alone because somebody dies on you is a completely different matter than being abandoned or rejected or ignored.

"I'm sorry," I murmured.

"Yeah, I was too. Sorry and mad and scared and lonely." His deep voice stopped abruptly and I heard him take a deep breath. "It took me a long time to stop blaming her for what went wrong between us and even longer to stop blaming myself, but I finally got it together and then I woke up one day and didn't miss her. I still thought about her sometimes, but she wasn't like a constant ache in my gut anymore. She was just a part of my life that was over."

I waited. I wasn't sure what all this had to do with the other night, but it didn't seem to be leading back to any analysis of my behavior, so I was prepared to listen until he tied up the loose ends for me.

"So when you kissed me like that . . ."

Like what?

"It brought up some feelings in me I haven't had in a long time and didn't think I'd ever have again."

Tell me about it!

He laughed a little then like he had gone too far to turn back now. "Cards on the table?"

"Of course." I wonder if anybody ever answers that question by saying, "Sure, all except the one I'm hiding in my boot."

"The truth is, I don't know any more about women than I did when my wife left me. I keep trying, but you all are some mysterious creatures."

"Thank you," I said, since I believe in acknowledging our magic rather than denying it.

He chuckled again. "I like you, Joyce. I know we haven't known each other long, but I feel something good happening between us, and I think you feel it too. But I know it can go a couple of different ways and I don't want to be pushing one way if you're pulling in another."

That made me smile. "I think I'd lose that one."

"I don't know about that, but I just want things to be clear between us, you know? Don't make me guess, all right?"

It was kind of funny in a way. I thought I had made everything pretty clear when I hung myself around his neck like a string of Christmas tree lights, but his history obviously made him wary of unspoken contracts with women who kissed him in the moonlight. *Truth*, I reminded myself. *Just tell him the truth.*

"I've been thinking about the other night too," I said.

"You have?" He sounded so relieved I wished I could kiss him again through the phone.

"The thing is," I said. "I've been by myself since my husband died, but I like you too, and I'd very much like to have . . ." What? Late-night conversation? Lightweight flirting? Unexpected laughter? Cuddling? Kissing? All of the above?

". . . a gentleman caller," I said finally, hoping that even if he had never read Tennessee Williams, the words were big enough to include all the possibilities he might be considering, but not so vague as to demand further definition. Not yet anyway.

"A gentleman caller?" He sounded hopeful but a little confused.

"You know," I said. "Somebody who likes to pick you up for dinner and take you to the movies and every now and then, you might even get carried away and kiss him good night."

I could hear him chuckling again. "I'd like that too," he said. "I'd like that a lot."

"Good," I said. "Then I'll see you at six-thirty."

"I won't be late."

Of course he wouldn't. No gentleman caller worthy of the name ever came late.

THIRTY-EIGHT

one of those nights

DINNER AT DOT'S IS always buffet, so we served ourselves and settled in a quiet corner with two steaming plates of
the best soul food for two hundred miles and two tall, red plastic
glasses of sweet tea with plenty of ice. I'm still old-school
enough to like the fact that the aesthetic in soul food restaurants
never changes. Red plastic glasses are as necessary as macaroni
and cheese if you're committed to *keeping it real.*

Nate took a swallow of his iced tea and smiled across the
table. I smiled back.

"Lynette Smitherman wanted me to tell you she's very sorry
for what happened the other night and she looks forward to
meeting you under less stressful circumstances."

"No apologies necessary," he said, buttering a golden corn
muffin. "If you can't fling things around when your heart is

breaking, you probably don't have much of a heart in the first place."

"She's volunteered to work on our film festival, so that'll give her something else to focus on." I took a bite of Dot's special-recipe candied yams dripping in butter and brown sugar and topped with a layer of tiny, lightly browned marshmallows. If sweets get you high, you would overdose at Dot's. I promised myself to walk twice my usual miles and took another bite.

"What film festival?"

"At The Circus," I said, realizing I hadn't told him about it yet. "We're having a film series in February. I've been using contemporary films as a starting point for some of our discussions and everybody really likes it. The festival will give us a chance to include more people in the conversation and maybe even raise a little money."

"How much are you charging?"

"Two dollars a show, five dollars for a weekend pass."

Nate was intrigued. "What kind of films are you showing?"

"*For us, by us,*" I said, quoting Tee. "Black films featuring black actresses."

"Let me guess who," he said.

"Okay." I was curious about who he'd pick.

"Let's see. They have to be strong, I know that. . . ." He frowned slightly, thinking. "Angela Bassett?"

I shook my head and he looked surprised. "How are you going to do strong women without Angela Bassett?"

"She almost made the cut," I said, "but we've shown *Waiting to Exhale* so much we're going to give it a rest, and *What's Love Got to Do with It?* isn't a black movie."

"What do you mean? There's hardly any white folks in it at all until the end."

"Tee's criteria require a black director."

"Who's Tee?"

I smiled. "You haven't met Tee yet. She works with me at The Circus and she's having a run of great ideas. The anti–Super Bowl party was one, now this festival."

"She's the one who had the toy gun, right?"

I nodded. "She picked all the movies too. Got any more guesses?"

"I'd say Whoopi, but she hasn't done a lot of movies that fit your guidelines either." He shrugged. "I give up."

I ticked them off quickly. "Halle Berry, Nia Long, Jada Pinkett Smith and Vivica A. Fox."

Nate nodded slowly and grinned. "Well, that's a bevy of beauties, all right. You shouldn't have any trouble bringing the brothers out."

Something in the way he said it kind of annoyed me. Sure, they're all beautiful women, but the casual assumption that that's the only reason men would come to see their work sort of pissed me off.

"The brothers won't be a problem," I said, adding some pepper sauce to my greens. "The festival's for women only."

His fork stopped halfway to his mouth with a load of baked chicken and dressing. "For women only?"

I nodded. "Most of our activities at The Circus are like that. It helps us keep our focus."

He put down the fork. "I don't get it. Guys can't even be in the audience?"

"We always have discussions afterward," I said. "That's a big part of what we do and it usually gets down to some pretty personal stuff. Women tend to open up more when there are no men around."

"But it's a public event. What are you going to do if some guys decide to show up?"

I offered Tee's argument. "How many guys do you know who are going to come to something billed as 'for women only'?"

"That's not the point, Joyce."

His tone had changed completely. Plus, he called me by my name in much the same manner Ezra Busbee had—to remind me who was in charge. I sighed and took a long, cold swallow of my tea.

In the initial stages of any relationship, personal or professional, men and women trying to talk without offending each other is like walking blindfolded across the interstate. You might make it to the other side unscathed, but I wouldn't bet on it. It's not that anybody's consciously doing anything wrong. It's just that the changes any women's movement worth its name should have produced never got beyond a few gatherings of radical feminists and some thoroughly cowed men whose connection to the rest of us remains tenuous at best. Since it's in our real lives that any real changes have got to take place, we're still at ground zero. And holding.

"What is the point, *Nate?*"

My tone should have alerted him to the possibility of dissent, but he plowed ahead.

"The point is, this festival sounds like a great idea, not just for women but for the guys I'm trying to work with at the school every day. I think you're limiting its potential positive impact by arbitrarily excluding males."

I raised my eyebrows. "We didn't do it arbitrarily. We did it because men always change the focus of any discussion until it's about them. How *they* feel. What *they* think. What *they* imagine the women in the room are thinking. I just don't have any interest in that anymore. No matter how much progress the girls make, the boys are stuck, always trying to be the center of the universe."

I shrugged the idea off like it was too ridiculous to be considered. "Or they don't care about anything except trying to sweet-talk some poor woman who's trying to listen or they get nervous because it's all too new and start being rowdy and disruptive because that's what they know best."

"I thought it was our job to teach them otherwise," Nate rumbled.

"That's *your* job," I said. "I work with young women."

"But what good does it do if the lessons only work when there's not any guys around?" he said, sounding exasperated. "Don't they have to be able to apply this new philosophy to the real world?"

Of course he was right, but I was too. We sat there for a minute pushing our food around and trying to find some common ground.

"It's not my decision," I said finally. "Tee's in charge and then the group votes."

He looked at me. "Is the vote final?"

"It is when they take it. So far, they're still in the planning stages."

"Then I need to make an appointment to talk to . . . Tee?"

She would have loved the idea of Nate asking for an appointment. *The West Wing* had nothing on The Sewing Circus!

"What do you want to talk with her about?"

He leaned across the table, wanting to convince me. "About another way of looking at this thing. About a way for me to bring some of my guys from the school over in a way that won't disrupt anything."

"I think she's pretty much made up her mind about that."

"Fifteen minutes is all I ask."

I hesitated. It would be a great chance for Tee to practice her negotiating skills with somebody other than me, and if he could convince her, including the boys might make for some interesting discussions. Besides, it really isn't my decision. It's theirs.

"All right," I said. "I'll ask her."

"Thank you!" He sat back, relieved, and grinned at me. "You make a brother work hard, you know that?"

I grinned back. We had gotten over our first real gender skirmish without charges of "male bashing" being bandied about and no personal animosity surfacing at crucial moments. That made me really happy.

"Didn't your mama ever teach you the rhyme about that?"

He shook his big smooth head. "Not that I recall."

"Man must work from sun to sun, but woman's work is never done."

That made him laugh out loud and throw up his hands. "You don't ever quit, do you?"

"Nope," I said. "But every now and then I take a night off, and you know what?"

His voice was a hopeful rumble. "What?"

"This is one of those nights."

THIRTY-NINE

this is a dream

I KNOW THIS IS a dream because I'm dancing. It's a party. No. A nightclub. A Cuban nightclub? It's a tiled balcony, I know that, and there's surf crashing near enough to hear it. There's music. Guitars. Other dancers are far enough away so that all I know of them is the echo of their laughter.

I am dancing with my Mitch and then Nate walks by and smiles, waves. I wave back and turn to Mitch, who is also waving.

"I like him," Mitch says, swirling me around expertly as if in the afterlife he has suddenly become Gregory Hines.

And I say, "I like him too."

And then Mitch leans over and kisses me. "I know, baby," he says. "Don't you think I already know?"

I woke up tasting the salt spray on my lips and listening for the sound of slow guitars.

FORTY

a payin' customer

I SAW NIKKI IN town today. She hasn't been around as much lately because her hours are still crazy at the club. The place seems to open early and close very late. She says they even have a lunch special. I wonder what it's called: *burger and a booty?* I resisted the temptation to ask her if she'd seen Junior, but she must have read my mind because she volunteered it.

"If I tell you something, will you promise not to tell Tee?"

"No," I said. That kind of preconfession bestowing of coconspirator status is always a trap. I never agree in advance to keep anybody's secrets but my own.

Nikki looked surprised, then she grinned and shook her head. "You a trip, Miz J. You don't never break. I bet somebody could wake you up in the middle of the night and you'd still be right on point."

I laughed. "I don't know about that. I'm just not very good at keeping secrets." Especially from Tomika. The effort required was not only superhuman but doomed to failure. She always finds out.

"Okay, well, how about don't tell her unless she ask you *specifically?*"

"What are you talking about?" These were kids' games. If she was old enough to take her clothes off for a living, she was old enough to take responsibility for whatever she was so reluctant to confess.

She glanced over her shoulder like she half expected to see Tee walking into the drugstore aisle where we were standing surrounded by fingernail polish and eyelash curlers and a dusty display of old school supplies. "Junior came into the club."

Her expression was a mixture of nervous triumph and cosmic confusion.

"When?"

"Two nights ago—but nothin' happened. That's what I'm tellin' you. He sat up front, but he couldn't do nothin', he couldn't say nothin', unless he *paid*. He was just another customer."

I wondered if that was really progress, but decided not to ask.

"Don't you think that's a trip?" Her smile was strained, waiting for my response. "Now he payin' for what he used to get free!"

The bell dinged as the front door to the small store opened and Nikki glanced up nervously. She knew this wasn't a positive thing, or she wouldn't be so nervous. There was more to this story. All I had to do was wait for the other shoe to drop.

"Why didn't you tell Tee?" I said.

She rolled her eyes. "Tee don't wanna hear nothin' 'bout Junior."

"I think it's dangerous," I said. "You should tell them not to let him in if he comes again."

She looked at me like I had taken leave of my senses. "As long as he a payin' customer, I don't get a vote on if he come in or not."

"Tell them he's harassing you."

If she had any doubts about my sanity, that removed them. She sighed. "Half the girls in there being harassed by somebody."

I wanted to tell her something encouraging; something wise and practical that would help her move from this phase to the next one with a minimum of risk, but nothing came to me, so I changed the subject.

"Are you going to be able to come to the festival?" I said. "You know we're going to do it up right."

"I gotta work," she said.

"Come late," I said. "Knowing how much Tee likes to talk about movies, we'll probably go till midnight."

"Good thing you not showin' Denzel," she said. "You'd be there all weekend."

We were both relieved to share the laugh.

"Well, I gotta go," she said.

I hugged her, and when she stepped away, she looked around one more time to make sure the coast was still clear and then lowered her voice.

"You know what's really weird?" she said, as if degrees of weirdness had been the topic under discussion.

"What?"

"Sometime, not all the time, but sometime, I still miss him."

"Junior?"

She nodded. "I know it's messed up, but that's the truth. We're supposed to tell the truth, right?"

Was that the sound of the other shoe hitting the floor?

"Right," I said. "But what do you miss?"

She shrugged helplessly. "That's the problem. I don't know! We just been together so long, you know? He the only man I ever had and it's like . . . it's like that oldies tune my mama play all the time."

"Which one?"

"I may not be the one you want, but I'm sho' nuff the one you need."

Jasmine was obviously still a Smokey Robinson fan. I looked at her daughter standing there searching for answers to her problems in the lyrics of old Motown tunes and wondered if I could do better. If she was simply missing Junior sexually, maybe a self-pleasuring ritual or two would be helpful. But if his absence was creating an emotional need too, more serious deprogramming was in order, and the cosmetics aisle was probably not the best place to do it.

"Nik," I said, "remember how hard it was for you to stop smoking?"

She nodded, the memory of nicotine patches and diversionary lemon drops fresh in her mind from her battle to quit last year.

"And remember how your body was telling you that you wanted cigarettes even though your brain knew they were killing you?"

"You sayin' I'm addicted to Junior?"

"Doesn't it feel kind of like that?"

She thought about it for a minute. "Sorta." She shook her head, looked around at the aisles full of remedies, pills, potions and lotions to cure what ailed you. "Think they got an anti-Junior patch up in here somewhere?"

I hugged her again. "Come by and talk to me next time you get a day off."

"It's a deal," she said, with her first genuine smile of the day.

I could tell she was relieved to be able to confess her ambivalence. I hadn't promised, but I don't think I'll mention it to Tee right away. Their living arrangement will help make Nik stronger, but that was only going to happen if their tenuous partnership could hold. Any sign of Junior on the horizon was not going to be a step in the right direction.

FORTY-ONE

undeniably different

TEE GREETED THE IDEA of working with Lynette Smitherman almost as unenthusiastically as she did Nate's request for an appointment. She had finally agreed to hear him out tomorrow afternoon, but she was adamant about Nettie.

"She don't wanna be with me," she said, frowning at me like she suspected my hand hidden in there somewhere. "She don't even know me."

"She'll get to know you," I said.

Tee frowned and tossed her braids with a defiant flick of her wrist. "That ain't my idea of a good time, Miz J. You like hangin' around with those old ladies. I don't."

"I'm not asking you to hang around with her. She wants to help. Somebody close to her just passed and she's trying to keep her mind off of it."

"When you get that old, somebody always gonna be dyin'," Tee sniffed with the arrogance that is only possible while you're still young enough to believe that in the history of the human race, you're going to be the first one who never gets old, never gets sick, and never, *ever*, dies.

"You're opening with *Introducing Dorothy Dandridge*, right?"

"You know we are."

Dissent made Tee snippy sometimes, but I didn't care. "Well, these ladies met her."

She was instantly impressed. "The real Dorothy Dandridge? Where?"

"At the premiere of *Carmen Jones*. You remember where Halle Berry steps out of that limo with that white fur and walks up the red carpet, suddenly a *star*?"

Tee nodded. Of course she remembered it. That scene is pivotal. The best moment of Dorothy's life and the worst. Her professional triumph marred by the betrayal of Otto Preminger, her lover and director, who appeared at the theater escorting his white wife. Not that escorting a *black* wife would have been any better, but all the questions raised would have been different. Not less hurtful, but undeniably *different*.

"You tellin' me they was at the premiere?"

"Not only that, they went to a party with her and a bunch of her famous friends right before."

She couldn't resist. Proximity to celebrity was almost as good as celebrity itself. Her imagination took what I gave her and ran with it until I delivered the coup de grâce. "They've even got photographs."

"Of the real Dorothy Dandridge?"

"Of everything that went on that night. The party, the premiere, everything. Lynette had a camera because they knew this was a once-in-a-lifetime thing."

"You think they'd let me see the pictures?" Tee said. "Maybe we could make a display or something."

"Let's go ask them."

She looked at me and something dawned on her. "You're not slick, Miz J. I see what you doin'. You tryin' to get me to take on this old lady 'cause she got some stuff I can use."

"Is it working?"

Her slow smile told me what I wanted to know and she reached for her coat. "So far, so good."

Once we got to the Smithermans', and I made the introductions, I was politely informed that I didn't need to stay since, as Lynette put it, they had to learn to talk among themselves right off, or they never would. Tee looked at me in a sudden panic at being left there alone, but I knew she could handle it, so I told her I'd be back in two hours and went back to The Circus.

Two hours later when I returned with Mavis in tow, Geneva had put together a little supper and set the table for the five of us. Lynette and Tee were sitting in front of the fire with their heads together, surrounded by photographs, clippings preserved in plastic and playbills spilling out of old folders. Mavis climbed into her mother's lap for a kiss and I caught the last line of what had obviously ended up being a serious strategy session.

"That's the way to maintain control of the situation, dear," Nettie said, patting Mavis's cold cheek affectionately. "Seen and not heard. That's the way to go."

"What are you two plotting about?" I said, wishing I had a camera to capture a picture of them, the old Idlewild and the emerging new one in what appeared to be a newly minted but absolutely mutual admiration society.

"We're not plotting," Tee said, grinning at Nettie and giving Mavis another squeeze. "We're organizing!"

"Well, whatever you're doing," Geneva said from the doorway, "stop doing it and come to supper. That child's hungry!"

"I'm hungry, Mama," Mavis said on cue, and we all laughed and headed for the table. Organizing is always a good thing, but Geneva's squash soufflé is even better.

FORTY-TWO

a yes-or-no question

WHEN WE WENT BACK to The Circus to pick up Tee's car, it wouldn't even pretend to turn over.

"This car is startin' to work my nerves," Tee said, giving the steering wheel a disapproving thump.

"I can drop you," I said.

"It can't be the battery. I just got a new battery three weeks ago!"

"Forget it," I said, settling Mavis in my backseat and opening the passenger door for Tee. "As good as things went today, you deserve a ride home."

"I've never met anybody like them before," she said.

"Then you're even. They've never met anybody like you before either."

We were so busy talking about the Smithermans, we didn't

see Junior's car until we pulled into Tee's yard. It was parked right beside Nikki's and the couple inside sat up quickly as our lights hit the rear window.

"Oh, hell no!" Tee said, getting out before I even stopped the car completely. She jerked open the passenger door of Junior's aging gray Buick and Nikki stumbled out of the car, adjusting her clothes. I could see Junior doing the same behind the wheel. Mavis remained blissfully asleep and I suddenly understood the value of a cell phone. In a war zone, emergency communications are an absolute necessity.

"Listen, Tee." Nikki was holding up both hands in front of her as if to ward off an anticipated blow. "The car was acting up when I got ready to leave the club and Junior . . . Junior just followed me home in case it broke down, you know, so I wouldn't be stranded on the road."

"So what were you doin'? Sayin' *thank you?*"

"Aw, Tee, you ain't got to go there." Nikki tried to look hurt.

Tee ignored that. "Tell him to get out of my yard."

"He goin' right now, Tee. Right, Junior? You already headin' out, right?"

Mavis murmured softly and I patted her shoulder gently. Nikki turned to look at Junior, and I could see the expression on her face: scared and confused. Hoping he'd go on home and not make a bad situation impossible; knowing he wouldn't.

He looked at her without blinking. "You *invited* me up in this muthafucka, remember?"

"I know, baby," she said, pleading. "But you gotta go now, okay?"

"*Baby?*" Tee's voice was outraged. "Since when you go back to callin' that nigga *baby?*"

"That ain't none a ya business," Junior said, stepping out on his side of the car but making no move toward us.

"It is if she doin' it in my yard," Tee said, her voice as icy as the ground.

I stepped out of the car, hoping there was safety—or at least increased intimidation—in numbers.

Junior narrowed his eyes and pointed a thick finger in Tee's direction. "You gonna get tired of gettin' in my business."

"I'm already tired of it," Tee said.

"Not as tired as you gonna be," he said.

"That's a crime." I spoke up quickly.

He turned toward me. "I ain't touched her!"

I could feel my heart beating in my throat. "You threatened her. That's enough."

"He didn't mean nothin'." Nik was flitting around helplessly, being careful to stay out of both Junior and Tee's reach. "I swear, he didn't, did you, baby?"

Always the pragmatist, *Baby* looked at us and decided that if I was telling the truth, we weren't worth the trouble.

"Fuck this," he said, climbing back into his car and peeling out of the yard in a hail of rock salt and day-old snow.

Tee looked at Nik with an expression I'd never seen before.

"Let's go inside," I said, unbuckling Mavis, who had slept through the whole thing. Tee seemed to be at a loss for words. So did Nikki, who was standing close by, trying to be invisible. "I'll put Mavis to bed while you two sort it out."

Tee looked at me. "She still asleep?"

I nodded.

"Good. I don't want her to see this kinda shit in her own damn yard!"

Tee was trying hard to stop cussing, especially around Mavis, but when she got mad, she lapsed back big time. Besides, Mavis was asleep, so all bets were effectively off.

"I'm really sorry," Nikki started apologizing again as Tee opened the door to the house and reached for her daughter.

"Why don't I put her to bed?" she said to me like Nikki hadn't spoken at all. "If I talk to this fool right now, I know I'm gonna say somethin' I'll be sorry for later."

"Sure," I said quickly. "Take your time."

Nikki, hearing what she probably thought of as a reprieve, even if it was only a few minutes long, shut up instantly so she wouldn't say anything to make Tee any madder before she disappeared into Mavis's room.

When we heard the door click behind them, Nik let out a rush of held breath and flopped down on the couch. "I have really fucked up now."

She didn't need me to add *you got that right,* so I put the kettle on and rummaged around Tee's kitchen cabinets to find some tea.

"You believe me, don't you?"

She was looking for an ally against what she feared would be a merciless recitation of the string of bad decisions that had led her to this moment.

"Are you telling the truth?"

She tried to look hurt, but I had seen her head pop up over that big front seat. I wasn't going for it any more than Tee was. "Of course."

Of course. It was going to be a long night. "You swore you were done with Junior," I said. "I was the witness, remember?"

She twisted her hands in her lap and frowned, reorganizing the lie. "I am done wit' him."

"Then why was he here?"

"I already tole you. My car was actin' up. He just gave me a ride!"

Her voice rose in indignant defense of the lie and Tee walked into the room quickly. Nikki shrank back against the couch and pressed her lips together like she was afraid anything she said could and would be used against her.

Tee looked at her for a long, silent moment. There was everything and nothing to be said between them. "Were you fuckin' Junior in my backyard?"

Nikki winced. "I tole you—"

"Save that bullshit! Were you fuckin' him? That's what I'm askin' you."

There was no place to hide. "Tee, I . . ."

"*Yes or no?*"

Nik's voice was a whisper. "Yes."

Tee didn't blink. "Then you gotta go."

"Aw-w-w-w, Tee, don't go there." Nikki's voice was a cross between a whine and a wheedle. "I'm sorry, okay? I said I'm sorry!"

Tomika shook her head. "That ain't good enough. I told you, I'm not havin' this shit around Mavis. You knew that. Now know *this*. I want you and all your stuff out of here tomorrow morning."

Panic was rising in Nikki's eyes. "Where I'ma go, huh? You know they rented my other place out."

Tomika was unmoved. "Your mama got a spare bedroom. Call her."

Nik stood up quickly, suddenly defiant in the face of her inevitable eviction. "Well, *fuck you*, then, Tee, okay? You gonna be all *toe the line* on me and shit, then just *fuck you!*"

"I didn't do it, Nik! You did!"

Conscious of Mavis, neither one raised her voice above an angry whisper. We spend so much time controlling what we feel—the pain and the joy—because our babies are sleeping in the next room. I wonder how much of it they absorb anyway; how much of it appears in their dreams.

"Yeah, I did it," Nikki hissed. "Because everybody ain't like you, Tee. Everybody can't just close that shit off and keep on like nothin' happened. Some of us need a man's hands, you know what I'm sayin'? You so busy savin' your shit for some imaginary Denzel Washington clone, you done forgot how good the real shit can be."

The teakettle was whistling weakly and I got up to turn it off.

"I ain't forgot nothin'," Tee said quietly. "But all you gotta remember is to get out my house before noon tomorrow."

Nikki snatched her purse off the couch and flung herself out of the room. "You ain't got to tell me twice!" She jerked open the door to the room she shared with Tee, but she didn't slam it behind her. She was pissed and confused but not crazy.

Left alone, Tee and I looked at each other.

"You okay?" I asked.

"Yeah. I'm cool."

I hadn't even taken off my coat. Things had happened so fast.

"I knew she was still messin' around with Junior. I can always tell."

The guilt of not telling her what Nikki had said about Junior coming by the club weighed on me. "You want me to stay awhile?"

She shook her head. "He ain't comin' back here tonight. It's tomorrow I got to start thinkin' about."

"You think she'll need a ride in the morning?"

Tee snorted. "Ain't nothin' wrong with that car."

"You're right," I said. "I guess not."

She walked me to the door. "You know what I was talkin' about before?"

"What?"

"About gettin' a real gun?"

"I remember."

"I'm thinkin' about it again."

FORTY-THREE

kind of blue

I SPENT MOST OF the next afternoon trying to talk Tee
out of her gun purchase and trying to get the sheriff's office to
take Junior's threat seriously. In both cases, I could have saved
my breath, so I was more than a little cranky when I pulled up in
front of the school to drop off some festival information for Nate.

The kids were gone by the time I got there and he was working in his office. He was wearing a beautiful camel-colored
sweater whose soft drape did nothing to hide the definition of
his chest muscles. Miles Davis's *Kind of Blue* was playing softly
on a CD player squeezed into the overcrowded bookshelf. His
music is so amazing, but I can't help listening for that mean
streak even on the sweetest tunes.

"Come in, come in," he said, coming from behind his desk to
greet me with a smile.

Our dinner at Dot's had lasted until they closed up and threw us out, still talking and laughing and getting to know each other. What we'd seen so far, we both liked. Now if we could just find a minute to explore it in peace! But not today.

"How's your day been?"

"I've had better," I said, all business.

My tone brought him up sharp. "I'm sorry. What happened?"

"Same old thing," I said. "But I wanted to drop off this stuff about the festival and let you know Tee's ready to meet with you as soon as you can give us a day and time."

"Slow down a minute," he said. "Are you okay?"

I stopped, took a deep breath and looked at him, being careful to stand far enough away to minimize the mandatory tilting of the head. "I'm fine."

"What are you so mad about?"

"I'm not mad."

He looked at me. "Mildly irritated? At least give me mildly irritated."

"Fine," I said. "I might be mildly irritated."

He nodded approvingly like at least we were making a little progress. "Any idea what might have produced this *mild irritation?*"

I shook my head.

He spread his arms wide. "If you don't like the sweater, just tell me. I'll go put on a suit."

That made me smile a little.

"And a tie!"

"It's not you," I said.

"Thank God! Then what?"

There was no reason not to tell him. "Tee's buying a gun."

He raised his eyebrows, immediately concerned. "Why?"

"Nikki brought Junior by the house and he threatened Tee when she told him to leave. She's scared."

"Well, nothing wrong with owning a gun if you know how to use it."

"Which she doesn't!"

"Then why don't you let me take her over to the firing range? If she's motivated, it won't take long to teach her."

That hadn't occurred to me and a wave of relief swept over me. "Are you serious?"

He shrugged. "If the problem is that she can't shoot a gun, that problem can be easily solved. What's she getting? A .38?"

To me the question of guns is always a huge moral dilemma, requiring much soul-searching and wringing of hands. Even when we had a real crack problem up here a few years ago, my brother-in-law practically had to beg me to keep a shotgun in the house.

"I . . . I don't know what kind she wants to get."

"Okay," he said. "I've got a couple she can try. Once she shoots them, it'll be easier for her to make up her mind."

A couple she can try? "How many guns do you have?"

He smiled. "A couple."

"Why?"

"I used to be a cop. Old habits are hard to break."

This whole conversation was making me feel so sad I thought I was going to burst into tears.

Nate's voice was a gentle rumble. "What's wrong?"

I didn't know if I could explain, but I had to try. "I just never thought I'd be arranging shooting lessons for one of my girls."

"Better to be safe than sorry."

That just made me feel worse. Is this the real price of freedom? And if it is, what if it's just too high?

"Do you feel free?" I said suddenly.

"Sure I do."

"Why?"

He thought for a minute. "Bottom line?"

"Bottom line."

"Because nobody can kick my ass."

"There you go," I said. "How many women can say that? Every man I see can probably kick mine."

"But those are the bad guys," he said, frowning. "All men aren't like that."

When you start talking about the bad stuff men do, the man present always want to be acknowledged as an exception. One of the good guys. I guess that's fair and I usually don't mind doing it, but sometimes I wish they didn't need to stop the conversation so often to be reassured. I didn't say anything.

He looked at me, and when he spoke, his voice was very gentle. "Can I apologize on behalf of the good guys for all crimes, real and imagined?"

I took another deep breath. "I'm sorry to be fussing at you about all this," I said, letting that *real or imagined* slide. "But just imagine if the situation was reversed."

"What do you mean?"

"I mean, what if every woman you saw could kick your ass?"

"I can't imagine it."

"Try."

"I can't imagine it."

I was speechless again. It is my feeling that trying to mold adult male behavior is a constant struggle in which consistency is everything. The reason so few men ever progress beyond the most basic understanding of who and what women really are is not that they get distracted. It's that we get tired and start letting them slide. Or we fall in love and our vision is so clouded by all that sweetness that we relax completely, convinced that this is the one relationship that will be able to avoid the sexist bullshit that has doomed all others. I know better. It's like that old movement song: freedom is a constant struggle.

"Well," I said, giving up, but irritated that even in his imagination he couldn't conceive of a vulnerability that I know in my bones, "if you could imagine it, you'd understand why sometimes when I get mad, it's important for you to hear what I say because the bad guys never will."

"Never say never," he said with that slow smile. "Things can change."

"I guess that's pretty much up to the good guys, isn't it?" I said, real sarcastic. "All five or six of you."

Now he was speechless, but I could tell he was thinking. "Something about this reminds me of how I felt the first time I made love in a black country," he said slowly. "Just knowing there weren't any white folks around for miles made it a whole different kind of exchange. Like not worrying about all that race stuff left a big space for something sweeter to walk in and sit down."

"The problem is, we don't have that option," I said, wondering what *something sweeter* looks like when it's up and walking about. "Most women aren't going to be making love anyplace where there's no men around."

He looked at me like he was starting to understand how complicated this stuff could be. "I think," he said, "I'm beginning to get your point."

FORTY-FOUR

in my mind's eye

WHEN TOMIKA CAME IN the next morning, she was grinning like the Cheshire cat and carrying a large manila envelope, which she dropped on my desk like I'd been waiting for it.

"Open it!"

"And good morning to you," I said.

"Good mornin', good mornin'." She waved at me impatiently. "Open it!"

The envelope was one of the old-fashioned kind where you wrap a string around a small round tab to close it. I unwrapped it quickly and pulled out an old copy of *Life* magazine.

"November 1, 1954," Tee crowed. "Is she killin' it or what?"

It was the famous cover shot with Dorothy Dandridge in full Carmen Jones regalia; hands on her hips, a sly smile, and enough sex appeal to make you squint.

"Where did you get it?" I said, unable to look away from Dorothy's saucy stare.

"Miz Smitherman gave it to me," Tee said breathlessly. "Can you believe it? I went by there to leave her a thank-you note and she had already pulled this out for me. She's had it all these years and she just gave it to me."

Tee was as excited as I've ever seen her. "She made me a list of all the stars that were at the dinner they went to before the show." She dug through her purse and unfolded a piece of crinkly pink stationery filled with Lynette's delicate handwriting. "When she started tellin' me who all was there, I had never heard of the people she was namin', but I could tell by the way she was sayin' it that they musta been big stars, so I acted like I knew who she was talkin' about."

I laughed. "She busted you fast, didn't she?"

Tee shook her head, embarrassed at the memory. "Fast? BAM! Faster than that! But she was cool about it. She told me not to pretend anything because it was too much work and didn't get you anyplace but further behind."

Lynette had a firm belief that anybody could learn anything once they quit pretending that they already knew it.

"So she wrote the names down for me. Look!" Tee smoothed out the paper and read the names out loud. "Count Basie, Sammy Davis, Jr., Diahann Carroll, Pearl Bailey and Lena Horne." She looked up, still enjoying the feel of their names, new in her mouth. "You ever heard of 'em?"

I nodded. "I even met Sammy Davis, Jr."

Tee was properly impressed. "For real?"

"My father took me backstage when he was doing a show in Detroit."

"How old were you?"

"Sixteen. He wanted Sammy Davis to come up here and perform at his club."

"Did he?"

"No," I said, remembering my father's disappointment. "But the show that night was amazing."

She picked up the magazine again, ran her fingers gently, respectfully, across the photograph. "Bein' that pretty didn't protect her at all, did it?"

"No, I don't guess it did."

"Think she'd a done better with a .22?"

I shook my head. "No. Do you?"

She sighed. "Deena been on me and on me about how dangerous it'll be for me to have a gun in the house while Mavis growin' up. She got all these stats about how many little kids find a gun in they own house and blow they own brains out." She paused for breath. "Now she tellin' me if I do get one, she can't let the twins come over 'cause they won't be safe."

"You change your mind?" I hadn't told her about Nate's offer yet. I figured I'd wait until they met. Maybe by then she would have changed her mind.

She shook her head, but slowly. Her braids swung, but they didn't dance. "You know on the list where it says we should know self-defense?"

I nodded.

"What kind of self-defense were you talkin' about?"

"I wish I knew," I said.

"Yeah," Tomika said, putting the treasured magazine carefully back into its ancient envelope. "I wish you did too."

FORTY-FIVE

the problem with
surrender

"THAT'S THE PROBLEM WITH black women," Bill said.

I was cooking dinner for him and Sister and she was running late at choir rehearsal. I groaned loudly and rolled my eyes. "Is that the topic for the evening?"

"The essence of true love is surrender." Bill would not be denied. "All the great poets agree on that. And if there is one thing a black woman will not do, it's surrender! No wonder nobody can stay together for longer than twenty minutes at a time!"

A friend of theirs from California had decided to divorce her third husband after a tumultuous five-year marriage during which they had separated and reunited twelve times before call-

ing it quits. Bill's theory was that the wife's unwillingness to surrender had doomed the union from the start.

"I didn't know we were at war," I said.

"Bullshit!" Bill said. "And you know it! Jack Kerouac wrote
'love is a duel' forty years ago and nothing substantive has
changed since then!"

"Do men have to surrender too?" I said, chopping vegetables.

"Of course not," he said patiently, like he was speaking to a
bright if rebellious child. "Men have to conquer, dominate, sub-
due. Look at the biology! *I will kick off! You will receive!*"

I groaned again and reached for my apron. "I thought football season was over."

"You know I'm right."

"I know I'm going to tell your wife on you when she gets here."

"She knows I'm right too. Sarah and Kwame should have
been together forever. He's crazy about that woman, but she
could never relax. Everything was combat with her. She could
never give him the benefit of the doubt."

"The benefit of the doubt about what?" I was flouring the
chicken. I don't eat meat anymore, but I was raving about dinner
at Dot's and Sister demanded some soul food, so fried chicken
was *required*. I had already cooked the collard greens, mac and
cheese and corn bread. We were going to make up for this high-
cholesterol feast by being more conscientious about diet for the
rest of the week, so I didn't feel *too* guilty. I embrace the concept
of moderation over abstinence. Less guilt-producing and, over
the long haul, probably just as effective.

"The benefit of the doubt about everything," Bill said, rum-
maging around in the refrigerator and pouring us each a glass of
white wine. "The essence of marriage is trust."

"Was he trustworthy?" I said, turning up the heat under my favorite cast-iron frying pan.

Bill looked hurt. "See? That's what I'm talking about. You immediately assume it's his fault!"

"No, I don't," I said, "but if she's not a madwoman, I do assume there's a reason for her behavior."

"That's what I'm trying to tell you," he said. "There doesn't have to be a reason. There's a free-floating rage that sisters carry that can lash out at any time, and it's lethal. Absolutely anathema to a long-term love affair."

Maybe Bill was onto something, but I wasn't about to confess and prove his theory. "What's free-floating rage got to do with surrender?"

"You ever try to make love when you're angry?"

He had a point there. Whenever I felt myself getting annoyed at Nate, all my appreciation of his overall fineness and undeniable sex appeal flew right out the window.

I took out the plates and the silverware and handed them to Bill. "Make yourself useful."

"You're trying to distract me." He grinned. "That means you know I'm right."

Sister opened the back door and stepped inside. "Right about what?"

"Come and get your husband," I said. "Quick!"

"Are you antagonizing the cook?" She gave him a quick kiss and hung her coat on the hook that ought to have her name on it.

"Every chance I get," he said, smiling at her. "But only with love, of course!"

"Of course." She turned to me. "What can I do to help?"

"Pour yourself a glass of wine," I said, handing Bill the napkins and the glasses. "You, on the other hand, have to work for your dinner."

"No problem," he said. "I know when I'm outnumbered. How about some music?"

"Great," I said.

"Any specific requests?"

My music is organized around my own madness and no other. People who alphabetize and catalog their collections have been driven to distraction by the fact that at my house, Maxwell is nowhere near Bob Marley, who isn't even in the same neighborhood as Johnny Mathis; but Bill was up for the challenge.

"Surprise me."

Sister took a sip of her wine and smiled. "This smells like my mama's house."

I turned the chicken, being careful not to splatter the grease. Only amateurs leave a trail. "I take that as a true compliment."

"Of the highest order," she said. "Is Brother Anderson joining us?"

She was trying to sound casual, but she was *dippin'*.

"I invited him," I said. "Unfortunately, he had a prior engagement."

"I'm surprised he didn't break it."

I laughed. "He couldn't. School board briefing."

I lifted out a perfect, golden-brown drumstick to drain on a nearby paper towel, stirred the greens and put the mac and cheese in the microwave. From the living room, Mahalia Jackson was singing "Jesus Met the Woman at the Well."

It was one of Bill's favorites because of the shockingly bluesy piano that accompanies her. I love the lyrics. It's always funny to me that the woman thinks she can fool Jesus. Almost as funny as me trying to fool Sister.

I took a sip of wine and wiped my hands on my apron. I wanted to say this right. "You know that moment when you meet a brother and you feel like he's open to another way of looking at things, even though he's never heard any of this stuff before in exactly the way you're saying it, but he really likes women and he'd love to understand them better because he knows that if he does, if he can just figure us out a little better, they—we!—will love him for it?"

"Sounds like me," Bill said, returning and draping an affectionate arm around Sister's shoulder. "Did Joyce tell you about my surrender theory?"

Sister held up her hand. "Please! No theories tonight!"

He tried to look hurt, but Sister just smiled and touched his cheek affectionately. "Even the Lord rested one day, sweetie."

I arranged the chicken on my mother's good platter.

"All right," he said, pretending to grumble. "No point in trying to enlighten Negroes about anything serious when they smell chicken!"

"You got that right!"

Sister said the blessing and I stood up to serve their plates. Everything had turned out perfectly, if I do say so myself, and our dinner conversation was pretty much limited to "Please pass the greens" and "Does anybody want that other wing?" I shooed them away from the cleanup, stacked the dishes for later and poured us all some tea.

"A perfect day," said Bill, looking for more music. He put on some Sidney Bechet and we all just sat there enjoying each other's company and listening to Brother Bechet's divine saxophone. I thought about Bill's surrender theory. How could we be expected to surrender? Things had gotten so bad Tee was buying a gun. Surrender wasn't in it.

"Penny for your thoughts," Sister said. I realized I'd been staring into the fire.

"Just woolgathering," I said, using my grandmother's favorite term for daydreaming.

"Woolgathering or worrying?" Sister knew a hedge when she heard one.

"I'm sorry," I said. "I was thinking about Tee."

"When I stopped by to see Nettie Smitherman this afternoon, she couldn't stop talking about her," Sister said. "The partnership must be working."

Bill laughed. "Now that's a match made in heaven. The only person who'll have a chance of out talking either one is the other!"

"She's going to buy a gun," I said.

They exchanged startled glances. "Tee?"

Bill's face clouded over. Back in Oakland, he'd lost one of his best students, a good friend and an older brother all to gun violence. Any talk of firearms was guaranteed to raise his blood pressure. "What for?"

"Junior threatened her."

"What did he say?"

"It doesn't matter," I said, unwilling to argue about whether or not the words he'd uttered constituted a real threat or just the heat of the moment. "The point is, he scared her and the sheriff's office acts like there's nothing they can do."

"You sound like you endorse the idea," Bill said, sounding accusatory.

"You know I don't," I snapped. "I hate guns, but what's she supposed to do?"

"What did the sheriff say?" Sister sounded really concerned. Her tone was as soothing to me as Bill's had been immediately irritating. This free-floating rage was getting to be a constant companion and I didn't like the feeling at all. I tried to match Sister's equanimity.

"They said there's not much they can do until he actually puts his hands on her."

"Do you think buying a gun will keep him from doing that?" Bill's tone had not improved.

"She's scared."

"What did you tell her?"

I sighed. This was not going to be the answer Bill wanted to hear, but we were all going to have to deal with the truth of the situation. "I told her if she was going to get a gun, she ought to know how to use it."

"What does that mean?"

"Nate's going to take her to the firing range."

Bill ran his hand over his face and looked at me like I had just lost my whole mind. "The firing range? What are you talking about, Joyce? You can't think this is a good idea!"

His voice was trembling with remembered pain and rising indignation.

"You know I don't!"

Bill stood up and started pacing. Sister's eyes followed him.

"You're supposed to say no!" he said, his face grim and tight. "You're supposed to say 'Guns don't solve anything!' 'Practice peace!' 'Thou shalt not kill!' You're supposed to say *something!*"

"Hang on a second, sweetie," Sister said softly.

Bill stopped pacing and sat down beside her slowly. "It's a terrible idea," he said, looking at me like I had been the one to bring it forward.

"You can't think it's any worse than I do," I said.

His mouth curled into a smile that wasn't one. "I'd be prepared to argue that."

Bill was not above reminding me what he had suffered, but, unfortunately, my own credentials in the suffering area are impeccable, so I didn't back off an inch.

"We're not talking about you," I said. "We're talking about Tee."

He looked at me. "I don't think I deserve that."

"Neither does she," I said.

Bill stood up quickly.

"Calm down, sweetie," Sister said, taking his hand like you do a kid's when you're crossing the street.

He took a deep breath. "I'm calm," he said, looking at me. "I just don't think I can talk about this anymore, okay?"

"Okay," I said, standing up too, but keeping my voice as calm as I could. "I'll handle it and keep you posted."

"Don't bother," he said.

That didn't leave me much room to be conciliatory, so I stopped trying. "All right," I said. "I won't."

Bill looked hurt. "Maybe we should call it a day," he said quietly to Sister.

She looked at him for a minute like she was trying to gauge his mood accurately. "Why don't you warm up the car, then, sweetie, and I'll be right there?"

Bill pulled his coat on slowly and turned to look at me when he got to the door. "Sometimes you seem to think you're the only one who loves these girls, but you're not."

"Talk is cheap," I said, and he drew back like I'd slapped him.

He grabbed his hat and scarf. "Thanks for an almost perfect evening," he said, and closed the door firmly behind him.

"I'm sorry," Sister said, watching Bill out the back window, but I waved away her apology.

"I don't need you to be sorry," I said. "I need you to tell me what to do for Tee."

She pulled her coat on and reached for her scarf. "You know what to do."

"No," I said. "I really don't."

"Go with her to the firing range," she said quietly. "She's got the right to feel safe."

I should have known she would understand. "I hate this."

She patted my shoulder. "Me too. That's why we've got to figure out something else *fast!*"

"Can't be fast enough for me," I said, opening the door for her and stepping out. "Think Bill will stay mad at me?"

She dropped her voice and kissed my cheek as if she were really saying good-bye. "Does he ever?"

He opened the door for her when she got to the car, but she smiled at him and said something I couldn't hear from where I was standing. Whatever it was, he looked at her and then back at me. She touched his shoulder with the slightest suggestion of an encouraging shove and he walked back across the yard, up the steps, wrapped his arms around me and hugged me tight; a real hug; a Bill hug.

"I'm sorry," he said. "It's not your fault or mine."

"Apology accepted," I said, hugging him back, wondering what Sister had said to change his mind so quickly. I knew we didn't have a real difference of opinion, but once Bill gets dug in behind a position, sometimes it can take days for him to let it go.

He leaned back and looked at me without taking his arm from around my shoulders. "So you're not mad at me?"

I smiled. "I can't be mad at you."

"Then tell me again why we're going home so early?"

"Because you're stubborn as a mule!"

"That may be the maybe," he said, "but I'm not too far gone to see the value of a strategic surrender."

"Especially when there's peach cobbler at stake," said Sister, herding us both back into the house.

I laughed. "Strategic surrender, huh?"

Bill looked properly sheepish. "That's the problem with surrender," he said. "Nobody ever lets you forget it."

"Don't worry," I said, dishing up the cobbler, glad we were all back on the same side. "Your secret is safe with me."

FORTY-SIX

the enforcer

I DIDN'T KNOW WHAT to expect from a meeting between Nate and Tee. She'd been on the phone several times with Nettie, but they were still *talking among themselves* and I was busy following up a few more funding leads that seemed promising. When he arrived on time, Tee was in the bathroom making last-minute braid adjustments, but his entrance was greeted with stunned silence by Deena and the kids, who stared at him openmouthed as if T. rex had just lumbered into the room, looking for lunch.

"Welcome," I said, wondering if I'd done the right thing by not warning Tee any more specifically than a fairly generic "he's tall." I could have added bald and smart and fit and fine, but I thought the basics should suffice.

When she walked into the office and saw him standing there,

taking up almost all the available space, her expression told me I was wrong. Her eyes and her mouth flew open simultaneously, and she was, for probably the first time since I've known her, speechless.

"Nate Anderson," I said, as he turned to face her. "This is Tomika Jackson. The festival was her idea and she's running the whole show for us. Tee, this is Nate."

"Good to meet you," Nate rumbled, holding out his big hand to shake hers. "I appreciate your taking the time."

"No problem," Tee said, trying to look him over without looking him over. "I am . . ." She paused like an actor searching for a line and I realized that's probably exactly what she was doing. "I'm looking forward to hearing what you have to say."

She nailed it and Nate looked as proud of her as I know I did. *You go, girl!*

"I promise I won't take much of your time," Nate said as we all sat down and Tee took out her yellow pad. She wrote everything down these days, which was great. We didn't have to remember anything.

"I'd like you to reconsider allowing males to attend your festival," he said, getting right to the point.

"Why?"

"Because I think they've got at least as much to learn as females, and left to their own devices, it's going to take a whole lot longer to teach them."

A convincing argument. Tee was usually open to alliances based on mutual self-interest, but right now, she looked unimpressed.

"Is that why they wanna come?" she said. "To learn something?"

Nate nodded. "Yes."

Tee consulted her legal pad and looked back at Nate. "How can we be sure of that?"

Nate looked a little surprised by the question. "I'm not sure I know what you mean."

"I mean"—Tee sounded firm but not unpleasant—"that when the guys usta come over here for activities and stuff, they'd always mess it up. That's why we stopped invitin' 'em."

Nate frowned. "Mess it up how?"

"All kinda ways," Tee said. "They come late. They come loud. They drunk when they get here or they tryin' to go out in the yard and smoke some reefer." Tee was picking up steam. "They hollerin' at the kids or pushin' they girlfriends around. All kinda stuff."

Nate was listening intently and her words seem to wound him. "I'm sorry to hear that," he rumbled.

"It was bad," she said. "Nobody could concentrate, and the thing is . . ."

She hesitated, searching for her lines again. "The thing is, we tryin' to change people's lives up in here. It's serious business and we take it real serious."

"I understand," Nate said. "And I respect your mission, but can I ask you to give the brothers one more try? I'll take responsibility for their behavior."

Tee looked a little skeptical. "How you gonna do that?"

"Anybody who doesn't act like he's got some sense will have to answer to me."

Tee sat back, considering the offer. I already loved it. I had an immediate mental picture of Nate tossing rowdy Lattimores out the back door like bad babies with the bathwater.

"That'll work," Tee said, slowly, "and we have one more house rule."

This was news to me. What house rule would that be?

"They can't talk durin' the discussion. Their participation . . ." She faltered slightly and consulted her legal pad quickly. "Their participation will be limited to viewin' and listenin'."

Nate's face mirrored my own surprise and I remembered Nettie's words: *Seen and not heard, dear. That's how you maintain control.* The partnership was working its show!

"Do you think that's fair?" Nate said.

Tee nodded, setting her braids into motion. "The main thing we can never get 'em to do is *listen*. They always busy arguin' their side of it, when most of the time, they ain't even got no side. This way, they ain't got no choice. They gotta hear us for a change!"

Nate looked at her for a minute, debating his options, then he sat back and grinned, shaking his head. "I wish I could say you're wrong about my brothers, but you're right. Listening is definitely not our strong point."

Tee grinned back at him, relieved that he understood; emboldened by her own ability to present her case and hold her own. She shot a glance at me and I winked my support.

"All right, then," Nate said. "Let me be sure I got it straight. The brothers are welcome as long as they don't act a fool, but they can't participate in the discussion *at all?*"

"And if anything jump off, they gotta answer to you," Tee added.

"It's a deal," he said, extending his hand again to shake hers across the table.

"You the witness, Miz J." Tee spoke to me directly for the first time since they sat down. Nate looked at me and I put my hand on top of theirs in a three-way shake of solidarity.

"Done!"

Tee's smile could have lit up every town in northern Michigan. Nate stood up and reached for his coat.

"Well, I'm going to get out of here before I agree to anything else," he said, smiling down at Tee.

"Thanks for comin' by," she said.

"It's a pleasure working with you," said Nate.

I picked up my sweater. "I'll walk you out," I said.

When we were standing at the back door out of earshot, Nate grinned at me. "You're not the only one around here who drives a hard bargain, I see."

"Each one, teach one," I said, laughing.

"She's got a lot of heart," he said. "Is she the one who wants to buy a gun?"

I nodded.

"That's a damn shame," he said. "But if she goes ahead with it, tell her I can take her to the range anytime she wants to go."

"Thanks," I said. "I'll tell her."

His smile returned. "Good."

As soon as I got back to the office, Tee and Deena exploded.

"How tall is he?"

"Is he really a teacher?"

"How long have you known *him?*"

Finally Tee shushed Deena and looked at me. "So what's the deal? You couldn't tell me the man was a *giant?*"

"He's not a giant."

They rolled their eyes. "Not in a room full of NBA players he's not, but around here, he's about as close as we get."

Deena sat down. "You know what my baby said the second he walked in the door? 'Giant, Mama! Look at the giant!' "

Tee had added tiny silver bells to the ends of several of the braids near her face and they were tinkling madly. "Out of the mouths of babes! I can't believe he's teachin' at the school!"

"He's a vice principal," I said, like his job description had anything to do with his overall appeal.

"*Whatever,*" Deena said, heading back out to where the kids were twittering about Nate among themselves, presumably in agreement on the fact that this was their first real giant, but everything seemed to be cool, so in the absence of fear, they could focus on wonder.

"So when were you gonna tell me?"

"Tell you what?" I said.

"That he was *fine,*" she said, echoing what I'd wanted to ask Sister that first night when he surprised me in the middle of my mambo. It was undeniable, so I decided to stop trying.

"Okay," I said. "He's fine."

"And *big!*" Tee said, like omitting it was tantamount to refuting the obvious.

"And big," I agreed, wishing we could change the subject, but knowing that was impossible.

"So is he married?"

"He's divorced," I said, "and he used to be a policeman."

"You like him?"

"He seems okay," I said.

"Okay, *okay,*" she said. "You better keep an eye out, Miz J. You might be up on your Denzel."

"How do you think the meeting went?" I said, changing the subject before she married us off.

"I think it went great," she said, "He couldn't believe I said they can come, but they can't say nothin'!"

I laughed. "I knew you and Nettie were going to be a formidable team, but this is above and beyond."

"You got that right!"

"Do you think the others will go for it?"

We had already announced it was for women only, but Tee grinned and tucked her hair behind her ears. "Sure they will. Who gonna pass up a chance to be in a room with a bunch of guys and they can't say a word? We could charge double for that!" She grinned at me again. "Especially since we got *the enforcer* to make sure nobody forgets the rules."

"Is that what he agreed to be?"

"He don't have to agree," she said. "All he gotta do is be there!"

the best kind of we

NATE WAS AS GOOD as his word. When Tee called him, he made us an appointment. When we got to the range and were assigned a lane with a target, he chose a gun for Tee from a small black bag he was carrying. It didn't clank when he walked, but when he put it down, it landed *solid*. I wondered how many guns were in there, but the idea of peeking made me nervous, so I just tried to stand as near Tee as I could and look supportive, whatever that means.

He showed her how to load the .38 Special, which he said was the smallest gun he owned, and how to hold it. Then he stood behind her, steadied her arm, and told her not to pull the trigger, but to *squeeze* it. While Nate was holding her wrist, she was able to hit the target four times.

"That was good," he said. "Now try it by yourself."

The kick of the gun jerked her hands up in a way it hadn't before and a look of panic came into her eyes. Nate just smiled.

"Relax and remember to hold your wrist steady, take aim and *squeeze* the trigger."

She nodded solemnly and looked at me while Nate went down to the last target in the row, as far away from us as he could get. There were two other men in their own shooting lanes, using the same three-step pattern: *steady, aim, squeeze.* I'm sure Nate was trying not to make Tee feel like he was looking over her shoulder while she practiced. What he didn't seem to understand was, she *wanted* him to look over her shoulder. We both did, but he was shooting a much bigger gun at a target much farther away than Tee's and we were on our own. I smiled at her in a way I hoped was encouraging. Tee took a deep breath, pointed the gun, closed her eyes and went for broke.

Nate took us back to The Circus after an interminable forty-five minutes during which, despite her best solo efforts, Tee never did hit anywhere near the man on the target again. I don't know who was more disappointed in how things had gone, him or Tee. I couldn't tell yet if I was disappointed or relieved, so I tried to stay neutral but positive, assuring them both that it hadn't been all that bad for a first-time effort.

When Tee went inside to collect Mavis, I stayed behind to thank Nate.

"Sorry it didn't go well," he said. "What now?"

"I don't know. At this point, I need to think it through and see what I can come up with, I guess."

I could have added *but first I need to get the sound of that gunfire out of my head.*

"I'm good for dinner at any restaurant within a fifty-mile radius," he said, smiling that slow smile.

I was tempted, but I needed to go home and regroup. "Can I take a rain check?"

"Sure," he said, looking genuinely disappointed. Things had been so crazy around here lately with Junior on the loose and the festival opening Friday that we'd barely seen each other, and when we did we were working. I missed him.

"Don't worry," he said. "We can figure this out."

That was the best kind of *we*. I just smiled.

"I have an idea," he said. "After the festival opens Friday night, how about I bring a bottle of champagne over to your house and we'll toast your success and see if we can grab a quiet minute for some non-work-related conversation."

"That would be great," I said, already feeling the bubbles tickling my nose. "I don't think I ever had a date that started at midnight."

"You don't have a curfew, do you?"

"Not on Friday nights."

Through the window, I could see Deena putting on the kids' coats; Tee turning off the inside lights, locking up. It was only five-thirty and it was already dark. In the soft light inside, they were a movie, lovely and laughing; unafraid. I realized it was beginning to snow.

We were standing very close together and Nate's voice was a soft rumble in the stillness. "I've been thinking about what you said about not feeling safe and free and I want to ask you something."

"Go ahead," I said, watching Tee scoop Mavis up in her arms and nuzzle her neck.

"If you did feel free, what would you do differently?"

I looked at him. "Everything."

"Can you be more specific?" he said, like he really wanted to know.

"I'd wear more red," I surprised myself by saying. "I'd wear a lot more red."

His voice dropped another few notches and became an impossibly sexy rumble. "Like that dress you had on at Bill and Sister's the night I met you?"

What was he talking about? "I was wearing black."

He looked surprised. "Are you sure?"

"I'm positive."

He laughed softly. "*My bad.* I could have sworn you were wearing red."

"Maybe it was the music." I laughed too.

"No," he said. "I think it was you."

And he leaned down for a kiss and I tilted my face up, up, up to meet him and the sky was indigo and the snow was soft as baby's breath and how could I ever get too busy to remember how to do this?

FORTY-EIGHT

on our way

THE FRIDAY NIGHT THE festival opened, we were all excited, but nobody was more excited than Tee. We expected a capacity crowd, including the ten brave male souls who came with Nate and who were prepared to remain segregated and silent throughout the postfilm discussion, although they were allowed to mingle and exchange pleasantries before and after.

All but two of them were members of Bill's workshop and he said they were shocked when he outlined the ground rules. He let them vent for an appropriate amount of time and then surprised himself by launching into a ten-minute educational diatribe on the crushing burden of sexist oppression borne by women worldwide, from cradle to grave, the role of all men in that shameful patriarchy, his students' personal responsibility to understand and fight against it, and, as part of that ongoing struggle, their absolutely sacred duty to learn how to listen to women when they talk, especially about themselves.

He said he felt like he was channeling the voices of all those women, me and Sister included, who had helped him see the light and become the liberated paragon of political correctness he is today. (His words!) By the time he finished his lecture, eight of them signed up for the trip and we were sold out.

Lynette Smitherman wasn't here yet, but she had been working on her Dorothy Dandridge remarks all week. She had also found time to take a small loaf of her special lemon bread by Nate's and he had set her mind at ease about any possible bad reaction to his happening upon her in what should have been a private moment. When he realized he had her to thank for the "silence is golden" rule regarding the boys, he told her he'd have to keep an eye on her in the future, which she told him wasn't likely since that was a full-time job.

Geneva had put together a small display with some photographs and clippings about Dorothy, including an autographed program from the premiere of *Carmen Jones*, which everybody touched with the proper amount of reverence and delight at finding it *here*. Tee was going to welcome everybody and I was going to lead the discussion afterward. Deena had the child care covered and Sister had brought over enough popcorn to supply all of Lake County.

By eight o'clock, even though Halle Berry hadn't accepted our invitation to attend, it looked like just about everybody else had. All our regulars were there, except Nikki. A group of girls came together from the high school because it was Black History Month and viewing a movie about Dorothy Dandridge was worth twenty points of extra credit.

Sheila Lattimore managed to catch a ride with Patrice. I was happy to see her, and I could tell she was glad to be back. By the time Sister arrived with Geneva and Nettie in tow, every chair was taken and people were scattered around the floor on pillows waiting for the show to start. The kids were set up in another room with *The Lion King,* and Simba was already frolicking around on the savannah, unaware that the voice of his beloved father is really James Earl Jones, who is also Luke Skywalker's daddy, which sort of makes them half brothers, but *that's not this story.*

When the Smitherman twins arrived with Sister, Tee saw them before I did and dashed into the office to get our desk chairs for them. They smiled their gratitude and kissed her, let her take their coats and settled in beside each other as excited as the kids in the other room singing "Circle of Life." Sherika Hill offered her chair to Sister and curled up on one of the floor cushions near enough to Regina to tease her and far enough away not to get swatted for it, and I went over to greet the new arrivals.

"I'm so glad you're here," I said, hugging Sister, then greeting Nettie and Gen.

"We wouldn't miss it," they said together, and Sister laughed. It was going to be a perfect night and we were all old enough to know it.

Tee, a stickler these days for starting at the time we say we're going to, blinked the lights like they do at the theater and stepped to the front of the room. She had pulled her braids off of her face and her eyes were shining with pride and anticipation.

"I'd like to welcome y'all," she said, "to the first annual Sewing Circus Film Festival for Free Women."

The room burst into spontaneous applause, and Tee blushed with pleasure. There are moments when everything comes together and you can actually see the results of your labor in the

faces of young girls who now unapologetically identify themselves as free women. Of course, we're not really there yet, but
like Sister keeps reminding me, the beginning of wisdom is to
call all things by their proper names. If that's really the case,
we're on our way.

FORTY-NINE

they can hear me now

WHEN THE LIGHTS CAME up at the end of the movie, there was a stunned silence. The Smitherman twins were wiping away tears, and they were not alone. The tragedy of Dandridge's life is so perfectly portrayed in the callousness of the police photographer taking photos of her naked body that we just sat there together for a minute absorbing it, our postfilm discussion questions forgotten in our shared despair at the waste of so much beauty and talent and heart.

"How come we not showin' *Carmen Jones*?" Tiffany said, finally, still sniffing.

"You voted not to," I reminded her. I had shown them a few minutes of it and they groaned and giggled and complained mightily about the strange music and the stilted language. When I suggested we show it as a companion piece to Berry's film, they voted it down unanimously, assuring me nobody would want to sit through it.

"Well, we were wrong," Patrice said quickly. "Let's vote again."

Before she could even state the question, everybody in the room raised a hand, even the boys, manfully silent but totally engaged. The Smitherman sisters nodded their approval and blew their noses delicately. Tee turned to them and her voice was gentle.

"Will you come back and watch it with us?"

"We would be honored," Lynette said, smiling.

Tee smiled back. "So would we. Miz J, your turn . . ."

We had passed out our questions and the discussion was lively and opinionated. At the end of the allotted time, the women in the room were exhilarated, the men were enlightened and the kids were ready to go home. To call the evening a huge success would be to diminish it with the inadequacy of understatement.

In the general flurry of coat gathering, baby bundling and securing of rides, I found Tee in the crowd.

"Not bad for the first one," I said as she zipped Mavis into her jacket.

She turned her face toward me and her smile was radiant. "It was great," she said, scooping up her daughter, whose sleepy head nestled contentedly on her mama's shoulder.

"I stand corrected," I said, kissing Mavis's warm cheek. "It was *great*."

"I'll be here early tomorrow," she said, heading out as Patrice corralled Lil' Sonny and Deena bundled up first one twin and then the other. Tiffany, holding Marquis by the hand, was riding with Regina, who was carrying Diamante, who had stayed awake through the whole movie, proving himself to be a true

Halle Berry fan even at a mere few months old. "We can talk then."

"Sleep in," I said. "You deserve it." And, if things go the way I hope they will at my midnight rendezvous, I'll be sleeping in too.

Surveying the swirl of activity, it's hard to say how happy it made me feel. I think Dorothy Dandridge would have loved it. To be taken seriously; to be understood and admired, analyzed, adored and truly mourned, so many years after her death would, I'm sure, have been a pure pleasure to her. It was almost like she had reached out and tapped Halle Berry on the shoulder like the spirits do in the movies and said, "Excuse me. I need you to help me tell my story. I think they can hear me now. Will you do it?" And she did. And so did we.

FIFTY

femme fatale

NATE HAD TO TAKE the guys home and drop off the van at the high school before keeping our late date. That gave me just enough time to go home and transform myself from dedicated social worker to femme fatale. I was definitely up for the challenge.

"Are we still on for tonight?" he had whispered as we passed each other at The Circus, working, as usual.

"We better be," I said, and he laughed deep in his chest in a way that made me blush in spite of myself.

He hasn't pressed me to do anything or explain anything, but I still felt a little nervous. The world had changed considerably since the last time I was dating, but I was nervous then too. People who long for their youth are usually people who have forgotten that it's just as hard to be fifteen as it is to be forty. You just have more energy and probably more optimism.

The trade-off is that you should be a whole lot smarter than you were in high school if you've been paying attention at all, especially in the areas of sex and love, which are, of course, the best windows to the human soul, and of such great complexity that even thinking you can figure any of it out is arrogant and foolhardy.

All that said, I wouldn't mind having back the skin I had at twenty-five, but short of that miracle, I wanted to look sexy without being obvious; age-appropriate but not dowdy; sensual but not slutty. Everything I pulled out looked too professional, too plain, too motherly, too tight, too casual, too dressy or just *strange,* and, of course, all black.

Finally, I decided on my favorite dress. It's not new, but it has, on occasion, when accessorized correctly, allowed me to feel almost sophisticated. I like the fact that it's long without being baggy and the scoop of the neckline shows the curve of my breasts. It's a little lower than I usually wear, but if you can't flash a little cleavage in your own house, then where can you flash it?

I put on my only pair of pretty panties with the demi-bra that matches them, slid into my dress, tied my braids with a bright blue scarf I borrowed from Sister and never intend to return, slipped on my best silver earrings and stood in front of the mirror to check the result of my efforts. I was rewarded with the sight of myself looking exactly like who I was: a free woman with a gentleman caller.

FIFTY-ONE

ass-kickin' clothes

I WAS GLAD HE brought red wine too. We put the champagne in the refrigerator and opened the Chianti first. Getting ready to make love for the first time in five years was giddy enough without champagne. The warm coziness of the Chianti in its little basket seemed more appropriate. He also brought a long box that he refused to let me open but promised to show me later.

"I felt like a kid coming here tonight," he said when we had settled in front of the fire within arm's length of each other but not touching. That's the other big difference this time around. At fifteen, delayed gratification is death. At forty, you've learned to enjoy the journey.

"Good," I said. "Then we're even."

"I think you might be a little bit ahead." He smiled. "You've already got answers to questions I've never even thought about. I listened to you up there tonight and I said, *This woman is on it.*"

I smiled back. "Don't worry. I'm prepared to tell you everything I know."

"I don't believe you."

His tone was so seductive that I took another sip of wine in self-defense. Did I even remember how to flirt?

"Why would I lie?"

He shrugged gracefully and slid closer to me in one smooth motion. "I don't know. There's always a good reason."

"Wrong." I said. "There's *never* a good reason."

"You're right, you're right!" he said, grinning and throwing up his hands in mock dismay. "See what I mean? I can't even seduce this woman without putting my foot in my mouth!"

I closed the remaining distance between us. "Is that what you're trying to do?"

"Absolutely," he said softly, and put his big arm around me.

I cuddled into the delicious curve of his body. "Good," I said. "Otherwise it's going to be a very long night."

He laughed against my mouth and his kiss was like a long, slow promise.

"How'd you get to be this way?" he whispered into my ear.

"I worked on it," I whispered back.

"Did you?" he said, kissing me again. His lips were warm and outrageously soft.

"Yes." I was feeling that kiss all the way down to my toes and realizing that five years is a long time between anything. I hope making love is like riding a bike: once you know how, you never forget it.

His lips were on my throat now, nibbling gently, and I could feel myself opening like one of those flowers Georgia O'Keeffe is so famous for painting and I wanted him. *It's been so long!*

"Tell me," he said, his lips brushing my ear. "Tell me what you want to do."

Everything, I wanted to say. *I want to do everything!* But before I could get the words out of my mouth, the phone rang. We both froze. The moment of truth. Is the life outside more important than this moment? Is anything anyone has to say more important than his fingers learning how to caress my breast? More important than my hand feeling the warmth of his thigh?

It had been so long since I had any reason to turn off the telephone, I hadn't even thought about it tonight. What if it was Tee? Or Nikki? What if Junior was on the move again?

Nate saw my hesitation and sat back slowly. "Get that if you need to," he said, brushing my cheek with his lips. "I'm not going anywhere."

"Maybe it's a wrong number," I said, reaching for the phone.

Sheila Lattimore's voice on the other end was a barely audible whisper. "Miz J? It's Sheila."

"I can't hardly hear you," I said, immediately on the alert. "Talk a little louder if you can."

"They right outside my room," she said.

I could hear angry voices, mostly male, shouting in the background. "What's happening?"

"Nik done tole Junior about the gun bein' a toy," she hissed urgently.

My face must have shown my distress because Nate moved over closer and touched my shoulder as if to say, *I'm here; don't worry.*

"He didn't believe her, so she said for him to ask me!"

I closed my eyes. "Are you okay?"

The background voices rose and someone was beating on her door. Sheila didn't say anything, but she didn't hang up. I could hear somebody, probably her mother, hollering Junior's name over and over. Then they must have pulled him away and I could hear their voices and the confusion receding.

"Sheila?"

"I didn't tell him nothin'," she said. Her voice sounded dead; resigned to the terror the night would surely bring. "But he gonna keep askin' me till I tell him what he wanna know, so I gotta get outta here!"

"Do you want me to come and get you?"

"Patrice comin' soon as Junior leave. The boys already over to her house anyway."

I tried not to sound as scared as I felt. "Where's Junior goin'?"

"He lookin' for Tee, Miz J. That's why I'm callin' you. *He lookin' for Tee.*"

My heart was in my throat. "Can you stay out of his way until Patrice gets there?"

"I'ma go out the window and meet her on Baldwin Road."

"Then hang up and go *now!*"

"Yes, ma'am," she whispered, but she didn't hang up the phone.

"Sheila?"

"Yeah?"

I knew what was worrying her, but she didn't have time to wonder about it now. "You did the right thing to call me. He's your brother, but Tee's your sister, remember?"

"I know."

"*Now go!*"

I clicked off the phone. Nate's face was a question mark.

"Junior knows about the toy gun. He's looking for Tee."

"Where is she?"

"I hope she's at home." I was already dialing her number, but her machine picked up. I didn't want to frighten her, but she needed to know.

"Nik told Junior about the gun," I said as calmly as I could. "Sheila says he's looking for you, so come over to my place as soon as you get this message. It doesn't matter what time, *just come!*" I hung up, hoping that was enough to convey the urgency I felt.

Nate was watching me. "What do you want to do?" He had asked almost this same question less than five minutes ago, but everything had changed and he knew it too.

"What I want is to see Tee drive up in my yard!" I said, looking out the window like she might be turning in at this very minute.

He nodded like that would be his first choice too.

A terrible thought occurred to me. "What if he's already at her house when she gets there? She won't know it until she drives up in the yard!"

Nate stood up and reached for his coat. "Why don't I go over there and wait for her so there's no chance of that happening?"

That was a great idea, but I didn't want to make it his fight unless he was prepared to voluntarily step into the ring. "She might have gone to Patrice's," I said, giving him a way out if that's what he was looking for. "What if she's not there?"

"Then I'll wait until she gets there and bring her here." He looked at me and smiled slowly, touched my cheek again, but softly, softly. "Don't worry."

"I won't," I said, worrying furiously. "I promise."

At the door, we kissed each other quickly.

"I want you to know," he said, "that this Lattimore clown is wreaking havoc with my love life."

I stood on tiptoe to kiss him again. "Mine too."

"Maybe I should just go over there and kick his ass and be done with it."

"Sounds good to me," I said, and it truly did.

"Only one problem." One more quick kiss.

"What's that?"

"These are not my ass-kickin' clothes!" he said, taking the back steps two at a time and heading for Tee's.

"Save me some of that wine," he called back over his shoulder, "and take a look in that box I brought and see what you think!"

In the sudden confusion, I had forgotten all about the surprise box. I went back inside, trying not to worry, and picked up the mysterious box from where Nate had propped it near the coffee table. I sat down and opened it slowly, pulled back the tissue paper and lifted out the most beautiful red dress I've ever seen.

"For the most fabulous free woman I know," said the card. "You'll always be safe with me."

Please let that be true, I thought, closing my eyes and dropping the dress back into its nest. *Please let that be true.*

FIFTY-TWO

one of those calls

WHEN THE PHONE RANG, I hoped it was Nate telling me everything was okay and he was headed this way with Tee and Mavis, *but I knew it wasn't.* There's always a different sound to the ring when it's one of those calls you don't want to answer because once you do, everything changes forever and you can never take it back, no matter how hard you cry or how loud you pray.

"Hello?"

"There's been an accident," the voice on the other end of the line said. "You should get here as quick as you can."

part

three

FIFTY-THREE

fighting for air

SHE SAID IT WAS Junior. We got the hospital center in Ludington just as they were taking her into surgery and she squeezed my hand hard and told me.

"It was Junior," she said. "I saw him!"

She had dropped Mavis at Patrice's and gone out to get them some ice cream to celebrate. When she started back, he fell in behind her. She tried to outrun him, but the faster she went, the faster he went until she took a curve too fast. Her car left the road, flipped over twice and hit a tree. She had a broken wrist, a broken leg and a couple of cracked ribs. She kept thanking God that Mavis hadn't been in the car. I did too. The doctor said there was nothing we could do there tonight and to come back in the morning.

We stepped out of the brightly lit hospital into the cold night air and it felt good against my face. In the darkness, Nate loomed large beside me and I took his arm, grateful for something to hold on to. This was a nightmare.

"Let's walk," he said, turning us toward Lake Michigan a few blocks away. That was the best thing about this town. All you had to do was hit Main Street and keep going, and before you know it, there's so much water a New Jersey gangster is said to have looked at it once and said admiringly, *I didn't know they had an ocean too.*

We walked in silence until the sidewalk ended in a small strip of snow-covered beach. We stopped and just stood there, looking out at the freezing water.

Nate put his arm around my shoulders and pulled me close. "You're trembling."

I could feel myself shaking in the circle of his embrace, but it wasn't the cold. I buried my face in his chest.

"I'm sorry, baby," he said, holding me tighter. "I'm so sorry."

"It's not your fault." My voice was muffled against his coat.

"Yes," he said, pulling back to look down into my face. "Yes, it is. That's what you were trying to tell me the other night and it's true. If I can't figure out how to protect you from Junior, what kind of man does that make me?"

"I don't know," I said.

I wasn't trying to be cruel, but it must have sounded harsher than I intended because he winced. I tried to apologize, but I couldn't say anything, not a word, and I wondered how much anger you can show somebody, how much hard man/woman truth you can tell and still expect him to hold your head, stroke your face and carry you around in his arms like you're his baby as well as his woman?

"You're still shivering," he whispered.

"I'm drowning," I said, no longer able to blink back the tears. "I think I'm drowning."

So he kissed me like our lives depended on it, long and deep and hard like he could pour his strength into me through sheer force of will. And we stood there in the cold wind and kissed and kissed until I wasn't sure I could stand by myself if he stepped away, because at that moment, that kiss seemed like the only thing that could possibly keep us alive until morning, and his arms around me the only thing that could keep me from going under.

So we held on, as formless as some strange underwater beings, and at the end of that kiss, we emerged; exhausted, unsatisfied, fighting for air.

FIFTY-FOUR

all emergencies

TEE WAS CRYING. HER leg was suspended in traction and her left wrist was splinted from her knuckles to her elbow. I was holding her good hand. Her face was still bruised and slightly swollen. All of this was of great concern to Tee, not because of the pain and discomfort she was enduring, but because she didn't want to alarm Mavis, who was staying with Deena until things got sorted out.

"I don't want her to see me like this," Tee was saying urgently. "All that's gonna do is scare her to death and I'm gonna be okay, so what's the point?"

She was getting agitated, which couldn't be good for her. She had insisted on calling Mavis this afternoon to reassure her daughter that everything was going to be okay. Mavis had begged to be allowed to come see her mama, and when Tee said no, she was inconsolable.

"It's only been a day," I said. "How about we wait until the swelling goes down a little and then you can decide?"

Tee had come through the surgery just fine, but she was pretty banged up from the accident. The doctor said she'd probably be there a week, which gave the sheriff time to locate Junior, who had disappeared without a trace.

I called Sister from the hospital so she could tell everybody what had happened and tell them to be careful. She promised to spend the day at The Circus to be sure nobody panicked. I tried to call Nikki, but her mother hadn't seen her, and when I called the club where she was working, they said the dancers aren't allowed to take personal calls. When I told him it was an emergency, he said, "they're all emergencies," and hung up the phone. I hoped Sister could reach her.

"She was *cryin'*," Tee said, sounding drowsy and miserable.

"She misses you," I said. "She's fine. Don't worry. We'll all take good care of her."

Tee tried to take a deep breath, but she had cracked and bruised her ribs and the effort made her wince. She closed her eyes. The painkillers they were giving her made her sleep a lot. They wanted her to lie still as much as she could, which is like wanting a tired two-year-old to stand in line quietly at the Kmart. Good idea, but it's not gonna happen.

"You need to get some sleep," I said. I had spent the day sitting with her, trying to reassure her that Junior would be in jail before she came home; trying to make myself believe it. "I'll be back tomorrow morning, okay?"

"Miz J." She opened her eyes, but I could tell she was drifting off. *Good.* "I'm not afraid of Junior, you know? I mean, I know he's dangerous and stuff. I know he was tryin' to hurt me, but that's what he's gonna have to do because I've had my fill of bein' scared, you know what I'm sayin'? Scared of my daddy. Scared of my brother. Scared of my uncles. Scared of Jimmy. *Scared all the time.*"

She yawned a huge yawn and her eyes drooped like a tired child. "But no more. You know why?" She squeezed my hand weakly. "Because all he can do is kill me, you know? And that ain't nothin' compared to bein' scared all the time. That ain't . . ." She yawned again and closed her eyes. "It ain't nothin'. . . ."

I kissed her cheek and tiptoed out. I had promised Nate I would call him at his house when I left the hospital, but right now, I was headed for Junior's.

FIFTY-FIVE

lifetime achievement

OF COURSE IT WAS a bad idea, but Tee lying in that hospital bed trying to talk herself out of being scared had made me feel crazy. I had to do *something*. I was convinced that Junior was hiding somewhere close, and if he was, his mother knew where.

Sheila hadn't been around since the accident, but Patrice talked to her. The Lattimores had closed ranks since Junior was now an official suspect with a warrant issued for his arrest, and Sheila wasn't allowed to communicate with the enemy camp, which was *us*.

Patrice was keeping Daryl and Duane as much as she could so they still came to day care. In all the confusion, nobody at the house seemed to miss them, or else four and five are too young to be an official part of a feud, even a blood feud. Sheila kept telling Patrice she was going to move out as soon as the police pick up Junior, but so far, she's still there, and he's still *somewhere*. I hoped my unannounced arrival didn't aggravate her circumstances, but I had no choice. I had to try to talk to her mother.

When I rang the bell, Jarvis opened the door. He looked shocked to see me.

"Hey, Jarvis," I said, stepping in around him. He was only fifteen and an official voice and sudden adult presence still startled him long enough for me to make my move. "I came by to see your mother. Is she home?"

"Yeah, she here," he said. *"Hey, Ma!"*

She didn't answer from whatever room she was in. The big color TV in the corner was showing a music video of a young woman in a thong and pasties wrapping herself seductively around a silver pole while young men in baggy clothes and gold teeth poured water and beer on her almost naked body. Men got arrested for that in New York City a couple of months ago and everybody wondered aloud where they learned to act so ugly.

Jarvis frowned and hollered a little louder. *"Mama!"*

She appeared in the doorway of a small bedroom. "Boy, what do you think you're—" Her eyes fell on me and she stopped midsentence and frowned.

Jarvis smirked at her reaction. "Miz Mitchell wanna see you."

"See me about what?" she said, advancing on me angrily. "Haven't you done enough?"

"I'm looking for your son," I said, trying to stay calm. "Any idea where I might be able to find him?"

She stopped inches from where I was standing. "You think I'm a fool? You think I'ma tell you a damn thing, knowin' you just gonna run back and tell the cops?" She leaned in even closer. "I ain't seen 'im. *Tell 'em that!*"

"They're going to find him sooner or later. The longer it takes, the harder they'll be on him," I said.

She sneered at me and stepped back a little. "They gonna be hard on 'im anyway. There ain't no place in this damn country for strong niggas. Niggas who don't bow down and kiss a cracker's ass!"

There weren't any white people around for miles, and as far as I know, none of them had required a booty smooch from Junior. "What does that have to do with this?"

"I wouldn't expect you to understand!" She spit the words at me. "My boys ain't no punks! I got five sons and ain't a one of them got sugar in his blood."

I realized suddenly that coming here was an even worse idea than I had thought. It was time to go. "All right," I said. "I'm sorry I bothered you."

"Yeah, you should be," she hissed. "If these girls would stop tryin' to trick my boys into havin' babies wit' 'em, they wouldn't be havin' all this trouble in the first place."

I reached for the door, but she snatched it open before I could touch it. "She brought this on herself. If she'da stayed outta my boy's business, wouldn't none of this happened."

That was going too far. I stepped out on the porch and looked at her. "If anything happens to Tomika Jackson, I'm going to hold you personally responsible."

Her eyes narrowed. "Ain't nobody got to force me to take responsibility for my kids! I always have and I always will!"

She said it like it was an accomplishment in which she took great pride. Her lifetime achievement: a house full of angry, abusive young men and one completely cowed young woman. She must be real proud of that, but I had had my fill. She slammed the door as I headed for my car.

Something made me look around before I drove off, and there was Sheila peeking out the front window. She raised her hand quickly, waved once and was gone.

FIFTY-SIX

a dangerous combination

IT'S AMAZING HOW QUICKLY it's possible to adjust
your routine to accommodate the unthinkable. It'd been three
days since Junior ran Tee off the road and he was still at large.
The state police put out a bulletin, but so far they hadn't been
able to find him. His car hadn't turned up, which was all the
proof Sheriff Tyler required to convince himself (and try to convince me!) that Junior was probably long gone to Chicago or
Detroit by now. An interesting theory, but Junior is not a rich
gangster, he's a broke thug. Going on the lam for him probably
means laying low on somebody's living-room couch until all this
blows over.

Deena and Patrice had really kept things going smoothly at
The Circus. Everybody was helping out more since I was still
spending a lot of time at the hospital. That was one of the real

revelations for me in the midst of all this. When it's time to step up, *they can step up*.

I was at the hospital Sunday night, but they still ran *Carmen Jones* for a capacity audience without a glitch. Afterward, Lynette and Geneva talked about the premiere and answered questions for almost an hour. Before they left, they gave Deena a letter for Tee that I delivered the next day.

My brave girl (it said in Lynette's spidery hand),
you are in our prayers and in our hearts. We hope you are doing what the doctors say and will be home soon. We are enclosing a few dollars in case you want some magazines to pass the time and nobody thought to bring them. We also recommend chocolate bars to keep up your morale. We like the ones with almonds. Stay strong!

Tee was delighted. Her spirits were much better since she and Mavis had established regular communication via the telephone and small notes I'd carry back and forth between them like Judith Exner shuttling dutifully between John Kennedy and Sam Giancana. Tee was almost ready to let Mavis see her, and I promised to bring her the day I got the okay.

The doctors said she was making excellent progress and might be able to come home in a couple of days, which was, on the one hand, great news, and, on the other, the source of a lot of stress for all of us. With Junior still roaming the woods, or whatever he was doing to stay out of sight, we couldn't guarantee that he wouldn't try to hurt Tee again once she got out of the hospital. She was going to be on crutches for at least another month and her level of vulnerability really worried me. I had suggested that she consider moving in with me, but she said she wanted to go home, so I let it slide. I had a few more days to convince her before she was actually going anywhere.

I hadn't seen Nate since the day after the accident. We spent that night in the hospital waiting room and he drove me home the next day, but since then, we'd just been missing each other. We kept leaving messages, and we were having dinner tomorrow with Sister and Bill, but the truth was, I didn't really want to see him yet. That free-floating rage Bill was talking about seemed to have taken up residence inside me and I didn't want to bring that to Nate. He doesn't deserve it no matter what the angry sister in my head keeps saying about how they all deserve it.

I keep thinking about what I could have done, what *we* could have done to keep this from happening. The more I thought about it, the more I realized that there didn't seem to be anything we could have done short of hiding in the bushes and blowing Junior's brains out as soon as we realized he was a threat, but that's no solution. Gandhi said "an eye for an eye leaves the whole world blind," and I believe it, but the helplessness I feel keeps churning around and coming out anger. Not at Junior, but at all the ones Nate calls "the good guys." What good are they if they can't protect us any better than this?

FIFTY-SEVEN

by any means necessary

BILL HAD MADE PASTA with spinach and tomatoes, a lemon roasted chicken and homemade rolls. He had chilled the wine and cued up Sweet Honey in the Rock to signify a safe space for high-strung women. When we walked in, he gave Nate that back-thumping chest-bump hug that passes for an affectionate brotherly greeting. For me, he had a warm squeeze.

"How's Tee?"

"She's amazing," I said. "Her leg is mending perfectly and she's already trying to talk them into taking the cast off her wrist."

"Thank God!" He hugged me again. "Well, then, let's make this evening a Tomika-free zone."

I froze. Men always have the option to think about this madness or not think about it. We don't. "What do you mean?"

"Nothing," he said. "Just that I'll bet if we try really hard, we can come up with something else to talk about for the next three hours. I think we all deserve a break."

Before I had a chance to ask him what the hell he meant by that, Sister came from the kitchen with kisses all around, a welcoming smile and four wineglasses. Bill took our coats and poured. I sipped my wine and tried to relax. Bill's comment had seemed inappropriate and insensitive to me, but I knew he'd been as concerned about Tee as the rest of us. Maybe it was just his way.

"Something smells great," Nate said, sitting beside me on the sofa.

"You got it wrong, brother," Bill said cheerfully. "*Everything* smells great."

"A cook without an ego is like a meal without hot sauce," Sister teased him, but then she looked at me hard. "You haven't been sleeping much, have you?"

I shook my head. "Not lately. Is it that obvious?"

"You're not going to do Tee any good if you fall asleep at the wheel on Baldwin Road," she said gently, not knowing she was breaking her husband's declaration of her living room as a Tomika-free zone.

"I offered to drive her," Nate said, sounding like he wanted Sister to know he had done his best, *but you know how she is.* I don't know why, but coming on the heels of Bill's weird pronouncement, it really pissed me off. I was beginning to realize that accepting this invitation was probably a bad idea.

"And I declined," I said. "I'm fine."

"The offer still stands," he said.

"I heard you the first time," I said, more sharply than I

meant to, feeling like Medusa with those snakes growing out of my head.

Bill raised his eyebrows. "A little testy, are we?"

Sister leaned over to kiss my cheek. "A sure sign of sleep deprivation."

"Relax, sweetie," said Bill. "You're among friends." He winked at Nate. "At least, as far as we know."

"So far so good," said Nate.

I smiled at him. A small smile, but it was the best I could do at the moment.

"How's your workshop going?" I said to Bill. We definitely needed a change of topic and Bill could always be counted upon to talk about himself for a few uninterrupted minutes. Maybe I could use the time to calm down.

He groaned. "They're hopeless! I asked them what they thought about the guy from Public Enemy saying rap is like a newspaper for the hip-hop nation. They seemed to endorse the idea as a concept, but when I asked them to try to write down some rap lyrics about a current event, none of them knew any. *Not one.* They weren't even sure what I mean by *current event.* When I said it's something you'd read in the newspaper, Ezell Henry said, 'Well, that's the problem right there. We don't read no newspapers!' " Bill shook his head and refilled his glass.

"You should have asked them to write about Junior running Tee off the road," I said.

Bill looked at Sister, who was looking at me. My comment just lay there, but I didn't care.

"It's a current event," I said. "Maybe you could help them think it through."

Bill frowned at me, his face darkening like a cloud. The two of us had declared an uneasy truce after our exchange about the trip to the firing range, but we hadn't settled anything and tonight both of us seemed to be full of strange energy. We used to call it bad vibes, but whatever you call it, I knew we were about to kill any possibility of a pleasant evening.

"It's a poetry workshop, Joyce, remember?" Bill's voice sounded sharp. "What could that possibly have to do with Junior?"

I set down my glass. "Well, what good is a poem right now if it doesn't have anything to do with Junior?" I said. "What's the point?"

"Calm down, sweetie," Sister said very gently. Her voice sounded like a summer breeze, but I brushed it right off.

"I am calm. I'm just saying I thought that was what black writers were supposed to do. *Tell the truth to the people.*"

"You don't have to lecture me," Bill snapped. "I'm not the enemy."

My face twisted into a tight little smile. "That's right," I said, looking at Nate. "You're one of the good guys."

Bill sat back in the chair and spread his arms in a gesture of supplication, but his face was harder than I wanted it to be. "I can't change the world with ten kids in a poetry workshop, Joyce. That's not my job."

"Then whose job is it?"

"You seem to have all the answers," he said. "Why don't you tell me?"

Nate reached out and took my hand, but I pulled it back. I didn't want comfort. I wanted clarity.

"All I know is this," I said. "Every day I drive over to the hospital and every day Tee asks me, 'Did they catch him?' And every day I have to say no. And then I get to The Circus and they ask me, 'Did they catch him?' And I have to say no and offer some encouragement by telling them something lame like all they have to fear is fear itself, when fear didn't run Tee off that road. *Junior did!*"

I stood up and walked over to the fireplace, trying to calm down, but determined to find a way to tell Bill how I felt. If he's really my friend, I have to be able to talk to him about something this important and he has to be able to listen. *Silence equals death.* Sister came to stand beside me, and when she put her arm around my waist, I know she could feel me trembling. Nate never took his eyes off me, but he didn't say anything.

"We're not cops," Bill said, not backing down any more than I was. "What do you want us to be? Vigilantes?"

He hardly got it out of his mouth before I answered him. "I want you to be men!"

I hated the sound of my own angry voice. Sister tightened her arm around my waist, but her eyes were on Bill.

"I thought you were the one who believed in the healing power of love," he said sarcastically. "Funny how as soon as you get scared enough, you go looking for somebody with a big gun to protect you by any means necessary."

"How can you . . ." I stopped before I could finish one more angry accusation. *Slow down. Take a breath.*

I looked at Sister, and there was such worry and concern on her face, I felt even worse. "I'm so sorry," I said softly, turning away from her, and then I started to cry. Nate stood up immediately and took me in his arms. He was talking to Sister and Bill, but he was holding me like we were all alone.

"Joyce and I have agreed that discussions of Brother Lattimore can be hell on your love life," he said. "I would like to expand that statement to say he is also the death of pleasant predinner conversation."

"Amen," said Sister, handing me a napkin to mop my eyes and reaching for Bill's hand. "Are you okay, sweetie?"

Bill shook his head and I heard him take a deep breath too. "I will be as soon as I get through being an asshole."

"Let's say a prayer," Sister said.

Sister will do that sometimes, just grab you and start praying like it doesn't require any more preparation than to bow your head and close your eyes and jabber away at will. I took Bill's other hand without looking at him and felt him give mine a small squeeze, although he didn't look at me either. I squeezed back hard. Bill's like my big brother. I can't stay mad at him. Plus, he was right. He's not the enemy. There is no enemy. There's just a lot of complicated human beings, some more damaged than others.

"Mother/father God," Sister said softly. "We ask for patience and for faith. We ask for courage and compassion. We rededicate ourselves to truth and the love that is strong enough to tell it. We say thank you for this and for all things and we say the name of our friend Tomika Jackson out loud—"

She paused and we all said Tee's name like an obedient Sunday school class. "Tomika Jackson."

"... to bring peace to her spirit, strength to her body and speed to her healing. *Thank you.*"

And we three murmured with her, clutching each other's hands; once again an unbroken circle. *"Thank you, thank you, thank you..."*

FIFTY-EIGHT

the specificity of
snowflakes

WHAT A NIGHT! AFTER Sister's prayer, Bill and I both apologized, not for our feelings, but for expressing them in such a combative way. I confessed to some of that free-floating *woman at the end of her last nerve* anger that is always easier to read about than to actually experience, and Bill confessed he'd been drinking wine all day because he couldn't bear to see how hurt I looked whenever I talked about Tee, knowing there was nothing he could do to make it better. Nate stayed close to me all night, and when he dropped me off at home, he kissed me like the good friend he was definitely proving himself to be and told me to call him if I needed to talk.

The snow was just starting to fall as I stood there watching his taillights disappear. The flakes were big and moist, falling so

softly you don't even know it until you step outside in the morning and everything is covered in a thick white blanket. It was a
beautiful night and I realized Nate was right. Junior was wreaking havoc on my peace of mind, my work, my friendships and
my brand-new-almost-a-love-life. There was no way I wanted to
be standing here alone tonight counting snowflakes.

I walked down the slope of the yard. The dock already had
its own blanket of snow and I took three giant steps to the end
of it, looking back with satisfaction at what could have been the
product of size six-and-a-half seven-league boots. I tipped back
my head and caught some of the big, wet flakes on my tongue.
The older I get, the more I am in awe of things I used to take
for granted, like the fact that each snowflake has a unique
design that appears only once throughout all eternity. How
amazing is that?

I was just standing there, watching the lake fill up with snow,
when Nate's car turned back into the yard and eased to a stop.
Had he forgotten something? The house was still dark and I
wondered if he would think I had already turned in. I don't
know why I didn't call out to him since I knew he couldn't see
me down here, but I didn't.

He stepped out of the car, walked quickly up to the back
porch, stuck something in the door and headed back so fast I was
afraid he'd get in before he heard me calling.

"Nate!"

He stopped and turned in the direction of my voice.

"Down here on the dock," I called. "Do you want me to
come up?"

"No," he said. "I'll come down."

He turned off his car and started toward me. I was always

struck by the economy of his stride. For such a big man, there was no lumbering, no wasted motion. I stood where I was and he walked out on the dock and stood beside me.

"You okay?" I said.

"I'm not sure," he said.

"What's wrong?"

"Nothing's wrong." He gestured back toward the house. "I left you a note."

"What does it say?"

He looked surprised at the question. "Oh, well . . ."

I waited.

"It's just something that I remembered from when I was a kid. You made me remember it. Tonight, I mean. Over at Sister's when you were trying to put into words how you felt about things." He stopped, hoping I understood. I didn't have a clue.

"Do you want me to read it now?" I said.

"No."

"Then tell me." It was so quiet, we were both whispering. There couldn't be a better place to share a secret.

He took a deep breath.

"Tell me."

"One time my father came back from Havana," he said, so quietly I could hardly hear him even in the silence. "It might have been the last time he went, I don't remember. What I do remember is that he brought my mother a dress, a *red dress*."

He hesitated again, and I slipped my arm through his and leaned a little closer. That seemed to reassure him and he smiled down at me in the darkness. "I was a kid, maybe five or six, but I remember him teasing her until she finally went upstairs and put it on. I could tell she didn't want to, but he kept on and kept on and finally, she did it. When she came back down, I didn't hardly recognize her."

He smiled a little at the memory. "My mother never wore red, *ever*, and this dress was about as red as you could get. It was silk or something and it sort of floated when she walked."

It was so quiet, I could hear the wind pushing the snow across the surface of the frozen lake.

"She was so beautiful that I looked at my father to see if he thought so too, and he had this funny look on his face that I'd never seen before. He went over to her and kissed her and then he picked her up and swung her around and around."

In my mind, I could see the skirt fluttering against her legs as they twirled. I hoped she was laughing at her husband's excitment. I hoped she shared it.

"Did she love the dress?"

He shook his head slowly. "She hated it."

My heart sank. I was hoping for a happy ending. "Why?"

"She said . . . she said it made her look like a whore. It didn't," he added quickly, "but that's what she said and then she turned around and ran upstairs and my father just stood there like she'd slapped him across the mouth and then he looked at me and shrugged and he said, 'I been married to that woman for ten years and I guess I don't know her at all.' "

He pulled me closer and I looked into his face.

"I don't want to be like my father," he said. "I want to know you, really know you. I want to know what you think and what you feel and what makes you laugh and what drives you crazy, and I'm trying, but the closer I get, the more mysterious you seem. I've never known a woman like you."

Under the circumstances, I thought a kiss was almost

required. His lips were cool and the snow on his face tickled my nose.

"I'll tell you what," he said softly, kissing my eyelids. "Why don't you save that red dress I gave you until you feel like it's safe to wear it and let me know."

"And then what?"

"And then I'll put on my best Sunday-go-to-meeting suit and come calling."

"It's a deal," I said, wondering when that would be. "It's a deal."

FIFTY-NINE

no chance

I HAD JUST FINISHED my morning meditation when Nikki pulled into the yard slowly as if she wasn't sure I'd be awake. The words to that old blues song popped into my head: *Don't you know I'm gonna be awake when you sleepin', and there when you ain't?*

Nobody had seen Nik since the accident. She called and left a teary message on my answering machine, all sobs and second-guessing, promising to come by and explain, but she never did. There was nothing to explain. Tee had known all along what would happen, which is the advantage of long-term friendships. Even when your friends act a fool, the ways they do it are rarely a surprise.

I stepped out on the porch and waved her inside. She walked slowly up the back steps and I felt sorry for her. She had been all

alone for a week with only fear and guilt and her mother's endless recriminations to sustain her. No wonder she looked shell-
shocked and skittish.

"I was drivin' by," she said. "I saw your car was still here."

I hugged her immediately and she hugged me back, relieved
and grateful that I didn't seem to be angry.

"Are you on your way to work," I said, "or can you sit for a
minute?"

"I quit that job," she said quickly. "I'm lookin' again."

"Then come in and have a cup of tea," I said, taking her arm
and practically pulling her inside.

I closed the door and watched her take off her coat and hang
it carefully on the hook closest to the door.

"You haven't seen Junior yet, have you?" I busied myself with
the tea, trying not to rush her if she had come to tell me something, or spook her if she hadn't.

She shook her head and her eyes filled with guilty tears. "I
didn't mean to tell him, Miz J! I swear I didn't mean to say a
word!"

I put down two cups of chamomile, pulled my chair up close
so we were almost sitting knee to knee and took her hands.
"What happened?" I said gently, hoping she might know something that would help us figure out where he was. "Just tell me
what happened."

Tears were running down her cheeks, but I don't think she
felt them at all. "After Tee put me out—and she was right to do
it," she added quickly. "I don't mean it like that!"

"I know. Go on."

"I went back to stay with my mama, so you know how I was
livin', and Junior kept comin' by the club, tellin' everybody I
was his woman. Wadn't nothin' I could do about it, but then he

ran outta money and he wanted me to get him in for free, like
they gonna let me just bring him around back and sneak him in
or somethin', so I said I couldn't do it and then I told him he
was gonna get me fired if he kept comin' around, and he just
went off."

She shuddered slightly at the memory and I held her hands
tightly.

"Is that when you told him?"

She shook her head. "No. I went on to work, but when I got
home that night, my mama had let him in, and they were sittin'
up in there, watchin' TV. Soon as I walked in, he jumped up and
started fussin' all over again and I told him he wadn't my man no
more, so he didn't have no right to be hollerin' up in my face and
he backhanded me across my mouth."

"Where was your mother?"

She shrugged. "Sittin' right there. When he hit me, she just
went in the back and closed her door."

I couldn't imagine leaving any woman, much less my daughter, to the tender mercies of Junior Lattimore. Being betrayed at
that level by your mother must be its own kind of hell.

"Then he said, 'You can't quit me, girl. You belong to me. I
made you a woman. How you gonna quit me?' And I said . . ."

"Go on."

"I said, 'Who you fuck first ain't got shit to do with makin'
you a woman.' Then he really started knockin' me around and I
heard my mom turn up the TV in her room so she wouldn't have
to hear it. She wadn't gonna help me or call anybody to help me,
so she didn't even want to know what he was doin' to me."

She withdrew her hands from mine, picked up her tea and
took a long swallow.

"So after a while he said, 'You such a bad bitch. What you

gonna do now, huh? What you gonna do?' And it made me mad. Tee always be tellin' me I got to learn to control my temper. She always be tellin' me that and tellin' me that."

She was crying again. I handed her a napkin.

"What did you do when you got mad?"

She stared down into her tea, ashamed now to relive the moment when she had put her friend at such risk with a few angry words. "I said, 'Oh, you real bad now, but if you so bad, how come you ran so fast when Tee point that toy gun at your ass?' "

She looked up at me and her voice trembled slightly. "I never meant to tell it, Miz J. I love Tee. She like a sister to me—*no!* She *is* a sister to me and I would die before I'd do anything to hurt her."

I picked up her hands again. "Do you remember the questions Sister wrote for the film festival?"

She nodded, clearly startled by the question.

" 'When did things go wrong?' " I said softly. "Remember that one?"

She thought for a minute. "When I told Junior Tee had the toy gun?"

I shook my head. "I don't think so."

She frowned and thought for a minute more and then I saw her understand the real question I was asking. I could also see that she knew the answer.

"When I went back to Junior and lied about it to Tee."

I nodded slowly. "It's always the lie," I said, remembering what we used to say in high school whenever anybody got caught doing something they had been lying to the rest of us about: If you can't admit it, you probably ought to quit it.

Nikki sniffed loudly and dabbed at her eyes.

"Why don't you come to the hospital with me?" I said.

Her panic returned instantly. She hadn't seen Tee since the accident. "Now?"

"I was on my way when you pulled up."

She stood up nervously and reached for her coat. "Tee don't wanna see me."

"Sure she does."

She wasn't sure if it was safe to be relieved yet. "She ain't mad?"

I shrugged. "I know she wants to see you. If she's mad, she won't stay mad."

That made her smile. "That means I just gotta wear it, right?"

I smiled back. "Right."

She hesitated but just for a minute. "Well, it ain't like I gotta get to work or nothin'."

"I've been meaning to talk to you about that," I said. "Why don't you ride with me?"

An hour later, Tee and Nikki had been through apologies, tears, fussing and forgiveness. I had offered Nik a job at The Circus filling in for Tee and she accepted, pending Tee's approval, which she received immediately and enthusiastically. Their friendship restored, they sat there looking at each other like neither one could believe their mutual good fortune. Good friends are hard to find.

Then Nik narrowed her eyes critically. "You know somethin', Tee?"

"What?"

"You need a new look."

Hair hadn't been a priority, but I had to admit, although I'd been tying her hair back in bright scarves, Tee's braids weren't looking so good. Some of them had come out, leaving various lengths of real hair behind. Some of them were unraveling at a rapid rate, poking their ragged ends out wherever, and I don't have to tell you we hadn't been keeping up with her edges, which had been thoroughly sweated out and were now framing her face in fuzz.

Tee tried to look hurt. "Is it that bad?" she said, her fingers fluttering over her hair, a frown of concern on her face. I was bringing Mavis for the first time tomorrow and she wanted to look as good as she could for her daughter.

"Pretty bad," Nik said, reaching into the unruly nest of Tee's braids and pulling away several that had been hanging on by a thread. "See what I'm sayin'?"

Tee frowned, using her good hand to point to the cast that made her right hand useless for combing hair. "You see I'm helpless here, right?"

Nikki grinned, looking around for the comb. "You ain't never been helpless in your life and you know it."

"And don't you forget it," Tee said.

"No chance," Nikki said, parting Tee's hair in a series of deft strokes and then leaning to kiss her friend's cheek lightly. "No chance at all."

SIXTY

love slave

THE NEXT DAY, BILL slipped a note in with the mail in my box at home. When I finally staggered in after taking Mavis to see her mama and presiding over my second tearful Tee reunion in as many days, the big envelope stuck out like a promise among the bills.

"Little Sister," it said in Bill's big chockablock printing style:

> After considering your suggestion that I try to be a more directly positive influence on the young brothers in my charge, even in regard to matters that do not seem to impact directly on my role as poet-in-residence, I asked them to create a character who was a good man. In arriving at the all-important common definition for such a rare

being, we utilized your model for free women. I thought
you might be interested in our thoughts on the matter. By
the way, please forgive my insensitivity the other night.
Too much wine is not good for writers even in the best of
times. In moments such as these, it is incumbent upon us
all to keep our wits about us.

He signed it, "your friend and love slave," and there was a
postscript at the bottom. "What would I do/without you/to keep
me/Honest?"

Bill's workshop had narrowed down to six boys, four juniors
and two seniors. Their list was entitled "For Men Only":

1. Tell the truth
2. Get a job
3. Show up on time
4. Pay your own bills
5. No hitting women & kids
6. No raping
7. Use a rubber
8. If you make a baby, be a father
9. Respect the old-timers
10. Bring the love (Bill's note: "I added that one.")

Of course you did, I thought, delighted by their efforts. That's
always the poet's job, isn't it?

SIXTY-ONE

guarding queens

TEE GETS OUT TOMORROW. I'm going to pick her up
at noon. I gave up on my efforts to get her to come stay with me,
but Geneva and Nettie Smitherman convinced her to come and
stay in one of their big downstairs bedrooms until she can get
around a little better. They even moved in a little daybed for
Mavis.

It's a perfect arrangement. Deena passes right by their house
on her way in every day, so she can pick up Mavis and drop her
off at night. Tee couldn't possibly get better care or livelier conversation than she would from the twins. They all seemed to be
looking forward to it, including Mavis, who had found in Gen
Smitherman a bedtime story devotee to rival her mother.

The only problem was, they still hadn't found Junior. There
had been a couple of break-ins reported, but nobody could prove

it was Junior holing up until the heat dies down, even though we all know it was him. I'm sure Sheila knows where he is, but she's hardly able to get out at all anymore. Patrice sees her every day when she picks up Duane and Daryl and said everything seems to be about the same at the Lattimore place, but I'm almost as worried about Sheila as I am about Tee and for the same reason: Junior.

Sheriff Tyler was sympathetic but told me for the umpteenth time that his hands were tied. He didn't have enough men to guard Tee or anybody else around the clock or to mount any kind of sustained search. By now, of course, I understood that. What I didn't understand was how I was supposed to tell Tee it was safe to come home when that was a lie. Nobody was safe around here. Not yet.

And why was that, I thought when I finally gave up on the sheriff doing anything more than looking concerned and headed for home. *Why was that?* Because, snapped the angry sister in residence just beneath my carefully cultivated peaceful exterior, because none of the brothers are prepared to accept responsibility. Because it never matters as much to them as it does to us. Because nobody can kick their asses and everybody can kick ours, especially if they're named Lattimore, especially if they're named Junior Lattimore, and why didn't Nate do something? Maybe it was time to ask him.

He came to the door before I rang his front bell. "I conjured you up!" he said, looking really happy to see me. "Come in, come in. You okay?"

"Fine," I said, sounding as stressed out as I felt.

"What's wrong?" His voice deepened with sudden concern. "Tee okay?"

"Coming home tomorrow," I said. "Remember?"

He let that pass. "That's why I called you. Did you get my message?"

I shook my head. "I've been in the sheriff's office all day trying to get him to take some responsibility for Tee's safety once she gets here. She's staying at the Smithermans' and—"

"I know," he broke in quickly, like he could feel me winding up, but I kept right on.

"They sure can't protect her," I said, starting to pace just a little. "They act like they don't even know what I'm talking about."

"I know what you're talking about," he said. "I already talked to Lynette."

That surprised me. "Talked to her about what?"

"About my idea. She loves it. They both do. They said it's about time."

I was getting more confused by the minute. "About time for what?"

"About time for some of the men around here to take some responsibility."

"Exactly!" I said.

"Exactly," he agreed, with a big slow grin. "Now that we agree on that, can I tell you the plan?"

"What plan?"

He drew me down beside him on the couch. "Tee's coming home tomorrow, and if Tyler can't guarantee her safety, then we will."

"Who's we?"

"Me and Bill and Buddy at the market and Tim at the hardware store and Brian up at the school."

"Sherika's Brian?"

Nate nodded. "We were talking about it the other day. He told me his girlfriend was really worried about Tee coming home." Nate grinned a little wider and covered my hands with his own. "Mine too, I said, so he said if I thought of anything we could do to let him know. He's agreed to take the shift between classes and football practice."

"What shift?"

"That's the idea," he said. "We're going to watch the Smitherman house in shifts around the clock until they find Junior, or we do."

Something in the way he said it made me think Junior would have better luck with Sheriff Tyler.

"I'm taking the first shift tomorrow. Then Bill. Then Buddy. Then Brian. If we each do a couple of hours at a time, we'll have it covered."

I just looked at him. I could imagine him and the others standing at attention outside the Smitherman place like the guards at Buckingham Palace and for the same purpose: guarding queens. Of course, they wouldn't have to stand outside and wear those funny hats and red jackets, but the principle was the same and just thinking about it made me so happy I started grinning from ear to ear.

"I think that's great," I said. "I was so mad when I drove up here. I wanted to fuss at you for not doing something, for not caring, for not figuring it out, and now . . ." I tried to find the words to express how this made me feel, but I couldn't.

"Thank you," I said.

"You don't have to thank me," he said. "This is my job."

"Because you used to be a cop?"

He shook his head slowly. "No, because I'm still a man."

SIXTY-TWO

but he was

LYNETTE AND GENEVA WERE all atwitter about the guard that Nate was going to place around their house. They had their own two shotguns, but knowing there were people assigned to keep watch over them made them feel much safer.

"I haven't felt this protected since Daddy died," Geneva said as she walked me to the door after I had dropped off some things for Tee's room. Lynette was busy making up the daybed with a set of brand-new *Lion King* sheets. They wanted Mavis to feel at home.

Lynette had asked me when exactly I thought we'd get back tomorrow so many times that I finally offered to stay the night so she could continue to ask me the same question at five-minute intervals until I left for the hospital in the morning, but I understood. We all felt relieved and we knew Tee would too.

"That Nate Anderson is a good man," Geneva said. She was trying to sound casual and having about as much success as her sister does. "Don't you think so?"

"I sure do," I said, giving her a good-bye hug and a wink. "Tall too!"

Her laugh followed me down the front steps. "See you tomorrow, dear. Drive carefully."

On the way home, I decided to do my walk, then call Nate and see if he wanted to come over for dinner. By the time I had changed my clothes and stepped out into the yard, I could feel the temperature dropping. I tucked my scarf in a little tighter and wondered how it felt to be hiding in the woods on a night like this. I wondered . . .

Junior turned into the yard so fast I thought he was going to hit the pine tree in front of the house. I jumped out of the way instinctively, which put his car between me and the back door. *Damn!* I thought about running, but the idea of being chased through the woods was even scarier than standing my ground. *What was he doing here?*

It didn't take long for him to tell me. He rocked the car to a stop, jumped out, strode around to the passenger side, jerked it open and dragged Sheila out by her arm. She was wearing gray sweats, no coat, and her eyes were swollen from crying or something worse.

"You want her?" he shouted. "You her mama now? You gonna be her family?"

What was he talking about? I tried to make eye contact with Sheila, but her eyes were rolling around in sheer panic. He jerked her roughly around the back of the car. Her legs crumpled and she almost fell. I started to move toward her to help,

although I don't know what I thought I was going to do once I
got to her.

Junior's voice brought me up sharp. "Where you goin'?"
That's when I saw the small silver pistol in his hand.

I stopped where I was. "Don't do this."

"Fuck you!" he shouted. Sheila winced and closed her eyes.
"You the one always makin' trouble! These bitches all got somethin' to say now 'cause of that shit you be teachin' 'em. Nik done
quit me. That other bitch pointed a gun at me, and this fool." He
shook her like a big rag doll. "This fool think she can take a side
against her own blood!"

He squeezed her arm harder and she whimpered softly.
Junior didn't care. "Talkin' about tellin' the cops where to find
my ass. Her own brother!"

He was ranting now. Sheila and I were a captive audience and
the words came tumbling out of his mouth like a river of poison.
He squinted at me and wagged the gun in my general direction.
I wondered suddenly if it was a real gun or simply another one of
his nephew's toys. I couldn't tell and I couldn't take a chance. He
was too angry and Sheila was too scared.

"My mama scoped it out first," he snarled. "She told me all
you bitches think you can just take a brother manhood but you
can't! 'Cause when you cut one down with your bitch ways and
your callin' the cops in and puttin' people behind bars and runnin' 'em out like they some kinda undesirable and shit, it don't
matta because another one gonna rise up in their place! You hear
me, bitch? Another one gonna rise up and another one and
another one until all you bitches bow down and act like you got
some sense. You understand me?"

I knew I couldn't reach the door in time to get to the phone inside the house and Sheila wasn't going to be able to help. He had either beaten her or scared her into submission, so it was just me and Junior in my snowy front yard, taking each other's measure one more time. I wondered if he had a plan or if he was making it up as he went along. If he was improvising, I might have a chance to change the direction of his solo.

"What do you want?" I said, wondering if he could even tell me.

"*I want you to stop fuckin' wit' me!*" he bellowed.

The sound of his shouting frightened Sheila into attempted action and she lunged suddenly against his restraining hand. He jerked her back so hard she lost her balance and fell to her knees, groveling pitifully in the snow.

"He gonna kill me!" she screamed. "Oh, God, Miz J, don't let him kill me!"

"Yeah, that's jus' what I'ma do," he hissed at her. "Ain't nobody callin' no cops on me and live to tell it." He turned back to me and smiled that twisted smile. "And since she learned that shit from you, I'ma let you watch."

He cocked the gun and pointed it at her head and I realized he really might do it *just because he could.*

"That's stupid," I said.

His eyes narrowed to disbelieving slits. "What the fuck you say?"

Now I was the one improvising, making it up as I went along, and I swear Miles Davis never worked harder. "I'm the one you want. You said it yourself."

He frowned, trying to remember. I prompted him, trying to keep my voice from shaking. Trying to sound as brave as I wanted Sheila to think I was.

"I'm the one who made her act this way, right?"

He lowered the gun to his side and considered what I was saying. "Yeah, so?"

"So if you mad enough to kill somebody . . ." I swallowed hard and spread my hands, palms up, like the answer was obvious. "I'm standing right here."

He narrowed his flat black eyes even more. "Oh, you that bad, huh? You ain't scared to die for this fool?" He pulled Sheila back up to her feet and I saw that she was staring at me. She wanted me to save her and that was exactly what I intended to do. Junior was a coward. He didn't know the meaning of standing up for your blood, but I did. He'd had us all scared to death, but all of a sudden, I wasn't scared of Junior anymore. I was more scared of being scared, and I was the only one who could do something about that.

"Don't be afraid," I said to Sheila. "You hear me? Don't you be afraid!"

"He's crazy, Miz J," Sheila whispered without taking her eyes off me.

I looked at her and I felt calm even though my heart was beating double time. Nobody had ever stood up for Sheila, ever. But this one time, she had backup, and so did Tee, and so did I. As long as we all stood together, Junior had no power over us at all.

"Don't be afraid of him," I said again. "He can't hurt us anymore."

"Shut up," Junior snarled. He seemed to be trying to figure out what to do next.

"If we stop being scared, everything changes." I was crooning to Sheila like it was a song. "Do you believe me?"

She hesitated, swallowed hard. "Yes."

"I said *shut up!*" Junior pushed her roughly aside and grabbed my arm. Sheila was scrambling around on her hands and knees, screaming at the top of her lungs, but all I could hear was the roaring in my ears like the ocean. Junior jerked me up against his side and pressed the gun against the side of my head. "Now what, bitch? What you got to say now?"

I closed my eyes and then I heard that unmistakable rumble. *"Drop it!"*

Nate was standing at the end of the driveway and he had a gun too. Junior whirled around without letting me go.

"I said drop it!"

"Fuck you," Junior said. "I ain't droppin' shit!"

Sheila stood frozen nearby, her eyes flickering from me to Junior, sobbing and shuddering, unsure where to look to avoid what she was convinced was going to be something terrible. I was watching Nate moving slowly toward Junior.

"That's close enough," Junior said.

Nate stopped on a dime. "You don't have a chance, young brother. Let the lady go and put the gun down *slowly*."

"I ain't your fuckin' brother." Junior spat the words at Nate. "And this bitch is goin' down."

I closed my eyes again. My legs felt like water, but I willed myself to keep standing. I knew Sheila was watching me. *I couldn't fall.*

"I'm warning you," Nate said slowly. "Put . . . the . . . gun . . . down."

"Or what?" Junior snarled. "You think you can shoot me before I smoke this bitch?"

I opened my eyes again, but Nate's eyes were locked on Junior.

"I don't think so, man," Junior taunted Nate, and I heard him cock the gun beside my ear. "You ain't that good!"

But he was.

SIXTY-THREE

that red dress

THE BULLET WENT THROUGH Junior's wrist as clean as a hole punch through paper. It went by my ear so close I swear I could hear it whistling "Dixie," although why that would be its tune of choice, I couldn't tell you. Turns out the Smitherman twins had just started on their dinner when they looked out of their kitchen window and saw what was going on in my front yard and called Nate. By the time the sheriff got here, Nate had stopped the bleeding in Junior's arm, tied his feet with the clothesline, wrapped Sheila in a blanket and cuddled me for long enough to be sure I knew I was okay. I was better than okay. Sheila and I were shaken up but otherwise unhurt. Junior was going to jail. He wasn't going to be able to bother any of us for a long, long time. We were finally safe, and it felt great.

The sheriff took our statements and the ambulance came to

get Junior. Nate left me on the phone to reassure the Smither-mans while he rode to the hospital behind that ambulance just to make sure there were no mishaps on the way. Patrice came to get Sheila and we hugged each other hard before she left.

"Don't worry," she said. "I ain't goin' back there at all. Patrice already got my boys at her house and ain't nothin' else back there I need."

I watched them drive away and tried to realize it was finally over. Tee would come home and we'd welcome her and drive her crazy fussing over her, until she made us stop and we all got back to the things we were doing before Junior started acting a fool. Especially in one critical area . . .

I went upstairs and ran myself a hot bath.

Breathing in, I know that I am breathing in.

Breathing out, I smile.

I soaked out the terrors of the day and got out feeling like somebody new. The phone rang while I was rubbing cocoa butter on my knees.

"Hello?"

"Joyce?" Nate rumbled on the other end. "How're you doing?"

"A little shaky," I said, "but I'm good. Where are you?"

"I'm at the jail," he said. "I want you to speak to a buddy of mine. Okay?"

"Okay," I said, disappointed. I was in no mood to give another statement about Junior to anybody.

"Ms. Mitchell?"

"Yes?"

"This is Sergeant Ford. Mr. Anderson just wanted me to let you know that the prisoner Lattimore has been treated at the hospital and released to our custody in good condition. He's in the maximum security area of our jail here right now and he's not going anywhere."

"Thank you," I said, trying not to smile. Nate wasn't taking any chances this time.

"You're welcome, ma'am," he said. "And anytime it would make you feel better to check on him, please feel free to call and ask for me."

"Thank you," I said again. "I will."

He handed the phone back to Nate. "You still there?"

"Of course."

"So you heard that, right?"

"I heard it."

"Do you feel safe now?" There might be sexier questions he could have asked me at this moment, but if there are, I couldn't tell you what they are.

"Oh, yeah," I said. "I feel very safe."

"Then will you do something for me?" he said.

"Yes," I said softly, feeling my body opening like a flower. "What do you want me to do?"

"Will you *please* go and put on that red dress so I can come calling?"

I looked at that dress, already lying across my bed like a scarlet silken promise. "I will," I said, wondering if surrender always felt so sweet. "I surely will."

SIXTY-FOUR

imagine

THAT NIGHT, I SLEPT like a baby. Nate did too. In the morning, just after sunrise, I woke up from a dream I couldn't quite remember, but wanted to, so I slid out of bed without waking him, went down to the kitchen and put on the teakettle. The mist was still hovering over the lake like a low-hanging cloud, but across the way, I could see the Smitherman twins already walking slowly down to the dock for their t'ai chi.

When I opened the window, it was so quiet, I could hear them laughing with each other just like they'd been doing for seventy-five years, and it was such a sweet sound that all of a sudden, I remembered my dream. So I grabbed a pen and wrote it down so I wouldn't get distracted by love or work or worry and forget that the first step is always to imagine . . .

Imagine it is dinnertime. Imagine we are sitting around a

campfire. *Imagine we are ancient, magical women who live in peace with all creatures, so that just beyond our cooking circle, the lions that we keep around as allies more than pets are yawning and settling their massive heads on their massive paws while we confer and confess, conducting our business as ancient, magical women often do, over steaming pots and sleeping children, a stone's throw from the mysterious male creatures with whom we share our blankets and our babies and our blood memories.*

Imagine our business includes culture and commerce and health care and technology and defense and diversions and endless discussions of what it means to fall in love and stay there. Imagine there is a full moon. Imagine there is peace and plenty and safety and spirit. Imagine what language we might speak. Imagine the sound of our laughter...